for Sonia,
happy reading!

firefly

Ice Born: Book One

firefly

Ice Born: Book One

from
The Secrets of Snow Valley

by

P. M. Pevato

S & H Publishing
Purcellville, VA

P.M.Pevato/S & H Publishing, Inc.
P. O. Box 456
Purcellville, VA 20134
books@sandhpublishing.com

Publisher's Note: This is a work of fiction. Names, characters, places, and
incidents are a product of the author's imagination. Any resemblance to actual
people, living or dead, or to businesses, or locales is completely coincidental.

Original cover art by Henrique de França
His illustration portfolio website is henriquedefranca.com

Summary: Most residents of the quiet alpine town of Snow Valley would scoff
at the idea of witches in their midst, yet a deadly war rages beneath the surface
as witch hunters stalk the local coven of emerging teen witches.

Firefly: Ice Born: Book One/ P. M. Pevato
ISBN 978-1-63320-022-7 – print edition
ISBN 978-1-63320-023-4 – ebook edition

iv

Dedicated to

Jean,

Linda,

and Farley

fair is foul

and foul is fair

hover through the

fog and filthy air

Macbeth, Act I Scene I

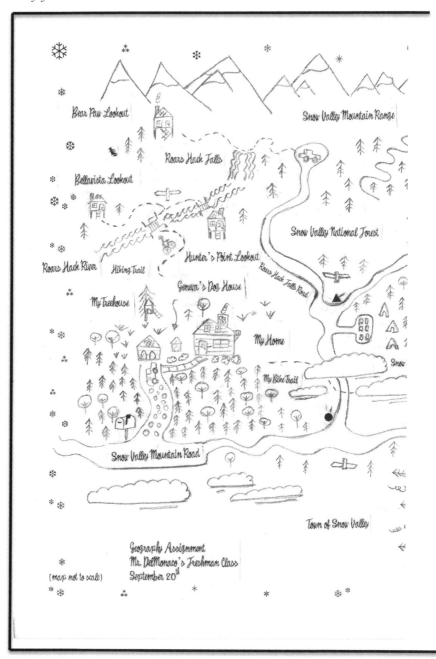

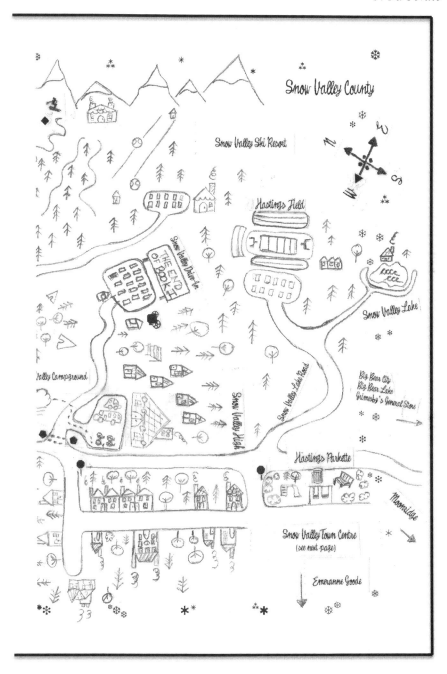

Firefly

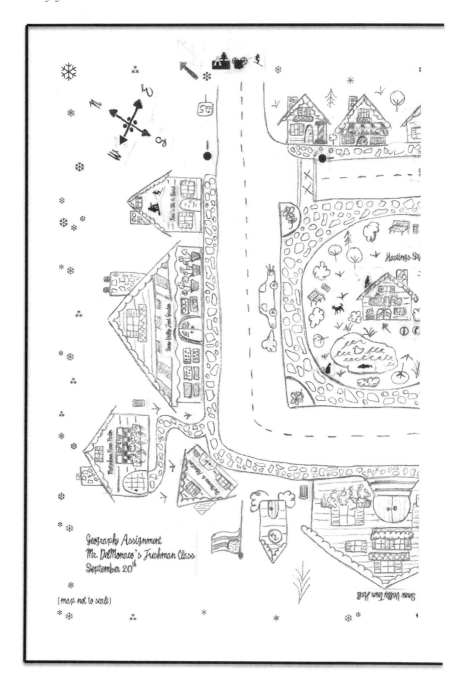

X

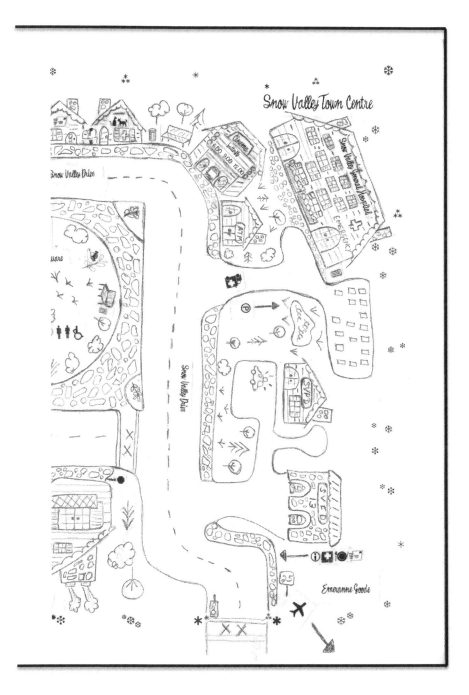

Table of Contents

Firefly Characters

THE SNOW VALLEY COVEN (ICE BORN)

The Ice Born witches of Snow Valley share the common power of premonition, known as the Ice Vision. The Coven members listed are all teenagers and close friends.

Emeranne Goode, or Ems

Her father, **John 'Jack' Goode Jr**, is Snow Valley County's Senior Forest Ranger. Jack's mother, Rosemary St. Marie, is Den Born. Em's mother, **Johanna 'Jo' Campbell**, lives in New York City, where she works as a milliner. Ems is telekinetic.

Carlton Cameron

His parents, **Putnam** and **Mackenzie**, run Cameron's Animal Hospital. Carlton researches history through transcendental travel and astral projection. His eccentricities and superior intellect set him apart from his high school classmates. Carlton's older brother, **Cuthbert**, is Snow Valley High School's star quarterback.

Ardelle Curry

Ardelle is gifted at weaving spells, is a talented knitter and seamstress. Her father, **Leonard Curry**, is Snow Valley's Fire Chief. Ironically, he has the ability to will his mind to start fires, the gift he passed on to Ardelle.

Morgan Hurst

Her parents are Ice Born. Morgan concocts potions and elixirs with dried herbs, flowers, and essential oils. She is also a talented artist who uses her artistic skills in magical ways. **Morgan** and **Ardelle** are budding fashion designers with their own label, *Curst Originals*.

Leland Kerr

His parents, **Simon** and **Charlsie Kerr**, are Ice Born. They own Kerr's New and Used Ski and Board. Leland is a gifted healer.

Gareth Garcia

His parents, **Diego** and **Carmen**, own Snow Valley Dry Cleaners and Alterations. The family moved to Snow Valley several years ago. They are hardworking, unfailingly friendly, and helpful to the townsfolk, although no one knows anything about their background. Gareth was paralyzed, two years ago, in a hit and run accident.

Selene Laveau

Raised by her Ice Born uncle, **Dr. Gavin Laveau** and his wife, **Callisto 'Callie' Laveau**, a nurse, Selene does not remember her parents. She is a descendent of voodoo priestess Marie Laveau of New Orleans. Selene is gifted with tarot cards and the Ouija board. Science, in particular chemistry, is her favorite subject.

THE FIRE BORN

One family of Fire Born, the **Bassetts**, settled in Snow Valley. The Bassetts own the Matterhorn Pizza Parlor and the entire family works for the business.

Bennett Bassett

A 'teenage' boy who remembers nothing of his mortal life before being brought into the Bassett family, **Bennett** is wracked with guilt and believes he is a monster. An artist and practicing poet, he delivers pizza for the Matterhorn.

Philippe Bassett

Head of the Bassett family, married to **Allora**. Philippe's children by his first marriage to **Charlotte** are **Miranda, Wallis, Giselle** and **Henry**. Allora is their stepmother. Philippe and Allora are Bennett's 'uncle' and 'aunt.' Allora has a son, **Terrowin Hanbury,** by her previous marriage to **Sir Terence Hanbury**.

THE DEN BORN

The Den Born, members of the Serrano Nation of Native Americans with deep ties to the land and wildlife of Snow Valley County, have protected generations of Ice Born.

River Vale

A smokejumper like his deceased father, **Basil,** River has been dating Selene for more than a year. His mother, **Rainn Storm Vale,** and his younger siblings, **Storm, Brooke, Meadow, Cedar** and **Woodruff 'Woods'**, aid and support the Coven as needed. Emeranne and River are related since Jack and Basil are cousins.

Byron Walker

His father is **Police Chief Orsonius Walker**, Den Born. His mother, **Evangeline**, is related to the Goodes and Vales through marriage. His great strength and unquenchable hunger are a source of both comfort and amusement to the Coven.

Lucas 'Luke' Stone
Emeranne's childhood friend. Luke's father, **Mohawk 'Moe' Stone**, is Jack's colleague in the Forest Service.

OTHER CHARACTERS

Zermatt and Geneva
Jack's loyal search and rescue Bernese Mountain Dogs.

Cooper 'Coop the Scoop' Kozalski
New to Snow Valley, an aggressive reporter for the *Snow Valley Standard*.

Roy and Delia Grimesby
They own Grimesby's General Store. Their daughter was **Violet**, Jo's best friend. Violet died in her teens.

Mayor Albrecht Kanz
His twin daughters, **Kandida** and **Alba**, are spoiled and self-centered. They both adore Bennett, and compete for his attention.

Principal Lipschitz
Runs Snow Valley High School. He actively dislikes Emeranne, whom he regards as a troublemaker. Teachers at the school include **Ms. Beltane, Mr. DelMonaco,** and **Mrs. Yin.**

Chapter One

Blizzard

EMERANNE

Even in a ferocious blizzard, Snow Valley kept her secrets well hidden.

I should know. Many fierce winter storms raged through the years without betraying the reason for the Valley's mysterious silence, until seven years ago, when a winter of particularly violent storms revealed a closely held secret. About me!

It was my fault Mom was on that treacherous road. She'd picked me up from school after dark. I was only nine years old, and served one more in a long string of detentions imposed by the school principal for reasons I considered ridiculous. Mom was later than usual because the traffic was bad. The snowstorm raged ever fiercer, yet she still came to get me.

It was my fault Mom drove up that slippery, snaking mountain road. It was my fault she was nearly killed. It was *so* my fault.

On the way home, Mom's red coupe was swallowed by an enormous snow squall on Snow Valley Mountain Road. We took turns rubbing the windshield every few minutes, but the road ahead of us was barely visible.

Snow pounded the glass before the car's whirring heater could carve out more than a circle the width of a small telescope lens, but that tiny opening was big enough to let me see a black eighteen-wheeled transport—out of control—coming right at us on the opposite side of the steep mountain road.

"Mom!" I shrieked. "Mom! Watch out!"

"What…what's wrong?" Mom asked. Then she saw the truck, and screamed my name: "Emeranne!"

Attention super-focused on events outside our car, I didn't have time to answer. I grabbed the seat belt and hung on for dear life. Puffs of snow scattered across the road and swirled helplessly in the skin-biting wind, but I wasn't frightened.

My breathing slowed. A thick blanket of fog surrounded me. Sound receded, leaving me with a sense of detachment and deep concentration. The clock on the dashboard was out of focus. I turned to Mom but could barely see her through the heavy fog. The clock and Mom faded away. Somehow, I broke through the mists to another space beyond my own world, a space where time and motion seemed suspended. I couldn't say for certain when the mists lifted, only that beyond the mists big trees had fallen down across the road, and Mom's small red car was flattened beneath the giant transport.

"Please please please," I breathed, "please don't hit us! Don't hit us! Miss our car, miss our car, miss our car! I don't want to die! I don't want my mom to die! Think positive, Emeranne! Think think think! See the transport! See the car! See the road! Everyone safe!"

The transport leaned into a sharp bend on the snowy road, skidded toward my mom's car—the road slick with black ice— and I gathered all my mental strength, all my considerable will, and focused my mind on what I wanted, what I demanded: the transport stopped, our car safe, our lives spared. I held my breath for a long, long minute…and watched through the windshield as the transport veered, then jackknifed, coming to rest on its side, blocking the road, but without hitting Mom's car.

When the mists shrouded me again, I floated within, as though I'd called the mists to return and carry me home. As the fog slowly fell away, I wandered back to my own world, heard Mom's gasps and saw the clock come back into focus. Wherever I'd travelled, I came back to find the rig's cab plowed into what looked like loaves of floury snow at the road's edge, where it came to a stop. Snow squalls twirled beneath the dark evening sky, the truck's headlights making snowflakes into ballet dancers unfurling furiously, colliding with drooping boughs piled across the road in the darkening sky.

Why weren't we dead? And what had I seen earlier when Mom and I didn't survive? I couldn't explain. We were alive, that's all that mattered.

Mom's hands were clamped on the steering wheel, her eyes fixed on the blocked road ahead. Through the windshield we watched as the truck driver forced his door open, climbed down and ran into the driving snow. His silhouette reflected pale yellow in the blurred light of the coupe's headlights. Halfway to the car, the driver turned his back to the wind, shielding his face, and half-stumbled backward from the force of the wind, his path guided by the headlight beams.

Holding on to his trapper's hat, he knock knock knocked on Mom's window. I could see his mouth moving, but couldn't hear what he said till Mom let go of the steering wheel and rolled her window down a scant inch. Out of breath, exhaling white vapors against the black sky, the driver panted, "You okay, lady?"

"Yes," she replied through chattering teeth.

"Wait here," the driver mouthed, raising one hand for emphasis.

Still in a daze, Mom blinked, nodded ever so slightly. Her eyes, round as snowballs, spoke before she did. "Emeranne, are you…?" The windshield wipers pounded. The coupe's engine rumbled.

"I'm fine Mom. I just feel a little weird." Then I told her what happened.

"You…you were *what?*"

"Inside a fog," I told Mom. "Everything went silent and you faded away. When the mists disappeared, I saw the accident, trees on the groud, the car crushed by the transport. Then I…I…"

"You what, Emeranne, you what?"

"And then I begged, really begged Mom, that the transport wouldn't hit us. And it stopped, Mom, it really did!"

She'd withdrawn her cell phone from her purse, but now she paused, then put it back. "Emeranne, you are never to breathe a word about this to anyone. Not to your dad, not to your friends. Do you understand?"

I wanted to ask why, but responded wordlessly with a slow nod of my head.

The truck driver tramped around our car, examining the sputtering and sighing coupe for damage. Mom opened her window enough to hear him say, "Looks all right! Just wait here, till I move my rig."

As soon as the road was cleared, Mom drove home in silence.

Mom never discused our near-fatal accident. In fact, she barely looked at me or spoke to me after that night in the blizzard. Occasionally, she managed a 'good morning,' or a 'have a nice day at school,' but beyond that? Nothing.

What had I done wrong? I thought she'd be happy that we escaped a damaged car, and possibly ourselves.

Dinners were awkward, when she joined my dad and me, which wasn't often. I kept my word, didn't say anything to anyone, and I guessed she hadn't told Dad either.

The wooden tree house Dad built in a sturdy back yard pine became my winter cave. Mom retreated to her studio on the top floor of the log cabin, burying herself in work, designing and sewing hat after hat after hat for her clients. I hibernated under layers of winter clothing and wool blankets.

And so this silent pact continued for the most the winter: me in my tree house, Mom in her studio. Eventually, though, I just *had* to know why she wouldn't talk to me. What had I done wrong? I'd wanted to save her. But the way she acted since the blizzard, it was as though I'd hurt her. I hoped things between us would change, but that hope faded as days went by. Eventually, I broke down and told Dad what happened, told him every detail.

When I finished, I held my breath, expecting to hear him say I needed to see a doctor, or that I shouldn't invent stories, or that at my age it wasn't unusual to have a vivid imagination. Or nightmares. *Was* it a nightmare?

But Dad didn't react as I'd expected. He sat me down in our tiny livingroom and added a few logs to the fire before sitting down in his worn red and black plaid armchair. Zermatt, his loyal search and rescue dog, snored on his rug.

"Ems," Dad said softly, "there's nothing wrong with you. I always knew, and your mom knew, too, especially when the detentions started."

I'd often had visions of events before they happened, and it didn't bother me—I didn't think I was unusual or special or unique. Instead, I figured I was cursed. At school, I was in trouble all the time, took the blame when teachers were locked in their staff room, test papers vanished, or the evil Kanz twins' backpacks spilled their contents in slushy snow.

Okay, I admit I'd *imagined* those things, but I didn't *actually* follow through. Yet, there I was, always at the scene of the crime.

"Your mom didn't want to say anything, but I've been expecting this day. I'd, hoped she would be here with me to tell you about—"

"Tell me what?" I interrupted.

Dad paused and inhaled deeply before continuing. "Ems, I want you to keep an open mind. I'm gonna tell you how you stopped the transport and—"

"I *stopped* the transport?"

He nodded. "That's right, you did. See, Ems, your mom should've told you that night, after she told *me* what happened first," he said, pointing his index finger to his chest. "Together we'd have told you…that's what we should've done." He rubbed one hand over his head. "No wonder it's been tense around here. I asked Jo what was going on, and she told me it was just mother-daughter growing pains."

I felt a surge of anger rise inside me. "She told you that?"

Dad slowly blinked his eyes. "Yeah, she did."

"Well, she made *me* promise I wouldn't say anything about the blizzard or the truck," I huffed.

Zermatt woofed as though he was dreaming. I turned my gaze to his rug. Eyes raised and forehead wrinkled, he looked worried. I reassured him, "it's okay, Matt."

Dad reached down with one hand to rub Matt's head. "You have every right to feel upset," he told me. "Your mom kept us both in the dark."

"So what's the big secret?" I asked.

"There's no easy way to say this, so I'm just going to put it out there, plain and simple. Your mom is part of the Snow Valley Coven."

"Coven?"

Dad sat perfectly calm, as as if he'd just told me snow was white. "Snow Valley has had an active Coven of witches going back centuries. We call them the Ice Born."

"Ice Born," I said feebly. "And you knew this all along?"

"Yup. Not everyone in Snow Valley knows, mind you. It's a well-kept secret."

"A secret," I mumbled. I couldn't believe what I was hearing. *No, this can't be true. I'm dreaming. Yeah, I'm dreaming... Witches are only in fairy tales—and are almost always wicked. That can't be my mother...or was he talking about me? No, I'm definitely not dreaming.*

He continued. "Ice Born witches share one power: premonition. It's also known as Ice Vision."

"You...you mean like...like..."

"Like seeing something that's gonna happen before it does."

"So," I said slowly. "You're not...not a witch."

"No," he replied before I could get the words out, "I'm not Ice Born. I don't have Ice Vision."

I didn't know what to say, so Dad filled the silence. "You'll become a member of the Coven when you turn sixteen."

Seven years, I thought to myself.

"That doesn't mean other powers won't show themselves once in a while. Like on the night of the blizzard," Dad said.

"*Other* powers?"

"Yup, Ems. Other powers," he repeated. "Hmmm...let me see. What did you say you did that night exactly?"

"I thought real hard about the transport. That it would stop, and miss Mom's car."

He nodded. "And it did."

"Yeah, it did."

"That means you may be able to move objects with your mind. If you could use your Ice Born intuition to see, then telekinesis to stop an eighteen-wheeled transport, I'd say you've got pretty strong powers already."

I didn't know what to say, except, "Mom too?"

"You mean, is she telekinetic?"

"Yes." I nodded in case he didn't hear my whisper.

"No," he replied. "She isn't. She's good with a needle, right?"

I nodded again.

"Your mom weaves spells. Good spells. Actually, *great* spells."

My head was spinning and I felt slightly nauseous. I was a monster, a wicked witch. No wonder I got detentions all the time! I was wicked. And cursed. But I didn't say any of that, I couldn't. "Weave spells?"

The way Dad told it was so casual, as though he talked about the weather. "Uh, thanks Dad. I need to…to go outside for a minute. Clear my head." I held back tears and ran out of the house through the side door off the kitchen. Matt sat up, Dad whispered a quiet word to him, and the dog followed me outdoors.

Dad knew exactly where I was headed. "Dress warm, Ems," he whispered.

I sat in my tree house for a long time and didn't notice the sunlight fade or the temperature drop. The only sounds I heard was Dad whistling for Matt and the screen door close. I cried for a while, then went over every detail of what happened on the night of the blizzard, until the only conclusion I could come to was that Dad had told me the truth. He had *never* lied to me. Ever.

Maybe I wasn't crazy after all.

When my stomach grumbled, I climbed down the ladder and went into the house through the side door. I could hear Mom and Dad talking. No, arguing. I didn't think they ever argued. At least, they'd never argued where I could hear them. I closed the door silently and listened, hoping Matt didn't hear me come inside.

Mom sounded distraught. "But you're not Ice Born!"

"You knew there was a fifty-fifty chance, Jo," Dad said.

I could practically hear her tears falling. "I don't want her to end up…end up like…like—"

"I know," soothed Dad. "I know."

I decided I'd heard enough, so I opened the side door again, and slammed it shut. I didn't want my parents fighting about me! Matt barked and dashed to the kitchen.

"Is that you, Ems?" I heard Dad say.

"Yeah," I shouted as I kicked off my winter boots. As if he sensed my confusion, Matt licked my cheek. "Good boy," I told him.

And that was that. I heard the wooden stairs creaking and a door closing upstairs. Dad came into the kitchen and made me a Swiss cheese and mushroom omelet for dinner. I could tell he wasn't much in a talking mood. Neither was I. After dinner I popped a movie into the DVD player. Dad and I watched a comedy, a good distraction, though neither of us laughed much. Later, I went upstairs to my bedroom, next to Mom's studio. I fell asleep with the sound of her sniffling.

The next day, I went downstairs for breakfast, expecting to find Mom reading the *Snow Valley Standard* over a cup of steaming coffee. But she wasn't there. I ran upstairs to Mom's studio. The door was locked.

I knocked on the door. "Mom?" I knocked again. "Mom?" I put one ear against the door. I heard nothing, not the rhythmic patter of Mom's sewing machine, not creaking floorboards, not Mom humming to a song on the radio.

Maybe she left early for a delivery? Mom often delivered hats to her personal clients and department stores where her hats were sold. She was extra busy because Christmas was less than one week away.

Where was Dad? I hurried down the stairs and into the kitchen. Dad might be chopping wood. I opened the kitchen door and peeked outside. The cold air bit my face. "Dad?" I looked around but didn't see Dad or Matt.

I ran to the front door. Mom's car was gone. Dad's Land Cruiser wasn't in the driveway, either. Mom and Dad never left me alone. What was going on?

I called Dad's office. Two back country skiers went missing, Dad's assistant told me. "No telling when he'll be back."

I hung up the phone and tried to eat a muffin but didn't feel hungry, so I sat alone in the livingroom. The house was so quiet. I didn't know what to do. I decided to call Morgan Hurst, one of my best friends. "Hi, it's Ems. I'm alone and don't know where Mom is, and Dad's at work." Morgan's mom picked me up within the hour. Mrs. Hurst left a note for Mom and a message at Dad's office.

I spent the day at Morgan's house. "Something's wrong," I said. Morgan nodded. Mrs. Hurst made several phone calls during the day. She lowered her voice if Morgan and I were nearby, or she'd quickly hang up the phone. Dad's assistant spoke with Mrs. Hurst. He was still on the mountainside. Mom didn't call all day. By nightfall, I gave up. "Emeranne, why don't you stay for a sleepover?" Mrs. Hurst tried to sound happy, but I could hear the layer of worry in her voice.

That night, I lay awake for a long time. Mom was busy, I convinced myself. She stayed in San Bernardino because she was too tired to drive home. That made sense. She didn't see Mrs. Hurst's note. Dad was working. How could he know I was left alone? Eventually, exhaustion from the combination of crying and worrying took over, and sleep found me.

The Dream came to me for the first time, that same night at Morgan's house.

I look out my bedroom window. A group of beautiful fireflies glow and hover near the dark forest behind the log cabin. I tiptoe downstairs, mindful that the last step creaks. Silently, silently, I open the side door off the kitchen, careful not to slam the springy screen door.

I can't help myself. I must know, must discover where the fireflies go, why they beckon me so. When they swirl behind the stand of massive pine trees, I take one deep breath and step into the dark forest, the ground thick with grass. Fallen pine needles tickle the soles of my feet. Without piercing my arms, I move pine boughs away from me, aided by light from the fireflies and the moonlit sky. Left and right and left again, one bare foot in front of the other.

Barefoot, I slide through the grass, cool and wet and aromatic. My lungs fill with scents of sweet clover and musky earth and damp pine cones. Tall, wild grass flosses my toes, tugs backwards, holds me, warns me.

Stay away from the dark forest...

I don't make a sound. I don't flinch. I wander quietly, quietly, deeper into the forest, guided by the pure light of a full moon and the fireflies' sparkly glow.

They form a perfectly round circle, then enter an apple grove enclosed within the thick woods. But there *isn't* an apple grove behind the log cabin. And yet, there it is, red apples and remnants of pinkish blossoms glistening under a full moon. Divided by a chattering brook as clear as ice, the narrow stream winds, caresses river rock, trickles and hums a melodic tune.

I spend a few blissful moments in the peaceful, improbable apple grove, a secret, a lie, a vision. I rest, recline on my back near the riverbank, cradled by the sweet grass, my skin brushed by tender moonlight drizzling through the branches. Surrounded by smiling red apple faces, a surge of gratitude sweeps through me. Sweet, chaste juiciness bursts within my mouth, strokes my taste buds.

In winter, I imagine the grove would generously provide withered fruit for snowbirds. Squirrels, their winter coats thick and tails extra fluffy, would flit and scurry up and down tree trunks and nestle among the snowy boughs. Pale blue waters would drift gently, gently, beneath a smashed windowpane of thin ice.

Moonlight disappears behind a dusty cloud. I rise, wipe pine needles from my comfy navy sweats and worn white T-shirt. In the darkness, I search for the fireflies and look above where they spin around and around, whirling dervishes in an evening meditation. I follow the fireflies, spinning and dancing, glowing with delight.

I nearly trip on a rotten log or branch or mound of moss. Slowly, my eyes adjust to the darkness and I see what I've stumbled upon. A boy rests on his back, asleep or unconscious or dead, his face obscure, out of focus, except for his eyelids. Afraid and exhilarated, cautious and reckless, I examine him. He is tall, six feet or more, a teenager, I think. Kneeling, I lean over his shoulders, watch his chest, place one ear on his heart, touch his wrist. I see, hear, feel nothing, nothing at all. No breath or heartbeat or pulse.

And he is cold. So, so cold.

When the cloud floats away, moonbeams strike his body like stage lights.

I want to scream, but I don't. I want to run, but I can't. My knees are frozen to the forest floor, my stomach aches with fear, and my heart beats rapidly.

When the moon slips behind clouds, the fireflies illuminate the boy's body.

Still kneeling, I reach out to touch him again, hold out my hand and straighten my arm, feeling for a pulse once more. Unexpectedly, he opens his eyes. They glimmer like tarnished silver, ashen and mysterious, shimmer like a pair of pewter goblets.

I still can't see his lips, but can imagine that he's smiling, smiling that I'm here with him, smiling into his silver eyes. His arms stretch, his hands reach out, lightly carress me. They brush my hands, my arms, my chin, my lips…

I wake up, beads of sweat thick on my forehead.

Mrs. Hurst drove me home after breakfast. Dad waited on the porch. Matt sat nearby. Both Dad and Matt looked worried.

"Come over anytime, Emeranne," Mrs. Hurst said. She exchanged a quick glance with Dad. They didn't have to speak. That glance told me everything I needed to know. I felt it, deep down. Mom was gone.

Christmas was a blur. Dad did his best to make the holidays as normal as possible. Presents under the tree, decorations scattered around the house, carrots and milk on the kitchen table. Yet, the log cabin felt empty.

During the day, I sat in front of my bedroom window, watching for Mom's red coupe. At night, when I lay in bed and my bedroom curtains lit up, I ran to the window, hoping the beams from headlights came from Mom's car. Every time, I was let down.

Sometimes, I sat outside Mom's studio with Matt, as if staring at the door would somehow bring Mom home.

"Ems," Dad said, "I don't think Mom is coming back."

"Why not?"

"I don't know."

"Did I…"

"No, Ems. It's not your fault."

"Maybe Mom left a note in her studio," I said.

"I don't have the key, Ems."

Eventually, I accepted Mom wasn't coming home.

The Dream haunted me for seven years following the day Mom left. Always the same details, the same abrupt end. I'd wake up, never knowing who he was, or why I dreamed about him. Why I dreamed about him—the boy with eyes as gray as a bleak winter sky.

Chapter Two

Murder on the Mountain

EMERANNE

By the time I started high school, I knew all the witches in Snow Valley.

What a relief to discover my best friends were future members of the Coven. I shared my mixed feelings and deepest fears, knowing my secrets were safe with them. Who else could I talk to? Mom abandoned Dad and me that night I told. She never called or wrote, and the subject was never discussed. Dad wasn't Ice Born, and I still felt guilty for Mom's leaving.

I discussed strange things since the snowstorm seven years ago, including my recurring dream.

"I've never seen fireflies in Snow Valley County," Morgan said.

"Fireflies are wondrous, magical beings," Selene Laveau said. "Ordinary by day, extraordinary at night. Fireflies are a symbolic reminder to look past physical appearances. How we appear on the outside doesn't always reflect who we are on the inside, where our spirit lives, shining from within to illuminate our friends and surroundings."

"Never judge a book by its cover," I said.

"Exactly," Selene said.

The Coven debated theories, but could not settle on a single explanation. Over the years, I learned how the powers of witchcraft I'd inherited from my ancestors worked, and how to control them.

For example, I'd struggled in math, my least favorite subject. One week before my freshman year began, math textbooks mysteriously turned up in our garage. As a result, I became the one and only student in Snow Valley High's history to receive multiple detentions before stepping a single foot on school grounds! To make matters worse, after the texts were removed from the garage, they turned to ashes in the delivery truck. And no evidence of a fire.

I'd been banned—for life!—from the Snow Valley Food Garden. One afternoon, while grocery shopping with my dad, a group of boys made rude faces at me. They stood in front of a pile of Roma tomatoes, two ninety-nine a pound. I pictured those pesky boys drowning beneath the pile of tomatoes, and just like that, the pyramid of blood-red tomatoes tumbled like an avalanche. I laughed so hard! Dad gave me a sharp look and nodded his head in the direction of the store manager, Mr. Sarducci, who had turned as red as the one Roma tomato I held in my hand. Busted. I couldn't admit I'd only *thought* about burying the boys, but Dad figured it was probably best not to say anything.

Apart from hanging out with my friends, mountain biking was my favorite activity. As soon as school was out, I biked Snow Valley Mountain's numerous trails snaking up and down behind the log cabin.

The first day of my summer holidays was worth a long bike ride up the mountain. I'd celebrate the end of my disastrous sophmore year at Snow Valley High and freedom from Principal Lipschitz, his penchant for tugging on his goatee and adjusting his pince-nez glasses when I'd angered him in some way, his ire satisfied only by assigning detention, served in a tenth circle of hell created exclusively for me.

16

Once I learned to control my powers, I didn't get into much trouble. But my reputation was already established, and Lipschitz kept an extra eye on me, waiting to pounce. He didn't need an excuse—or evidence—to assign detention after detention. Dad argued with Lipschitz, but there really wasn't much he could do.

My most effective antidote to Mr. Lipschitz was the forest.

One sunny and fresh Saturday morning, above the permanent bank of clouds, floating veils of mist stroked my face, a pleasant wind tossed my long hair spilling from the sides of my bike helmet, its reflectors a prism of neon yellow, green, silver, opal. Pine needles scraped my bare arms, buttery sunlight spun past me, a glistening disco ball in the silent, mystical forest. Radiant beads clung to my eyelashes. Blue holes punched through the green forest canopy.

In the far distance, much higher than my location, Roars Hack Falls bubbled and sprayed furiously. I crossed the wooden bridge over Roars Hack River and listened to the babbling water gush over boulders large and small, feeling as though the rolling waves on the river's surface weren't waves but watery hands warning me. Something was wrong, but I couldn't see what it was. I had nothing, no Ice Vision, only a warning in my gut.

Stay away from the dark forest...

Near the river the curvy trail split and I had a choice. I could go left to Bellavista Lookout or right to Hunter's Point. I turned left. Was it sheer chance? Was it fate? One thing I knew for sure. It wasn't an Ice Vision.

It was that fork in the road that made all the difference. It marked a turning point in my day, my week, my year—maybe even my life.

The clear blue sky turned cold, and the last fragments of daylight were extinguished by a thick, suffocating mask of gloomy smoke. Pine trees swayed and recoiled, threading their needles through the forest's patchwork fabric in shades of melted chocolate and bruised peach. The smell of burning pine smoke stung my eyes. *Fire!* The scorched wind tasted of damp earth, sweet pine, and spiced cider.

My bike skidded when I pressed the brakes. I needed to turn back. Unless…my palms moved swiftly around my waist. Nothing. No cell phone. Damn! I'd have to hurry before the blaze spread further. The mountain bike's thick tires drew a fan on the ground as I prepared myself for a frantic ride home. Just as I was about to push off, an eerie sound reached my ears. I slowed my breath to listen. Another scream. I turned my head and looked over my shoulder. Was a hiker in danger at the lookout? An animal wouldn't scream like that. I glanced down the mountain, then behind. I couldn't leave now. What if someone needed help? Was hurt?

Before I could change my mind, I swung my bike around. Pedaling harder and harder, breathing shallowly, I rode higher up the mountain, deeper into Snow Valley National Forest, closer to Bellavista Lookout. The smell of fire grew stronger. Even so, I pushed through choking smoke and intense heat nearing the lookout. Every time I inched nearer, a violent wind slapped my face, pushed back, threatened my bare skin. Over and over, I heard Dad's voice in my head: *Never ride your bike to that area of the woods.*

I wasn't supposed to be here, high up Snow Valley Mountain, where the cloudbank floated below steep, jagged peaks and endless crevasses and rivers of ice and fingers of snow.

Ems, he'd say in his deep, authoritative voice, the second he found out I'd broken the only rule he'd imposed upon me, *didn't I remind you a thousand times? Didn't I say it enough? Never ride your bike to that area of the woods?* He'd shake his head disapprovingly, wrinkle his forehead, rake calloused fingers through his windswept black wavy hair peppered with white.

Why not? I'd asked myself this morning. *Why not take a quick ride up, through the wilderness, on one of the mountain trails?* After all, I wasn't a child. In four months, I'd be sixteen. Practically a grown up.

Never ride your bike to that area of the woods…

The cries faded by the time I emerged from the overgrown hiking trail, braked, and wiped trickles of sweat from my forehead. Was I too late?

I froze on the spot. A body was tied to one of the tower's thick wooden posts.

I threw my bike down mid-way between the wood line and the black tower of flames, tore off my helmet, ripped my blue and white bandanna from my head and placed it over my mouth and nose and as much of my stinging eyes as possible. Then I ran. I needed to help save him, or her. Maybe it wasn't too late. Maybe the person passed out from the smoke. As I ran, the smoke threw me to the ground, where I dropped to my knees and clawed my way toward the lookout.

Acrid smoke belched from a raging blaze and choked my words. I lifted my chin and assessed the encroaching blaze: orange and pink pillars of fire with pale blue centers spit all around. Flailing boughs entangled a stinging breeze. Tiny insects plunged in drunken spirals, twigs cracked and spit. Birds fluttered their wings, silenced their sweet songs, and made haste, flying away.

Somehow, through the black smoke and spreading fire I caught a glimpse of the person tied to the lookout.

"No," I mumbled. "*No,*" I cried. "*NO!*" I screamed.

Her body limp, minutes away from being swallowed by the fire, I caught a fleeting glimpse of her face and the wind moved her hair, and recognized the person bound by rope was Charlsie Kerr, an Ice Born witch.

The numbing combination of disbelief, fear, and shock gave me chills despite the heat surrounding me. My eyes burned and watered. I whipped the bandanna from my face and retched uncontrollably, while flames jumped over my head. The flames landed farther behind me, near an uprooted tree untouched by fire, a knotted mess of twisted roots and a fallen trunk covered with emerald moss. I crawled toward the forest's edge, knowing I was too late. Knowing she was dead.

I edged past my bike, catching a glimpse of my distorted reflection on the bike's polished titanium frame. A stranger's gaze stared back, shades of green boughs and brown trunks mixed with dark shadows and orange flames. Pine needles pierced my palms and dug into my knees. I didn't care. I wasn't the witch burning in the fire. I wasn't the murdered Ice Born witch. I wasn't Charlsie Kerr. I wasn't…I couldn't complete the thought.

What was happening? Everything was getting dark. Even the flames that crackled around me lost their light as I sank into darkness.

The Dream claimed me, but this time there was no moonlight and no fireflies. The evening sky was so dark I barely saw the boy's body lying on the ground. I felt a chill running down my spine as I approached him. It felt wrong, all wrong. My heart raced faster and faster until, without warning, the boy's eyelids opened and he sat up. I stopped breathing long enough to feel disoriented, to disbelieve what I saw. The boy's eyes weren't gray this time; instead, they were angry and orange, as though a bonfire burned inside and extended toward me, reaching for my arms, pulling me closer and closer to the inferno.

I screamed and stepped away, but caught my foot on a root, which sent me tumbling. My hands hit the ground first as I tried to break my fall. When I looked up, the boy stood over me, and a bone-chilling laugh escaped his lips, while his eyes continued to burn ferociously. I lifted my hands to shield my eyes and protect my head. My palms ached and smelled like rusted nails, as though a thousand thumbtacks lined the ground. An invisible force drew me toward the boy, pulling me into the blaze, pulling me, suspending my body in mid air. No matter how hard I tried, my powers didn't work. I couldn't stop him from drawing me into the fire until I was nearly consumed.

Blaring sirens and whirring helicopters saved me from the boy's fiery eyes and, for a moment, I didn't know where I was, until I opened my stinging eyes, and wiped pine needles and long strings of tangled black hair from my face. When I stared down at my body, tattooed with pine needles, my white T-shirt was soiled blood red and earth brown and ash black.

I must have laid on my side with my head resting on a mossy part of the trunk I'd seen earlier. I continued to move my gaze down my legs to my running shoes, sat up and looked beyond my shoes, past the bandanna I must have dropped as I ran to the forest's edge. I rubbed my burning eyes a few times, certain my mind invented drag marks on the ground, two parallel lines cut through the pine needles, stretching from where I remember falling to where I woke up, on the spot where firefighters found me and carried me to safety. I blinked a few times, refocusing my eyes, but the drag marks were sharper in focus. Somehow, I'd managed to crawl away from the burning lookout.

I couldn't say the same for Mrs. Kerr, a seasoned witch whose body lay lifeless and burned at the base of Bellavista Lookout, an Ice Born witch who must not have foreseen her death through an Ice Vision. The following day, I learned that none of the Snow Valley witches had seen the danger.

A few days after Mrs. Kerr's funeral, Dad and I sat in the livingroom with Matt, now retired from service, and Geneva, Dad's new search and rescue canine partner. He picked up the remote control for the flat screen television and changed the channel to KSNO, the only local television station. Breaking news covered Mrs. Kerr's death. Reporters swarmed as close to the crime scene as possible, tied off by yellow police tape. Every angle was examined, every perspective, and a myriad theories were proposed.

News reports recounted disturbing similarities between Mrs. Kerr's death and another murder in Snow Valley, back when Mom and Dad were high school sweethearts, when Violet Grimesby was burned on the same spot where Bellavista Lookout stood, and had been rebuilt once already. Today, the commemorative plaque in Violet's name was destroyed, like her life, and now Mrs. Kerr's too. If I felt this disturbed, as though a part of me was ripped out, as though a part of me died, imagine how Leland Kerr felt, having lost his mother. Leland was one of my best friends, and a member of the young Coven.

A news conference with Police Chief Walker was in progress. He pledged to restore calm and protect the public's safety. Dad asked Chief Walker to withhold information regarding my presence on the mountain. A man of his word, Chief Walker refrained from providing details of the crime, including the fact that I'd discovered Mrs. Kerr's lifeless body.

"To preserve the integrity of the investigation," justified Chief Walker to the disgruntled reporters who aggressively pressed for more information. Dozens of vans with huge satellite dishes on the roof could be seen in the background, parked in front of the police station. Media flocked from near and far to tiny Snow Valley, eager for an exclusive with anyone who may have witnessed the fire.

"Has the San Bernardino County Sheriff's office stepped in to assist in the investigation?" asked a reporter from Big Bear City.

"Is it true the body was bound?" inquired a young, eager male *LA Times* reporter.

"Can you confirm the time of death?" pushed a local KSNO reporter, her voice shrill.

A *Fawnskin Star* reporter waved her iPhone in front of Chief Walker's face. "Why was Mrs Kerr on the mountain?"

A KTLA reporter addressed Fire Chief Curry. "Was the crime scene preserved, given that water and flame retardant doused the fire?"

"When you gonna release the name of the girl who found Mrs Kerr?"

The reporters fell ominously silent and turned their heads to the back of the crowd.

The remote control slipped from Dad's hand.

Chief Walker strained his head for a better view of the source. His shaking fingers fumbled while adjusting his police cap. "Whoever gave you that idea?" he asked irately, directing his question to a rather scruffy looking reporter wearing a wrinkled beige trench coat and a threadbare hat.

"Why, *you* did, Chief. Saw you escortin' a teenage girl outta the police station's back door last night. Long black hair straighter than this here pencil of mine. About five five more or less? Local girl, maybe? Now why else would you do that, Chief?" grinned the reporter, shifting a cigar stub from one side of his mouth to the other.

The reporters shouted demands for more details, and they repeated the scruffy reporter's assertions.

"Who was she?" persisted the *Fawnskin Star* reporter.

"That's police business. None of yours," declared Chief Walker. "No further questions."

The rowdy press conference ended abruptly. Dad picked up the remote control and turned off the television. "Cooper Kozalski." His voice shook with suppressed anger.

"Who?" I asked.

"Orsonius called this morning. Told me about this overzealous crime reporter new to the *Snow Valley Standard.* Calls himself Coop the Scoop."

"Really?" A light bulb flashed in my head. Of course. I smacked my forehead with the palm of my hand. "Dad, does this reporter, Coop the Scoop or whatever, does he drive an old yellow Mustang convertible?"

"Dunno, Ems. Why?"

"A yellow Mustang followed us from the police station parking lot."

"Figures," he growled. "If Kozalski starts diggin' around, he's gonna trigger more panic in town. Like we need it," he said, rubbing his unshaven face.

For now, my identity was kept under wraps. So, too, was the fact that Mrs. Kerr was an Ice Born witch whose powers failed to save her life.

Dad suggested that the teenage members of the Coven not meet until things died down. One thing was clear: each member was in grave danger, our generation and those before us.

In search of a distraction, I went upstairs for the rest of the afternoon and tried to clean my bedroom until I gave up. By the end of the week, I'd developed a severe case of log cabin fever, so I begged my dad to let me attend a town hall meeting until finally he gave in.

Dad dropped me off at Snow Valley Dry Cleaners and Alterations, where my friends waited for me in the back room. "No one had an Ice Vision?" asked Morgan, nervously twisting her dark brown ponytail into a curly question mark. "I didn't see anything, otherwise I'd have...have—"

"Neither did I," sighed Leland, his pale mournful eyes downcast and sullen, still waves in the ocean, in contrast to his hair, all beach and gleaming sand. "If I'd been there with her, maybe, just maybe..."

"Don't do it, Leland, please don't beat yourself up. Do you think whoever did this would've let you walk in and heal her? You'd have met the same fate," I said sadly.

Gareth Garcia pushed the tires of his wheelchair closer to the group. Paralyzed by a hit and run driver, Gareth's powers had not yet surfaced. The Coven assumed his paralysis delayed the development of his powers. "Does anyone know why your mom was at Bellavista Lookout?"

Leland shook his head. "The last time I saw Mom alive, she carried flowers and waved at me with the bouquet before she drove away."

Ardelle Curry's kind, hazel eyes dissolved into syrupy tears slowly dripping beneath her horn-rimmed glasses. "Oh, Leland," she said, stifling sobs. Tenderly, Leland put his hand on Ardelle's quivering shoulder. "The flowers were for Violet, for the anniversary of her death."

The Coven remained silent for several minutes until Carlton Cameron broke the silence and fumed, "Not a single one of us experienced an Ice Vision." His intense blue eyes burned with rage. "I promise you one thing: I'm going to get to the bottom of this!"

Gareth turned to Carlton. "What are you thinking? Could it have been..."

"Witch hunters? That's certainly one theory."

"There haven't been witch hunters in Snow Valley for decades. The Ice Born hadn't detected any in all those years," Morgan said.

Leland sighed deeply, heavily. "Maybe Mom's powers faded more than she'd anticipated."

We all knew this would happen eventually, that the Coven's Ice Born parents would slowly lose their powers as the younger Coven became stronger.

Byron Walker bowed his head, spilling long, thick dreadlocks around his massive shoulders. A Den Born, Byron and his Serrano ancestors protected Snow Valley's witches. This giant bear of a teenager with dinner plate sized hands growled, his baritone voice boomed and echoed around rows and rows of plastic covered clothes on an electric coat-hanger system. Byron was related to me and the Vales, my cousins from Moonridge, through marriage. "The Scent failed us, too. If witch hunters *have* returned, I'm going to tear them to shreds!"

"Byron, we'll help Chief Walker as much as we can. Off the record, of course," winked Carlton.

"You got that right," growled Bryon, smacking his huge fist into his palm.

"Don't forget about my dad, he's already helping out as much as he can," reminded Ardelle, referring to Fire Chief Curry.

"Whatever it was, whoever blocked Ice Visions and the Scent, we better find out and find out soon, or else…" Carlton hesitated, the whirring motor propelled plastic covered clothes on hangers toward the front counter, the only sound.

We all knew what Carlton was about to say: *Or else one of us could be next.*

"Thank you and have a nice day," we heard Mrs. Garcia say to a customer.

Morgan narrowed her sea foam eyes. "Do you think Mrs Kerr's death was a warning?"

Carlton pressed his long fingertips together. "Let's hope we never find out."

"We need to consult the Spirits," declared Selene, her voice as raspy as usual. She rested purple nails on her caramel toned chin, narrowed her violet eyes.

"Better head out, hear what Mayor Kanz has to say," suggested Gareth, "even though he hasn't a clue what's really going on."

Morgan pulled my hood up to cover my head. "Best to keep a low profile."

Snow Valley's town square resembled a traditional European ski village. The town hall was modeled after a famous hotel in the Swiss Alps. Storefronts colluded with this Switzerland-in-Snow-Valley deception, along with the tidy square and wooden balconies and window boxes spilling with red geraniums in the summer. This tiny alpine town brimmed with skiers during the winter. Rustic vacation homes dotted the rugged landscape surrounding Snow Valley National Forest. Residents and vacationers alike shopped along Snow Valley Drive where they bought fresh produce at Snow Valley Food Garden, ate at the Matterhorn Pizza Parlor, picked up pet food at Cameron's Animal Hospital and strolled through Hastings Square.

We walked by Kerr's New and Used Ski and Board, Leland's family-owned store. The window display was draped in black, darker than threatening clouds. A beautiful photo of Mrs. Kerr was enclosed in a silver frame. Taken on her wedding day, she looked like an angel. Long hair of finely spun copper. A garland of pretty blue and white flowers on her head. A wispy white dress as delicate as a spider web after a soft rain.

In front of the window memorial, a homeless man with a twisted upper lip strummed his battered guitar covered with various stickers. "Occupy This," read one, accompanied by a rude gesture. Wild, filthy orange dreadlocks spilled from beneath a stained Angels baseball cap. He asked passers-by for spare change. A red velvet-lined guitar case was wide open, a few bills and coins scattered inside. I threw in three coins that clinked as each fell into the case. When I looked back to see him again, he'd disappeared.

With less than two thousand residents, I recognized most people gathered in Hastings Square, including older generations of the Coven, members who'd mentored their children and children's children, passing responsibilities from one generation to the next.

Politely sending us a nod and a wave, Giselle Bassett and her youngest sibling, Henry, stood nearby. Mrs. Kerr's death could adversely affect business in town, especially Kerr's, Cameron's, the Food Garden, and the Bassett family's Matterhorn. Snow Valley seemed peaceful, but was not immune to crime. The responsibility of Snow Valley's pristine image rested on the shoulders of Mayor Albrecht Kanz, nervously preparing his address, tapping and testing and adjusting a screeching microphone at his official-looking podium marked with the town's coat of arms.

From the top of Snow Valley Town Hall's rustic wooden steps, with Chiefs Curry and Walker by his side, Mayor Kanz fielded questions, besieged by angry residents demanding full disclosure of the murder and a speedy arrest.

A large, boisterous crowd filled the square. Some voices shouted, others mumbled complaints. All shared the same sentiment: profound anger.

"My business is gonna suffer," bellowed Mr. Baumann, owner of Snow Valley Drive-In.

"It's like that Grimesby girl all over again," gruffly shouted Albert Assam, his wife Angie by his side shaking her head. They had closed their barbershop and hair salon to attend.

Mayor Kanz pleaded with the enraged crowd, begging residents to stay calm, and to allow the police to continue the murder investigation. The Mayor asked residents to report any suspicious activity they'd noticed over the past few days.

Struggling to pull a cooler on wheels through the angry crowd, a strange looking woman wearing a long black dress and a black veil draped around her head and spilling around her shoulders, gestured toward her cooler. Some shook their heads politely or dismissed her like an annoying mosquito or ignored her completely.

The woman held up bottled water above her veiled head. "You vant drink?" She spoke quickly, in a thick accent. Her eyes sparkled, lined heavily in charcoal.

A man's brusque voice rose above the noisy crowd. The voice I'd heard on television. The one that had asked Chief Walker about the local girl with long dark hair leaving the police station. This time, the untidily dressed reporter held a megaphone in one hand, a tattered notepad in the other.

"When're you gonna tell us the truth? When're you gonna reveal the name of that girl leavin' the station? I saw her being driven away in a beat up ole' Land Cruiser. Know the one I mean?"

Chief Walker exchanged a nervous glance with Chief Curry, sharing unspoken thoughts. Mayor Kanz wore a confused look on his spray-tanned face.

Knots filled my stomach, ice rushed through my veins.

"Yeah, thought so," continued Coop the Scoop, nodding his head smugly. "Anyone else know who I'm talkin' 'bout?"

"That's gotta be Ranger Goode's truck," someone shouted.

"Yeah, Emeranne's dad," shrilled others.

"Figures she'd be caught up in this mess," agreed others, nodding their heads.

"Ranger Jack's here…I just seen him," said a bossy junior from Snow Valley High.

People in the crowd twisted their heads this way and that. From the sidewalk, I saw Dad's tall frame above the throng of people who, by now, formed a circle around him.

"Let's get Ems outta here," urged Byron, my personal bodyguard, guiding me toward the cleaners and shoving me through the wooden front door so hard I almost tripped.

Carlton pulled out his cell phone as he ran to Mr. and Mrs. Garcia, speaking in hushed tones. Mr. Garcia locked the front door, turned the Closed sign around and drew the blinds. I stood dumbfounded, my feet glued to the shiny black tiled floor.

"Your dad's on his way," Carlton told me, having received a text message.

The crowd chanted my name. *Ems Goode! Ems Goode!*

This was a modern day witch hunt.

"Like mother, like daughter," a woman screamed, her voice so loud it carried through the dry cleaner's windows.

"Apple doesn't fall far from the tree," another agreed.

"Ems, we'll do a quick boundary spell and keep the Coven safe." Morgan pulled my hand into a circle. Selene scribbled various symbols upon the floor inside the circle with Mrs. Garcia's white tailor's chalk. She chanted incantations, spilled chunks of salt Mr. Garcia stored for the sidewalks in winter, making small circles and wavy lines and piles of various sizes. In a trance, Selene lifted her head and hands to the ceiling, swayed and turned around and spun until she fell to her knees, shaking.

The Coven chanted, too, at first in a whisper, then louder and more intense until the invocation was complete.

"Quick, Ems, change clothes with me," urged Morgan, jerking her head toward the bathroom. I didn't ask questions, removed my worn red Forty-Niners hoodie, and exchanged mine with Morgan's T-shirt. She rushed out the bathroom door to the front of the store with the hood pulled over her head.

"Over here," instructed Carlton, holding the back door open for me. A police cruiser waited in front of the Matterhorn. "Ems, you're going to Moonridge for the summer," was all he said.

Chapter Three

Headlines

EMERANNE

"Get in," ordered the officer seated on the passenger's side.

I opened the back door, jumped in and slammed the door, never daring to look back as the cruiser raced away. Although I didn't see anyone near the Matterhorn, I had a strange feeling I'd been watched by those silver eyes I saw again and again and again in the Dream. Watched from the silence of the forest. Watched by the eyes of the ancient trees, trees that guarded many secrets of those who'd passed through the forest's charcoal doors toward its shadowy crypt of mysteries.

Hastings Square disappeared as the cruiser turned the corner and headed out of town.

I'd never felt more alone in my life.

One of the officers looked over his shoulder when I'd snorted a little louder than I'd intended. That's because my powers showed vans parked on the side of Snow Valley Mountain Road, where eager reporters waited outside for my imminent arrival in Dad's now-infamous Land Cruiser. Except, of course, it was Morgan in my hoodie instead of me.

When the police cruiser turned off the highway, my anxiety decreased.

It took about an hour for the cruiser to approach the impoverished reservation. Welcome To Moonridge, Home Of The Serrano Nation, read the green and white road sign. The cruiser passed a store where tourists mingled, looking at traditional crafts hand-made by Serrano women using the same methods passed down from previous generations.

Minutes later, the cruiser turned onto a gravel driveway and parked in front of a small home with wooden siding stained dark brown. My cousin, River Vale, waited on the porch, seated on a rough timber bench. As soon as River saw the cruiser, he ran toward it, and opened the cruiser's back door. I waved to the officers as the cruiser backed out of the driveway.

River hugged me and said, "Good to see you, Ems."

"You too," I said.

"Wish it was under better circumstances."

I sighed. "Yeah. Me too. And it's been too long. How are things with you?"

"I'm a smokejumper now," River said proudly. His piercing black eyes and gorgeous copper skin tones shimmered in the daylight, as if his skin were on fire.

River's Serrano ancestors were renowned for their fearless abilities to climb towering trees, scale steep mountainsides in Snow Valley County, jump from helicopters, and skydive effortlessly—without experiencing any symptoms of vertigo. Many Serranos were recruited by the local fire department and trained as smokejumpers, or in the case of River's late father, Basil, joined Snow Valley Mountain Search and Rescue team.

Dad's mother, Rosemary St. Marie and Basil's mother, Sage St. Marie, were sisters who were born and raised in the same house where Rainn Vale now struggled to raise six children on her own. Basil's photo, taken in traditional Serrano costume, hung on the livingroom wall's faded green and brown wallpaper. Dad helped Rainn as much as he could on his limited salary.

Rainn made extra money weaving baskets and spinning clay for hand painted pottery just like her mother did before her.

However, smokejumping or traditional crafts weren't the Serranos only talents. Members of the Serrano Nation kept the traditional belief that their deceased ancestors reincarnated as grizzly bears, thought long extinct in California.

But not in the proud nation's view, or in the Snow Valley Coven's experience.

They were Den Born, who with the help of their ancestors, for centuries protected consecutive Snow Valley Covens, guiding the only creature able to destroy immortal witch hunters—a gigantic grizzly bear, its claws able to shred, its long teeth able to crush, maul and destroy witch hunters. Until Violet—and now.

Serrano legend holds that departed ancestors reincarnate as Spirit Bears. Whenever the Den Born's Scent picks up an immortal witch hunter's presence, the Den Born gather in the Elders' Spirit Lodge. The Elders form a drumming circle around younger, stronger Den Born–including River and Byron–to guide them on their Dream Journey. This journey takes the Den Born on a quest. Each Den Born visualizes meeting one of his or her ancestors, and asks the Spirit Bear to find and destroy the witch hunter. One by one, the young Den Born mount Spirit Bears and from that moment on, the grizzly takes over.

River got right to the point. "What's up with the Coven's Ice Vision?"

I shrugged. "What about the Scent?"

"No idea, Ems," he said, his deep bass voice sad. "The Elders seek guidance from their ancestors, but so far have no answers."

"I wasn't supposed to be there, you know, Dad warned me not to go there, but I did anyway." I choked back tears. "And now, everything's a mess."

"It'll pass, Ems."

"I hope so."

"But how could this happen? It's so infuriating," scowled River through clenched teeth, "Why didn't the Scent warn me about the hunter's snare? The filthy hunter responsible will be sorry," he fumed. "I promise."

"That's what Byron said," I told him. "Something more like tearing the hunter to shreds."

"Yeah, I'll be happy to help," River answered.

My cousins welcomed me with warmth and affection. Except for daily conversations with River, my cousins never asked questions about the Lookout Murder. The oldest of six children, nineteen-year-old River rarely let me out of his sight. His younger siblings watched over me when River left early for work.

Twelve-year-old Woods, the youngest of the Vales, did the yard work while his four older sisters helped their mother, Rainn Vale, with chores. I pitched in, except for cooking. Much to my embarrassment, even the youngest sister, Cedar, told me I'd be doing them all a favor if I stayed out of the kitchen.

Like the Snow Valley Coven, the Den Born met regularly in the Spirit Lodge to discuss this dilemma, but none could sense what had stifled their keen powers of detection for tracking witch hunters. River thought it best for me to avoid these discussions, carried out in the Spirit Lodge. I agreed. I didn't want to be reminded of the horrid fire that took Charlsie Kerr's life. Or the fact that none of us saw it, had premonition about it, or could stop it.

The Dream haunted me on my first night in Moonridge. This time, a girl lay beside the boy. Her face was a windowpane on a rainy day, dripping with water and foggy with steam. I pressed my hands against the glass, misty from my warm breath, and hoped her face would appear when the rain stopped. Waiting for both faces to come into focus.

Storm woke me, held me, caressed my hair and reassured me, "It's a dream. Only a dream, Ems." But I wasn't convinced.

One afternoon, while waiting for River at Moonridge's only gas station, I read the headline through the *Moonridge Mail* newspaper box window: GOODE RIDDANCE, it said.

Snow Valley's sole witness to the Lookout Murder skips town. Reliable sources say she has gone into hiding, fearful for her life, read the caption below my freshman school photo that, like most school photos, wasn't the most flattering.

"Ignore it, Ems," advised River, leading me away gently by my clenched fist.

Apart from chores, I passed the time going for short walks around the reservation. My dad called me daily but didn't say much about the Lookout Murder.

"Get your mind cleared before school," he encouraged.

Selene visited regularly, a pattern that wouldn't be considered unusual or raise suspicion as she and River had been dating for over a year. So no curious reporter followed her. Selene updated me on the latest news to prepare me for September—the dreaded month of my return to Snow Valley High.

My Ice Born power of premonition, the Ice Vision, warned me Cooper Kozalski and throngs of other reporters waited eagerly to interview me. At summer's end, Coop the Scoop discovered my hideout. I don't know how he did, but he did. By then, it was time to go home, back to school, back to reality, back to Principal Lipschitz's accusing eyes glaring through his pince-nez.

River drove me home in his family's rusty two-toned tan and brown Volkswagen van. The day was young, sunny and warm. The last day of August. I rolled down the window, stretched my neck, and breathed in the pine-scented air. The Lookout Murder seemed far away, until I spotted a car following the van.

"What the—"

"Ems?"

"How did he find me?"

"Who?"

"Coop the Scoop."

River looked in the rear view mirror. Cooper Kozalski's beat up yellow Mustang convertible was close behind. Every time River accelerated, so did Coop.

"Don't bother, River. He won't give up. Let me take care of him." I imagined the Mustang ran out of gas, or its muffler dragging on the road, or both.

Minutes later, River looked in the rear view mirror again and chuckled. "Looks like we lost him, Ems. Car trouble or something." He winked. "Nice one."

I looked over my shoulder. Sure enough, Coop the Scoop stood outside his car on the highway's gravel shoulder, hat in one hand, scratching his messy hair with the other.

As River approached my home, dozens of reporters waited at the end of the our driveway, none permitted on the property where the log cabin was set deep behind thick stands of pines. I rolled up my window. River turned off Snow Valley Mountain Road. Reporters surrounded the van, competed for a spot at my window. "Ms Goode! Ms Goode!"

I turned to River. "Someone tipped off Coop and the other reporters, I bet."

"Who would do that?"

I shrugged. "Dunno."

River slowed the van down to avoid hitting reporters, who posed many questions as the van inched forward.

"Is it true you found Mrs Kerr barely alive?"

"What were her last words?"

"Can you confirm you've identified the killer?"

"What's your comment on Cooper Kozalski's latest exclusive?"

"Ignore them, Ems," said River, as calm as usual. "It'll pass."

"It's harder than you think River," I confessed. "And I've turned Dad's life upside down."

"Don't beat yourself up. Jack's got thick skin. And we're gonna find that vile monster who did this to Charlsie."

River dropped me off, gave my arm a reassuring pat and left for work. I heard reporters shouting my name.

Dad waited for me at the front door. Matt and Geneva barked and wagged their tails.

Dad frowned. "Damn reporters and their huge lenses. Coop the Scoop warned Chief Walker he's gonna leak another exclusive by Labor Day. Wouldn't name the source, he said, keepin' it confidential, to protect the source. Source my—" Dad bit off the sentence, but his disgust was evident. As predicted, the Labor Day *Sunday Standard* had another Coop the Scoop exclusive citing sources close to the investigation.

GOODE GRIEF read the latest headline. *History has a strange way of repeating…began the article. Nowhere is this maxim more evident than in Snow Valley, an idyllic alpine village with dark secrets. Secrets from its haunted past. Under tragic circumstances, a hitherto mysterious girl on a solo ride up one of the mountain trails came across a local resident, Charlsie Kerr, who lost her life in a devastating fire on imposing Snow Valley Mountain…*

Graphically, the article described Mrs. Kerr's lifeless body. The valiant efforts to contain the fire. And my presence.

"Put your life in danger, that moron and two-bit paper," Dad said, his voice hard.

Chiefs Curry and Walker were furious, too.

But that's not all. Coop the Scoop went farther.

Emeranne Goode is said to be distraught and heavily medicated after witnessing the horrific murder at Bellavista Lookout. The Chief Medical Examiner's official autopsy confirms the victim was tortured. One source claims Ms. Goode sat frozen with fear as the dreadful scene played out before her eyes. Other sources close to the fifteen-year-old describe her state of mind as 'unstable' and 'unpredictable'. Ms. Goode has not provided a statement of what she witnessed. To make matters worse, by an ineffable twist of fate, Ms. Goode's biological mother, Johanna 'Jo' Campbell of New York City, found herself in the same circumstances two decades ago. Ms. Campbell discovered the burned and mutilated body of Violet Grimesby in exactly the same location as her daughter's discovery twenty years on.

Neither Ms. Goode nor Ms. Campbell was available for comment.

"Liar!" I screamed, throwing the paper down after scanning the article.

"I know, Ems."

"I wasn't hiding! I'm not heavily medicated either. Distraught, sure. Who wouldn't be?"

"I know, Ems," Dad repeated. "As long as he doesn't dig too far. Find out about the Coven. And when the Coven meets, make sure no one can listen in."

"Dad, do you think that…that…Mom…"

"What Ems? That your mom heard about the murder?"

"Yeah, just curious. And Mom is mentioned in the article, too, so maybe she read about it online."

"Don't think about it, Ems."

"Yeah, I know, but sometimes I wonder…"

"Me too, Ems. Me too."

Swayed by Coop the Scoop's article, Mayor Kanz requested an interview. "Forthwith," demanded the Mayor, according to Dad, who refused to return the Mayor's phone calls.

Following the publication of Cooper Kozalski's exclusive, residents panicked. Although Chief Walker knew the likely killer was a witch hunter, his duty was first and foremost to serve and protect the public. His office was flooded with anonymous tips after a ten thousand dollar reward for credible leads was offered. But no arrests were made, no suspects identified.

Outrageous stories circulated in the newspapers, on blogs and social media sites, quoting statements I'd never made. One even claimed I was involved in a devil-worshipping cult and ran away, unable to take responsibility for the ritual killing.

More important to sell newspapers than to report the truth, I fumed silently.

On Labor Day, Mayor Kanz held another emergency meeting, this time inside the town hall. I didn't dare show my face. According to Dad, tempers flared. Parents demanded a resolution to the Lookout Murder before their children returned to school. Otherwise, they'd insist on resignations from Mayor Kanz and Chief Walker. A mob atmosphere filled the circular council chambers, filled to capacity with irate taxpayers.

Morgan texted me that a cell phone video of the meeting was uploaded on YouTube.

A series of angry remarks were shouted from the crowd. "You weren't elected to sit around and twirl your thumbs."

"Your investigation is a joke!"

"Gotta rely on reporters to keep us in the loop."

"Summer's almost over and we ain't got nothin' figured out, no one arrested."

"Where's that Goode girl? Let's hear what she's got to say for herself!"

The insults continued until everyone had their turn at the

microphone. In the end, Mayor Kanz and Chief Walker promised more transparency, increased patrols and an accelerated investigation, though I wasn't sure what more could be done to find a witch hunter.

Finally, Dad walked up to the microphone. The entire crowd fell silent. He confirmed I'd found Mrs. Kerr, but reassured residents I wasn't a witness or on medication. He'd appreciate if everyone would leave me alone. And encouraged everyone not to believe everything they read.

"You all know me and my dedication to the people of this town. I give you my word, Emeranne is goin' through hell. Please, leave her be."

I had the first day of my junior year to think about. I knew I'd get odd looks at school. Looks that said, *there's Emeranne again, the freak who discovered Mrs. Kerr's dead body.*

On Tuesday morning, I showered and changed into faded jeans and a T-shirt and wrapped my old Forty-Niners hoodie around my hips, the one that Dad's brother, Uncle Vince, gave me a few years ago, the same hoodie Morgan wore to divert the relentless press.

My pencil case was still in my old navy backpack from freshman year. All I'd need were gym shorts, runners, tank top. I picked up my backpack from my bedroom's wooden floor. I paused on the landing to look over my shoulder at Mom's locked studio door. Were answers to my many questions surrounding Charlsie's death held behind that door, I wondered? I didn't have time this morning, but kept that thought in the back of my mind.

Downstairs, I found a note on the harvest table.

Ems,
Picked up your class schedule
Bought you a new notebook and bike helmet

Recharged your cell
Left money for lunch
Be extra careful
    Love
        Dad, Matt & Geneva

I gulped down a heaping bowl of Sugar Crisps and milk and put my bowl, spoon and glass in the dishwasher. And paused to spin the kitchen witch hanging at the window.

With my overflowing backpack slung on one shoulder, my new bike helmet in one hand–I'd lost mine in the fire–and the new notebook, I rushed out the door, determined to be early on my first day of school. I always rode my mountain bike to school until Snow Valley's early winter made biking impossible.

The bike ride down the mountain was my favorite part of the day. When brisk morning air slapped my face, when little fluffy clouds resembling melted marshmallows on twigs by the campfire drifted across a banana yellow sun, when green shades resembling abstract murals swooshed by – neon sorbet, sweet pea, crunchy celery, emerald forest, honeydew jade, citrus lime, blackened olive – sharing gallery space with distinct signs of autumn. I imagined beautiful colors soon to come, colors like Twizzler red and golden egg yolk, pumpkin orange and gingersnap rust, toasted marshmallow and indigo ink.

Vivid layers of sun-kissed brown, golden sunflower and bonfire red dyed the crisp early light. I reached the steamy cloudbank and veered toward my short cut, sailing past more trees. Mustard toned oaks, stands of tall regal pine, rippling poplar leaves. With challenging inclines, sudden dips and tricky curves, the bumpy ride continued south to the school's backyard.

I loved the rush from riding down these hills, the feeling that left my stomach behind at the hill's brow long after I'd descended, the sweet scent of damp pine needles.

Within minutes, far from the mountain's white frosted peaks, Snow Valley High's cedar-shingled roof came into view. The main building was a single story post and beam wooden structure, its grounds lovingly maintained to preserve the surrounding natural beauty. The school occupied a former hunting lodge originally owned by A. Watson Hastings, a Texan oil magnate, who built the lodge a century ago for private guests.

High ceilings, honey brown walls, floor to roof windows and a warm, inviting lounge area with a fieldstone fireplace created more of a resort atmosphere than formal learning environment. The lodge's dining hall and study were the school's cafeteria and library, moonlighting as Snow Valley's only banquet hall and public library. Wooden lockers lined the main lodge's rustic hallways. Outdoors, several single-room sleep cabins were transformed into small classrooms, big enough for one long table and two benches. A blackboard hung behind each teacher's plain wooden desk and chair.

My pace slowed as I veered toward the school's bicycle parking and raised my chin to the sky, transformed from ice blue to ominous purple.

In the main lodge's foyer hung the portrait of A. Watson Hastings, smoking a huge cigar and posing with his favorite hunting dog, a bloodhound named Caligula. The built-in glass cases lining both sides of the foyer were filled with Snow Valley High's vast collection of athletic awards. Despite a small student body, the school was home to the nationally ranked Wizards football team. Homecoming week was a big deal. Every September, alumni returned for the annual game against Big Bear High Grizzlies.

It was a habit of mine to start the day admiring one trophy in particular, made of wood and metal. A statue of a Wizard holding a football in one arm and wand in the other, sat on three wooden layers, around which a number of gold stars were engraved with the names of former football players. John 'Jack' Goode Jr MVP was engraved on one of those stars. The framed color glossy photo next to the trophy was Dad's unmistakable face smiling back at me.

I zipped my backpack open to retrieve my class schedule. Locker number one-thirteen, near the main office, so Principal Lipschitz could keep his beady eyes on me. I groaned.

Late last night, an Ice Vision warned me what I was in for today. Fortunately, my Coven knew the truth about Charlsie Kerr. Unfortunately, those facts could never be reported.

I closed my locker and sighed, not quite ready to face the day.

Chapter Four

Sketch

BENNETT

"Bennett!" I turned at the sound of my name. My cousin Wallis Bassett caught up with me, and we headed to the art room. I sensed Emeranne's presence behind me, setting up her easel and casting furtive glances in my direction when she thought no one was looking.

I arrived in Snow Valley at the beginning of summer, shortly before the murder. I'd felt bad for her when she couldn't leave her house after Mrs. Kerr's murder, confined to the little isolated log cabin on the mountain. It wasn't fair. But I knew that life wasn't fair. And I should know, condemned as I'd been to this existence, an existence I'd never wanted, never anticipated. Death would have been better.

Seven centuries ago, I died. Died on scorching sand, the day a burning sun perched high in the clear blue sky. The day when a sea breeze coated my throat with brine and salt and stroked my legs, back and forth, back and forth.

I'd died but wasn't brought back to life. Instead, I'd been cursed for an eternity. An eternal existence with no end, no limit, no boundaries of time or space. My existence couldn't be compared to anything known to humankind. It wasn't really life—and yet it was.

I was an anomaly, a mathematical equation without a solution. An experiment without a resolution. An immortal without boundaries. Mortals, I thought, were so damn lucky. Mortals knew about life—and death, theirs a finite time on earth.

I read the newspaper articles all summer long, followed the unwarranted and occasional outrageous suspicions surrounding Emeranne, a girl who'd ridden her bike up Snow Valley Mountain on a warm summer day. That should have been it. The end of her day, her story.

Just a teenage girl on a mountain bike, celebrating freedom from school. Instead, she'd discovered the burning body of Charlsie Kerr.

A mother, wife, daughter, aunt, niece, friend. A witch. A dead witch.

And a member of the Coven, just like her son, Leland Kerr.

Customers at the Matterhorn gossiped all summer long about the Lookout Murder and didn't hide their suspicions about Emeranne. The things they said. Accused her of. I wanted to yell out at the top of my lungs, *It wasn't her fault!* But I couldn't. So the gossip continued.

I don't know how Emeranne kept it together on the first day of school, how she remained stoic and strong, knowing students whispered behind her back. Or said what they felt without bothering to whisper when she passed their lockers in the hallway. Emeranne was at once mystifying and uncomplicated, a shattered vase without visible cracks.

One reporter was unduly harsh. His aggressive pursuit of Emeranne worried me. I'd have to keep close tabs on Cooper Kozalski. I needed to keep a watchful eye on her, knowing she was more than just a girl on a mountain bike celebrating summer holidays. Much, much more…

Students whispered about retired Mrs. Summerhill's replacement as the new teacher walked into the classroom wearing tan leather boots and a matching wrap dress that showed off her petite frame. I raised my eyebrows. *Nice.* Wallis kicked my leg and glared. I returned a *what? I didn't do anything* glance.

The new teacher's smile was pure poetry. "My name is Ms Beltane. Welcome to junior art class. It's a great pleasure to be Snow Valley High's newest teacher."

Ms. Beltane discussed art supplies required–brushes, paints, palettes, sketchpads, canvases–and reviewed basic techniques. Boys gazed longingly at Ms. Beltane, spellbound by her attractive caramel colored eyes, her chic lipstick, a soft neutral shade, her shimmering complexion, dark and mystifying. "Fat chance, guys," I mumbled. Wallis kicked my leg again and gave me one of her *be civil or else* looks. I shot her an exaggerated smile.

There was something familiar about the new teacher. Hmmm. Let me think. I sniffed the air discreetly. A vaguely familiar scent was distributed by an open window breeze, a scent that always brought me back to southern India, a mix of jasmine and patchouli maybe? A woman I'd met in Keralia wore the same scent. A women I'd met in the eighteen eighties.

She was the exact opposite of how Wallis had described the retired art teacher. Mrs. Summerhill smelled of faded roses and wore a shade of red lipstick that made her teeth look yellow. Dirty tissues dropped to the floor from the sleeves of her old-fashioned synthetic dresses, usually in big flowery prints that made her look like the overstuffed sofas and wing chairs arranged around the fireplace at the old Bassett pub, the Fox and Hound, in Stratford-Upon-Avon.

The Bassetts were the only family I had, but we didn't always travel as a group. It was too noticeable to have the same family appear together, but we always managed to keep in touch.

No matter where I went or what lives I lived, I always came back to be with them.

When you've lived as long as I have, school won't be at the top of the priority list. Not even the bottom. In fact, school wasn't on my list at all. Snowboarding, mountain climbing, skydiving, bungee jumping without the bungee, those were *definitely* on my list. The more dangerous the better.

Usually we pretended I was home schooled, but that would have made us appear strange in Snow Valley. One thing immortals learn early is that appearing strange can get you in a lot of trouble. So, here I am, back in high school.

Snow Valley was a popular vacation spot in the winter. In this lifetime, the Bassetts owned the Matterhorn Pizza Parlor where I worked after school and on weekends, waiting tables, bussing, washing dishes, mopping the floor, putting out the garbage and delivering pizza. I rarely skied on weekends because the Matterhorn was way too busy and the phone didn't stop ringing for take out.

I yawned, wondering how I was going to get through one more school day. And this was only the first day of junior year. I twirled the dark ring on my right hand.

Boredom shifted my gaze around the classroom. Big mistake. From across the room, Kandida and Alba Kanz batted their fake eyelashes and tossed toothy smiles in my direction. They were so annoying. Following me around at school and eating at the Matterhorn all summer. Girls like that made me regret coming to school, but I had no choice in the matter. *To avoid suspicion*, Allora reminded me, almost daily.

What's another day when I've had so many?

The Kanz twins always stared. I knew that look. Puppy love, high school crush, starry-eyed adoration. Every Saturday night, they ate at the same booth, ordered the same gluten free crust, zero calorie soda, frozen vanilla yogurt parfait. And they waited for me, sometimes for hours, until my shift was over, hoping I'd join them at a midnight showing of a stupid romantic chick flick playing at Snow Valley Cinema.

And every Saturday night, I gave them the same response: tired, busy, working early the next morning. Or my cousins covered for me and made up lame excuses, saving me from the agony of spending more than one minute around the twins' screeching, high-pitched voices. But they didn't give up, constantly competing for my attention, pushing one another out of the way to sit closer to me, flirting and giggling. I mean, they practically threw themselves at me.

It's partly my fault, I have to admit, because sometimes, just for laughs, I flirted back. I know I know, it was kinda mean of me but hey, a guy needed to have a bit of fun once in a while around here.

"For today's assignment you are required to sketch how you see yourself, your own image," instructed Ms. Beltane. For the remainder of the class, the only sounds comprised of black pencils scratching and crosshatching and smudging on paper.

I leaned down and reached into my knapsack for my leather bound journal and thumbed through to a blank page. I used the journal to record some of my deepest, darkest thoughts. Sometimes my entries were just prose, but other times a form of poetry ran through me and I had to write it down. I flipped back to one of my drawings, the outline of a girl with long hair. Over the centuries, her outfits changed–peasant dresses, Elizabethan collars, Antoinette wigs, Victorian ball gowns, and oddly, armor and chainmail–but one feature remained the same. She didn't have any defined facial features. I'd tried to see the face, but I couldn't. When I'd added features, they never fit.

How did I see myself? Should I be honest and draw a monster?

When I'd finished a rough outline in my journal, I wrote

48

four words beneath the sketch and put the pencil down on the easel's tray.

i

My hand seemed disconnected from my mind. I don't know where this drawing came from. Even so, I drew a more detailed version on the art paper. I scratched and smudged. As I drew, somehow I felt Emeranne's eyes on me, stealing innocent looks between easels.

am

Wallis sneezed and turned to me. For a moment I put my pencil down, pulled out a white handkerchief from my pocket and handed it to her, then resumed drawing.

a

A chair scraped the floor behind me. From the corner of my eye, I watched Emeranne shift in her chair and take a peek at my sketch. She gasped and dropped her pencil that bounced a few times and rolled until it stopped under my easel.

I didn't think my sketch was *that* bad.

Why did Emeranne drop her pencil? Did my drawing upset Emeranne and if so why? I looked over at Wallis and raised my eyebrows. She opened her mouth slightly and dropped her chin as discreetly as possible. I looked at my sketch again. Had Emeranne guessed what I was? Had she seen the part mortals didn't see, the secret part, hidden deep inside?

The part no one saw except me. I leaned down and picked up Emeranne's pencil. Slowly, I turned around and extended my arm toward her. The look on her face reflected what I already knew. The look summed up in one word.

monster

Chapter Five

Snakes of Fire

EMERANNE

Emeranne. I heard my name whispered behind me. The sound seemed to echo from every surface of the room. I couldn't close my ears to the whispers. The strange looks in the hallways didn't stop. What were they looking at? Did they think I wanted to discover a murder? Finally, the buzzer blared, signaling the end of morning classes. I fished for lunch money in my backpack and entered the cafeteria's windowless lobby through one of two archways on either side of the dining hall's massive wooden doors. In what was once a fancy lounge for guests to gather and engage in light conversation and pre-dinner drinks, the expansive room remained much like it had in those days, surrounded by warm wood paneling. Upholstered benches ran all along the paneled walls, from corner to corner.

I raised my chin and turned my head back and forth along the wall where framed black and white photos hung, photos of the original lounge. Women wore elegant evening gowns and elbow length gloves. Their hair was pinned up with jewel-encrusted combs. Their gloves, covered with sparkling bracelets and chunky rings, held pencil thin cigarette holders and fragile looking glasses shaped like half moons on the tip of an icicle.

Women raised their glasses, their flawless faces giddy. I could almost hear their laughter and clinking glasses.

Standing at the bar directly opposite the dining room doors, men in tuxedos smoked cigars and raised tumblers to their lips. Many photos featured A. Watson Hastings leaning against the bar, eyes closed and mouth wide open—apparently engaged in jovial conversation or some hilarious joke—puffing on a long cigar. Rings of pale smoke travelled above the bar.

Today, A. Watson Hastings and his cigars and scotch and guests and long bar were replaced with No Smoking signs, water fountains, screeching students and more padded bench seats where the bar used to be. That's where I sat, amid growing chatter, waiting for my friends until the dining hall's massive wooden doors opened. The entrance hall rapidly filled with hungry students, many of whom lowered their voices when they spotted me sitting alone.

I leaned left, then right, hoping for a glimpse of my friends. Within minutes, Ardelle and Morgan entered from the left archway, Selene from the right, sidling around small clusters of huddled students.

"At back on bench," read my text message to Morgan.

Carlton, Leland and Bryon followed Gareth, who carved a pathway toward me as students politely moved out of his way. When the dining hall doors opened, I bought my lunch and joined the Coven at our usual round table as far away from other students as possible. The table pushed up against tall windows that framed a perfect view of green and brown dappled sunlight streaming through rippling leaves and russet tree trunks.

In hushed tones, I recounted the uncanny resemblance of Bennett's sketch to the boy in my dream.

"Or *wished* it was him," teased Byron.

Morgan leaned toward me. "Are you still having the same dream?"

"Yeah," I answered. "Ever since the blizzard."

Gareth wheeled his chair sideways to face me. "Ems, exactly which blizzard might that be, if you don't mind me asking?"

"Uh, the one, you know, the one when I stopped the transport."

Ardelle gasped. "Are you sure it's the same boy?"

"*Shhhhh*, keep your voice down!" Morgan whispered.

"The lunchroom is pretty noisy, don't worry," Carlton assured her.

"Still, you can't be too careful," she replied quietly.

"You're right, Morgan," agreed Carlton.

Ardelle lowered her voice and asked me again. "Are you sure the boy in your dream is similar to Bennett's sketch?"

"Yeah," I replied, adding, "I hope I'm wrong."

"He actually sketched the same boy in your dreams?" Carlton kept probing.

"As opposed to the boy *of* your dreams," joked Byron.

"That's enough for today, Byron." Morgan frowned and tightened her mouth.

Carlton closed his eyes and pressed his fingertips together. "It is possible, after all Bennett is new to Snow Valley." The Coven shook their heads and sat silently.

"We need to consult the Spirits," said Selene in a tone grittier than usual.

"Something we should've done months ago," said Leland.

"Are you sure you're ready?" Carlton raised his eyebrows.

Ardelle adjusted her horn-rimmed glasses and tossed her thick red hair. Rays of sunshine spilled through the panes of glass, setting her hair on fire. "Wouldn't we raise suspicion? What if we attract the hunter somehow? What if—"

"What if you *relax* for once?" Byron said to her. "We don't even know for sure it *is* a hunter."

"Byron, you know how Ardelle gets during times like this," Morgan said.

"Yeah, don't I," he grumbled. Morgan shot him a quick look and he backed off.

"We can't wait any longer," said Carlton firmly. "It must be done."

"Agreed," confirmed Selene. "We have no other choice."

"Agreed," Ardelle echoed, though her sad eyes were trained on Leland.

"So, are we all in agreement?" Carlton asked. No one disagreed. "Okay then."

"Let's meet tonight at my place," I suggested. "Dad's been working late ever since…" I left unfinished what I was about to say, *ever since Mrs. Kerr's death.*

Leland's mouth twitched. "It's okay. I know she's…she's gone."

Carlton drew a long, long breath. "Are you ready to—?"

"Yes," replied Leland. "I'll have what you need."

The buzzer sounded. Lunch was over.

Selene broke the sad, lonely silence. "So after school? At Ems'?"

"Tonight." Morgan nodded.

"Tonight," Carlton repeated.

Byron carried a stack of pizza boxes stamped the Matterhorn into the house. Morgan and Ardelle set the long kitchen harvest table with plates and cutlery and glasses. With a hungry look in his eyes, Byron flipped one of the pizza boxes open.

"This one's mine," he declared. "*All* mine!"

"Just pass the rest around, will ya?" Gareth teased. "Before you eat every single piece!"

"Bennett and Wallis were working," said Leland.

"Ems, I have a message for you," Byron said. "'Tell Emeranne that Bennett says hi.'"

"Ems, you have a new admirer." Ardelle giggled.

I shrugged, pretending to be disinterested.

"Bennett and Wallis look more like twins than cousins," commented Gareth.

Ardelle nodded. "They could be twins *and* models, they're both so tall and athletic looking, both have dark brown curly hair. Except hers is so long."

"What about the rest of them? How well does anyone know the Bassetts?" asked Selene.

Byron looked up and said, "They're kinda quiet, and work a lot at the Matterhorn."

"We know Henry from football practice," Leland said. "He's a nice guy."

"He's the freshman, the new cornerback, cracks me up," added Byron.

"Not like the oldest sister, you know the one I'm talking about? The one who manages the Matterhorn," I said.

"Miranda," said Selene. "Ems is right, she's not so friendly."

"That's for sure," agreed Ardelle. "I always say hi to her at the Matterhorn, and she just stares at me."

"Eat up everyone," urged Selene, switching gears. "It's almost spell time."

In between chews and sips of soda, the Coven talked about the dilemma: why wasn't an Ice Vision triggered? Were there any rational explanations? Possible theories?

"And let's not forget the Scent didn't work for the Serranos, either. Something's definitely wrong," I reminded them.

"Yeah, what's the deal with Scent, Byron? River told me no one in Moonridge was warned," asked Selene. "Any thoughts?"

"Nothing. Absolutely nothing," growled Byron.

"Then again, have the Ice Born always been warned?"

Ardelle asked.

"No, not always," Morgan said, then, "don't forget about Violet Grimesby twenty years ago."

Leland's head was bent over his plate of untouched pizza. "And my mom."

With one index finger on his temple, Carlton asked, "Our Ice Vision hasn't warned the Coven of any danger posed by the Bassetts, has it?"

"No, not that I know of, but I can only speak for myself," replied Selene.

"Why would they have anything to do with…" Morgan's voice trailed off. For an extended moment, the Coven sat silently, mulling those unspoken words.

"Is it because of the sketch?" I asked.

"Yeah. Maybe. I don't know," answered a frustrated Gareth.

"Leland," I said gently. "If this is too much, too soon—"

He shook his head. "We have to find out…so, so others won't die. Our only choice is to find these damn murderers."

Rising, Selene rubbed her hands together and asked, "Did anyone prepare the fire?"

Byron smacked his forehead. "Crap," he said and darted out kitchen door. Minutes later, his massive arms were loaded with firewood.

Ardelle and Morgan cleared the plates and cups on the harvest table and loaded the dishwasher. I boiled a pot of water. Byron turned to Ardelle and said, "The flue is open. Now do your thing."

Ardelle's hazel eyes lit up and her freckled nose wrinkled. She dashed to the livingroom and waved her hands. The logs burst into flames. Balls of paper curled blue and orange and black. Bark on the logs crackled and hissed.

Byron whistled. "I never get tired of watching that!"

Firefly

The Coven gathered around the fieldstone fireplace. The faintest splinter of moonlight found its way through the livingroom curtains.

"Leland," whispered Morgan. "Do you have—?"

"Yeah," he said, leaving the livingroom for a minute. Leland returned with a Ziploc bag and handed it to Morgan, who tenderly opened the bag and withdrew a hairbrush and pulled a few hairs. Then her eyes met Leland's, blue and sad and tentative. "If you want to back out…"

"No," he said firmly. "It must be done," and lowered his head. Morgan cut a few locks of his sandy hair and mixed them with Charlsie's. Ardelle retrieved a needle from her sewing kit. Leland held out his hand. Ardelle pricked his index finger and let the blood fall into a tiny vile.

Morgan and Selene came prepared for tonight's activities. Selene assembled her Spirit Board on the coffee table, waved a poppet in the air, and mumbled incomprehensible incantations.

"Selene learned this in New Orleans over the summer from her aunt, traditional spells tracing all the way back through her mother's lineage to her famous ancestor, Marie Laveau," said Morgan.

I knew her Spirit Board was a collector's item handed down in Selene's family from one generation of voodoo priestesses to the next. Its color resembled a light pine table with random dark brown knots. Faded black letters, numbers, symbols and words filled the board. Black stars in circles dotted the edges.

Morgan mixed a number of special herbs she'd collected around Snow Valley during a full moon, then sprinkled them in her mortar and pestle with hair and a few drops of blood from the vile and ground everything together. The Coven passed the bowl around. At last, Selene finished chanting. I poured the bowl's contents into the pot of hot water, whispering words taught by the Coven's previous generation and passed along to the emerging Coven.

Selene inhaled and placed her hands above the Spirit Board's planchette, moving it carefully, carefully. She looked down, noting every letter until the planchette pointed to Goodbye on the ancient board.

"By the pricking of my thumbs, something wicked this way comes," she exhaled, her raspy voice controlled and unwavering.

"Three witches from Macbeth," Ardelle whispered.

Together, we stared at the swaying flames, holding our breath while the fire raged. Suddenly, the fire cast forth two faces, contorted by mad, murderous flames. One male. One female. Charcoal eyes sunken deep in their heads, hair blowing as if by a strong wind. The female's eyes were a deeper shade and her hair was longer than the male's. Both appeared to have hair dark and curly from the smoke outlining their prominent features. The woman's face was long and thin, with a petite nose and full lips, twisted in an evil sneer. The man's jaw was square, his neck thick and his nose aquiline.

He turned his head slightly, grinning at his accomplice, and hissed in a deep, chilling voice, "I have killed the one whose hair you burned."

"And I have burned the one whose child offered his blood," laughed the woman.

"Beware," the faces warned in unison, "for one of your Coven shall be next." And then the faces dissolved within the flames. Their eyes were the last features to disappear. Raging flames shot out of their eye sockets, threatening to stab us like a poker just removed from fire.

Ardelle shrieked. Bryon growled. "Who are they?" asked Morgan in an undertone.

Carlton cleared his throat. "Witch hunters."

I turned to Carlton. "So it was witch hunters after all. We

should have had a warning, why didn't we?"

"Have you ever seen them before?" Morgan asked.

Slowly shaking his head, Leland stared blankly at the swaying blaze. Selene grasped Leland's hand. Byron laid his massive arm around Leland's narrow shoulders. I thought Leland would break down. Instead, he said, "Don't ever forget their faces. Because when I see these sadistic witch hunting monsters, I'm going to destroy them both with my bare hands."

"You got that right," growled Byron. "Count me in. When I'm done, they'll look like they've been run through a wood chipper *and* a paper shredder."

Carlton rested his chin on his fingertips, pressed together, eyelids closed, deep in thought. "Morgan, grab your sketch book and pencils," he said in a voice low and solemn. "We need to sketch their features while their images from the fire are fresh in our minds."

She obliged quickly. Sketching furiously, Morgan drew both faces exactly as they'd appeared in the fire moments ago, adding her own special details, details marking the hunters for the Coven to identify. She drew two sets of hands encircled with flames winding like a summer sunset above Snow Valley Mountain's jagged peaks, fire snaking around each wrist, flames shooting upward toward elbows. Morgan scratched flames into flesh, tongues of fire on skin, coiling black chains binding bone.

"And now," Carlton declared, "let's join together for the last step, the final incantation, cutting into flesh and bone, snakes of fire, red and orange and black, around their wrists, up their arms, forever scarred."

The Coven whispered together, whispered the magical words that would physically mark the witch hunters, tear into their skin, rip apart their flesh, char bone until nothing was left except a pile of ashes.

Carlton turned around slowly and looked at each member of

the Coven. "It's done. From this moment on, we'll be able to see the permanent scarring we've inflicted. And then we'll know who did this," he said, and looked directly at Leland, "who did this to your mother."

It was only a matter of time before the witch hunters responsible for Charlsie Kerr's murder would be caught, identified by scarred wrists visible only to the Coven.

All night long, I lay awake, unable to sleep or maybe afraid to sleep. I closed my teary eyes and pictured Bennett's sketch in art class. Was it just a coincidence? I had my doubts. Deep down, I knew there'd never been any coincidences in Snow Valley. I thought about those two evil faces in the fireplace. Who were they? Where were they from? Would they return?

Chills ran up and down my spine. I pulled the duvet over my head, but hiding did nothing to prevent the Dream from haunting me that night.

The male's face from the fire was now superimposed on the boy's face in the Dream. An inferno blazed in the boy's eyes and his arms were covered with snakes of fire. The fireflies flew away, leaving the girl alone, as frozen as an icicle. So still that I was certain she was dead. I tried to warn her, tried to tell her, *Get up! Run! Run for your life!* But just like one of those nightmares where I can't run no matter how hard I try, the girl didn't hear me, as though my words were stuck in my throat.

When I told my friends about the Dream the next day at school, they didn't think it was anything to worry about. According to Carlton, my recurring nightmares "represented my subconscious fears, layered with the male suspect's image."

I had my doubts.

Chapter Six

Coop the Scoop

EMERANNE

On Friday, I rode to school extra early and waited for my friends in Snow Valley High's cozy reading room in the library. A few details needed to be finalized for the next day's camping trip to Big Bear Lake where we planned to celebrate our sixteenth birthdays together.

Amidst several magazines strewn on a pine coffee table, an unfolded map was piled on a stack of *National Geographic* magazines nearest my reach. I picked it up and plunked down on one of the comfy sofas. I held up the tattered map, examined the earth's active volcanoes, and drew the map closer to my face. One area was singled out by a text box, a group of islands in southern Italy.

Aeolian Islands, I mouthed a few times, uncertain of the proper pronunciation.

Stromboli, Vulcano, Vulcanello, site of one of Italy's three active volcanoes.

Vulcan, Roman God of Fire, is said to reside beneath the islands. To appease his fiery spirit, residents still offer bonfires and fireworks at festivals in honor of Vulcan.

I wondered if the faces in the fire were related to Vulcan. I shivered at the thought.

A gruff voice called my name and a finger persistently tapped the map shielding my face. "That you hidin' behind the map, Emeranne Goode?"

I lowered the map to see who tapped it. Wearing a tattered, stained camel-colored trench coat without a belt there stood the one person I'd managed to avoid until now.

Cooper Kozalski.

His drab coat was unbuttoned, revealing a yellow check shirt, no tie, baggy green trousers and one of his coat's belt loops dangled by a thread. Coop the Scoop's facial features weren't any tidier, matching his overall ill-kept appearance. He had a few days' stubble on his face. A tangled moustache covered his upper lip where an unlit cigar stump was wedged in his mouth. He held a rumpled coil top notebook in one hand and a pencil in the other. Thinning, light brown hair, disheveled and probably uncombed for days, spilled out from beneath a cream crumpled hat with a small brim frayed around the edges.

"You Emeranne Goode?" he asked again.

"Who wants to know?" I pretended not to recognize him.

He chuckled. "You're a hard girl to track down."

"And you say that like it's a bad thing."

He chuckled again and bit his cigar stub.

"There's no smoking on school premises," I cautioned.

"Oh, yeah, I actually don't smoke. Just kinda like the idea of smokin' without health risks. Lung cancer and all. I chew cigars stubs instead," he explained, shifting the stump from one side of his mouth to the other.

"Isn't chewing tobacco just as bad?"

"Oh, yeah, well I only chew on the stub, see? Not like a baseball star." He winked.

"Smoking, chewing, whatever. You shouldn't be in school

with a cigar in your mouth. It's a bad example. Even if you're not smoking."

Coop cleared his throat several times. "You got me there, kid. Can't argue with you, you're smarter'n me that's for sure. Let me introduce myself—"

"Don't bother."

This joker approached me in school, without my dad around or any other adult present. How did he get into the school and past control-freak Lipschitz? Visitors had to sign in.

He cleared his throat again. "I'm investigatin' the murder from early July—"

"More like spreading rumors."

"Don't be all angry," he replied, stroking his moustache.

"All angry? When someone spreads lies about me, I'm gonna be angry."

"Oh, c'mon kid. Just doin' my job."

"Not very well," I said in an undertone.

"Well, the reason I wanna speak with you is gonna kinda sound silly, ya know, but—"

"You want to print more garbage? More lies?"

"Well, now, I can't figure out what happened on that mountain. Thought you'd wanna help me out, seeing as you're real smart, whaddaya say, kid?" I didn't answer again. He groveled nervously, shifting his cigar stub more frequently. "I got only a few questions, figgerin' out the sequence of events, 's all, I promise. Then I'll leave ya alone."

"What exactly do you want to know? There's nothing more I can tell you about the fires. Except I wasn't hiding in the forest. Didn't witness anything. And was never on medication. Are you going to print a retraction? Or not?"

"Oh, sure kid. Whaddever you want."

"You wrote a bunch of lies…"

"Had my sources, kid."

"Really? Like who?"

"Can't name 'em. To protect 'em, see."

"You weren't concerned about protecting me, were you?"

Cooper shifted awkwardly on his feet. "Got my job to do."

"Your job? Hey, genius, what about my safety? The killer or killers might believe what you wrote, that I'd witnessed the Lookout Murder. Did you think about that when you wrote all those lies?"

"Killers? Did you say killers? So you do know sumthin', don't ya, kid?

"Don't quote me, I'm warning you, or else—"

"Or else what?"

I didn't finished what I wanted to say. *Or else I'll curse you.*

"Well, gotta write what's been dug up, see."

"I bet you do," I grumbled. "Sold a lot of papers, didn't it?"

Cooper ignored my last comment. "I'll give you an exclusive. In the *Standard*. Nice picture of you. IN MY OWN WORDS by Emeranne Goode, with Cooper Kozalski, of course."

"Of course," I repeated sarcastically. "I can't help you and have nothing more to say, unless you'd like to continue with my dad present," I warned.

"Oh gee that's not necessary. No need to call adults in on this, now is there? Just wantin' to check my story. Make sure I got all the facts straight, 's all, cuz I'm not so good on facts and need a lotta help, from smart kids like you, 's all." He winked again, laughing heavily.

"You're right. About not being so good on facts. That's the only sensible thing you've said so far, Mr Kozalski."

He winked a third time.

"Something in your eyes, Mr Kozalski?"

He ignored me. "My crime investigations ain't over. Far from it. And see here, two items were found at the burned lookout. Recognize either?" Cooper held up what appeared to be a tattered piece of white cloth and a photo of a gleaming, ornate silver square-shaped item. He removed a similar one from his coat pocket. The item glistened in the sunlight. Coop flipped the top open, and ran his thumb along a round black disc. A bright, bluish-orange flame emerged.

"Recognize this hankie? Or the lighter in the photo?"

"Should I?"

"Not necessarily. Merely wonderin' if you'd ever seen 'em before, 's all," he queried, handing me his own lighter after flipping the top closed to extinguish the flickering orange flame. I held the lighter in my hand. Turned it around in my fingers.

"No. Never." Except...I bit my lip. Bennett had given Wallis a white hankie in art class.

"What it is?" said Cooper. "You got that look in yer eyes."

"What look?"

"You know what I mean," he said in a low growl.

"No, I'm afraid I don't," I said flatly.

"Yeah right. And ya don't know who PHB is? I'm guessing it's the same person, cuz the hankie has the letter B, see here," he said, unfolding the torn, stained hankie.

B? For Bennett? For Bassett? I swallowed. "Nope," I replied through clenched teeth.

Coop raised his index finger, about to ask me another question, when I saw Carlton approaching. I closed my eyes and exhaled slowly.

"If you'd like, we can continue this unauthorized interview in the main office. I'd be happy to let Principal Lipschitz know that a newspaper reporter from the *Snow Valley Standard* interrogated me in the library without an adult present. And we wouldn't want that would we? Like you said, I'm only a kid."

I omitted that Principal Lipschitz was unlikely to object to Coop's clandestine actions.

Cooper stood silently. A sinister chuckle escaped his lips between intense chews on his cigar stump. He lifted both hands in apparent surrender. When Carlton entered the reading room, Coop the Scoop threw him a rather nasty glare before he left, snickering on his way out.

"What was that all about?" Carlton asked. "Was he bothering you, Ems?"

"Oh, you don't know the half of it," I replied, sending Chief Walker a quick text about the crime scene evidence in Coop the Scoop's possession.

Byron and the Coven assembled in the reading room minutes after Coop the Scoop left. I recounted his visit word for word. With only a few minutes left before the bell rang, Carlton passed a list around, allocating responsibilities for food supplies and camping gear.

"Let's get out of here in case that fool of a reporter comes back for more," he said.

"Let him try, Ems," growled Byron. "Let him try."

Other than a near-detention from Principal Lipschitz for breaking the School Dress Code when, in class, I'd covered my head with my Forty-Niners hoodie, I was glad Friday morning passed by quickly. Morgan and Ardelle needed sleeping bags and met their mothers for a quick shopping excursion at lunchtime. Selene spent lunch hour toiling over an optional science class experiment, something about distilling various herbs and flowers.

Carlton was excused from afternoon classes in order to prepare for the trip. Unlike me, he wouldn't suffer missing school. Dressed head to toe in white—a V-neck white cable knit pullover with navy stripes, trousers, tennis shoes and visor—he mentioned Wimbledon and something about Roger Federer eating his heart out. He departed with a perfectly executed pirouette. I assumed Carlton had been on one of his astral traveling adventures. Lucky Carlton, the only member of the Coven with powers of astral travel and projection.

Gareth worked out in the recreation centre, training for a wheelchair race in Big Bear City next spring. Leland and Byron tossed a football around outside during lunch. I sat nearby on one of the picnic tables.

Nibbling on translucent green grapes, I examined both sketches. Chief Walker photocopied and distributed copies to members of the older Coven in case anyone recognized the witch hunters' faces. The deep sound of Byron's authoritative voice resonated through the cool September air.

"Hold the football with your fingers between the laces, like this," he instructed, "to get a wicked spiral."

"Ready?" Leland asked politely. Byron ran to the forest's edge.

"Yeah," confirmed Byron. Leland threw the football high in the air. It spiraled perfectly into Byron's outstretched hands. "Nice throw, dude," complimented Byron.

"Yeah, nice throw. And great catch," said a third voice. I looked up from the picnic table. Ben casually slid into a seat across from me, straddling his legs on either side of the bench.

BENNETT

"Hi, Emeranne. It is Emeranne, isn't it?" I knew her name perfectly well. After all, her name and photo had been in the papers all summer.

"Yeah, I'm Emeranne." She sounded wary and barely looked at me before returning her eyes to the arc of the football, then stifled a gasp as though she'd just remembered something important, and lowered her glance to the picnic table. My eyes skipped to the table where a large manila envelope nestled beneath pencil sketches. Emeranne covered the sketches with the envelope and brushed them away from me with her forearm.

I knew those faces. Crawling up from their hands to their forearms were flames or snakes.

"We've not been formally introduced. I'm Bennett Bassett. You can call me Ben, if you like. Mind if I join you?"

"No, I don't mind. And you can call me Ems."

The football whizzed by. Left. Right. Left. Right.

Her eyes were glued on the football's ping-pong patterns. That's what girls always do when they like you, I'd learned over the centuries. They ignore you, pretend they don't care.

We sat for a few quiet, contemplative minutes, watching the football. I removed a perfectly round, unblemished apple from my backpack and carved it with a pocketknife. I spun the apple around. Its fire engine red skin fell away like petals from dying apple blossoms swaying in a cool, late spring rain. I sliced the apple in equally proportioned wedges until an hourglass core lay exposed on the picnic table.

"Want a piece?"

"Um, sure," she said, avoiding my eyes.

I handed her a perfect morsel. Emeranne bit into a juicy, glistening wedge. Her moist lips wrapped around it. She chewed, closed her eyes, inhaled deeply before swallowing.

"You seem close to your male friends. Dating anyone?" I asked, catching her off guard.

"No," she blurted. Softening her defensive response, she elaborated, "we're more like siblings."

More like a Coven, I thought. "So, no boyfriend?" I couldn't help myself. I liked to make girls blush.

"No," was all she said, nervously peeling a piece of faded paint from the wooden picnic table and crushing the sliver between her fingers. Her face turned redder and redder.

"Anything interesting happen today?"

She seemed to debate my question, thoughtfully weighing the pros and cons. Finally, she made up her mind. "Yeah. Had a visit from Cooper Kozalski, a reporter from the *Snow Valley Standard*. He's been a pain all summer, ever since…"

"The Lookout Murder. I read about it in the papers. A tragedy."

"So you heard?"

"Yes, I moved here at the beginning of the summer." Right before the murder, a fact I kept to myself. "So about this reporter, Cooper, he came here? To the school?"

"Yeah," she said, finally peeking at me from beneath long, dark eyelashes.

"What did he want?"

"To talk about the Lookout Murder."

"I'm sorry, sorry about what, what—"

"Thanks," she said quickly, not letting me finish what I'd wanted to say to her for months. *It's not your fault.*

"And what did you say?" I asked, quickly shifting the topic.

"Say to Cooper?" Emeranne asked. I nodded and she continued. "Not much. I told him that his articles were false and I'd never hidden in the woods or saw the murderer."

"Anything else?" I prompted and fixed my gaze on her. I knew girls couldn't resist this. I knew it wasn't fair, but hey, I needed more information.

"He showed me a white hankie, tattered and stained," she shrugged indifferently. "And a photo of an old lighter, apparently from Bellavista Lookout. I have no idea how he got hold of crime scene evidence."

I didn't answer. Emeranne cast her eyes down and lowered her voice. "There were initials on both. B and PHB. Cooper asked if I'd seen the hankie before or knew who PHB was."

"And?"

"I told him the truth. That I didn't."

"He shouldn't be bothering you," I said crossly, raising my voice. "This is tantamount to harassment."

"I don't feel harassed," she replied defensively. "I'm glad I had the chance to tell him how I felt, that he put me in danger and is a total liar."

Byron and Leland paused for a moment, distracted by our escalating voices.

I decided to change the subject. "What are you doing on the weekend?"

"Camping with my friends," she said.

"You're lucky," I groaned. "I'm working, as usual."

"Do you work every weekend?"

"Yeah. Just about." I twisted my ring around and caught Emeranne staring at my hand. "It's snowflake obsidian."

"Uh, what?" she said, startled.

"Snowflake obsidian. My ring, that's the stone, in case you were wondering."

"No, I wasn't wondering, um, but it's nice. I've never seen a stone like that before," she said, rushing her words. "It looks rare."

"It is." I replied. *Millions of years*, I wanted to tell her but instead I said, "I had to scale a volcano to find the rock that produced the stone."

At first, Emeranne wore a puzzled look, until she laughed. "Yeah, right, I bet you did."

Yes I really did. Instead I said, "Of course not."

The bell rang. Protectively, Byron and Leland hesitated before running inside the main lodge after Emeranne threw them a reassuring glance.

I continued to chat all the way to her science class about little things. Things like the changing weather. Snow Valley's beautiful scenery. The cool mountain air. Then I did something

I suspected no boy had ever done before. I opened the classroom door for her. She held her breath and avoided my eyes. Chivalry went out of fashion along time ago, but I liked some customs from my past.

"Have fun camping with your friends," I said, leaving Emeranne inside the door. Her green eyes glimmered like two frozen emeralds.

I still got it, I smiled to myself, *after all these centuries.*

A serious talk with my family was urgent. The rogue hunters could blow our cover and, what was more, had no business meddling in the assignment my family had been given.

To destroy the Snow Valley Coven once and for all.

Chapter Seven

Poachers

BENNETT

"We've got a problem," I reported to my *de facto* family, seated around the largest round table in the Matterhorn. Seven white dinner plates sat empty but for a few crusts here and there, red pizza sauce stains, napkins crumpled and discarded and piled in heaps of frustration.

I was the orphan nephew according to official records. Unofficially, I was no such thing.

I turned the Open red fluorescent sign off where it hung in the Matterhorn's window above red and white checkered curtains.

Philippe Bassett ran his fingers through close cropped, bobby pin straight hair. "What happened now, Bennett?"

Allora, Philippe's second wife, didn't pose a question. "It has to do with Charlsie Kerr's death," she concluded.

"We were never ordered to touch the older Coven," Philippe said.

"That doesn't mean *all* Fire Born complied with orders," Miranda said darkly.

Philippe shot Miranda a cautionary glare.

I continued, doing my very best to suppress my rage toward Miranda. "The young Coven obtained sketches of Octavia and Ulric."

Giselle held her breath and looked directly at me, turning her head in the process, two thick, perfectly plaited braids of tawny hair swung about. "How?"

I shook my head. "No idea."

"Octavia? As in my *niece* Octavia?"

"I'm afraid so, Philippe," I replied. Philippe crossed his arms and lowered his chin.

"I never liked Ulric." Henry shook his dirty blond hair. "Major fail."

Philippe glanced at his son, Henry, who resembled his father the most out of his four children, then said to me, "Where did you see—?"

"I sat with Emeranne Goode during lunch. She tried to hide the sketches. Before she did, I managed to see them." Miranda snorted and tossed her long hair. I ignored her. "She claimed the sketches were Morgan's random drawings. I didn't press for more information."

"Too coincidental," Wallis said.

"And the arms were marked with what looked like tongues of flames," I added.

"Talented, this young Snow Valley Coven," remarked Allora. "They've scarred Octavia and Ulric with snakes of fire. I haven't seen that curse in a long time. The Coven will be able to identify them by the tracings, visible only in the Coven's eyes."

Philippe frowned. "This is serious. We should have sensed their presence."

"You know what this means. We have Fire Born poachers among us," added Allora. She pressed her fingers to her temples and closed her eyelids over her eyes, two different tones of gray. "Our powers were blocked somehow."

72

"Can this mean—?" Giselle started to say.

I cut in. "Our serum?"

Wallis bit her lip. "Maybe," she replied. "You know, I didn't think much of it at the time. I walked in on Carlton Cameron and Selene Laveau two days ago in the science lab, scrambling to hide an experiment from me. I spotted liquid mercury in a Bunsen burner and a mortar and pestle filled with black powder. I thought maybe they weren't supposed to be in there or something and took me for a teacher when they heard me open the door."

"Was it *argentum vivum*?" Giselle asked.

"Not exactly," answered Wallis. "Our science and geography curricula feature the study of volcanoes, so there'll be experiments with mercury, cinnabar and obsidian, if I remember correctly," she said.

"Guess they're getting a head start," assumed Henry.

"Or not," added Giselle, nervously tugging on her obsidian pendant.

"Yeah, they need it, the idiots," Miranda laughed.

Henry narrowed his eyes. "What if they've figured out our secret?"

"I doubt it," Miranda laughed. "They're way too stupid."

"Miranda," Philippe said. "Manners." She answered with a rude face.

So mature, I mouthed to her. Miranda glared back.

Allora reached across her chest and grasped her opposite arm. On the inside, at the bend in her elbow, she traced her index finger over a cluster of scars. "Do you think—?"

Wallis interjected. "That they know? How could they?"

Giselle inhaled a shallow, quick breath. "Know what we need to exist?"

"Emeranne was curious about my ring, so I told her it was snowflake obsidian," I admitted. "But I don't think she has any idea how the stone supports our immortality."

"She's so clueless, that b—"

"Shut up, Miranda!" I screamed.

"Why didn't you just tell her about Mount Shasta, too?" Miranda challenged.

"Miranda! Enough!" Philippe shouted, not one to raise his voice often. Miranda shrank, but I saw the hatred in her steely eyes.

Allora pressed her pale peach lips in a thin line. "Do you know what this means?"

"Total screwedville," moaned Henry, wiping a napkin stained red across his mouth.

Examining burgundy nail polish and tossing her shoulder length hair that resembled a vast wheat field in autumn, Miranda remarked tonelessly. "Well said, Henry." Her obsidian earrings caught the light and sparkled brighter than icicles melting under the winter sun.

"The issue at hand," said Philippe, clearing his throat, "is how we respond. If we pursue Octavia and Ulric we'll assuredly invite unwanted scrutiny from the Varangian Guard and be forced to explain why this new Coven hasn't been destroyed."

"Yet," modified Miranda.

Allora bowed her head and held it in her hands. Long saffron hair shielded her heart-shaped face. She exhaled, countering, "On the other hand, if we do nothing, eventually the Guard will pay us a visit. And destroy the Coven themselves."

"We delayed for so long we're running out of excuses to throw the Guard off our scent," Wallis said, worrying with her obsidian bracelet.

"I don't know," admitted Philippe. "I keep telling the Guard we haven't gained the Coven's trust. Maybe the Guard sent the poachers."

"But that's our task, isn't it? Gain the young Coven's trust?" asked a bewildered Henry.

"Assimilate. Infiltrate. Eliminate," added Miranda bluntly.

I clenched my fists. "But we've hesitated, I've hesitated. And you know why?" No one said a word, so I answered my own question. "We're having second thoughts," More silence. I continued, barely whispering, "Deep down, from the beginning, did anyone truly want this?"

"Speak for yourself, loverboy. I'm not having any doubts," Miranda huffed.

Philippe and Allora swapped fleeting looks. Henry cast his ashen eyes down.

"Not…not really," admitted Giselle. "But what choice were any of us given?"

"This…this immortal existence," stammered Wallis in a low voice. "Or—"

"Death," declared Miranda callously, raising one perfectly shaped golden eyebrow.

"I know," admitted Allora, breaking the escalating tension, "I know we've, all of us, at one point or another, doubted ourselves and what we'd become, what we must do, but—"

"But what?" I interrupted. "Who decided what we can or can't do? Has this existence been a life? Because it certainly hasn't been an existence to be proud of for me these past seven centuries."

"Speak for yourself," hissed Miranda again.

Philippe knit his eyebrows and drew a long, long breath. "Truth be told, we couldn't carry out our last assignments, could we? And now Terrowin, forced into hiding." His sad voice broke off, his sorrowful eyes rested upon Allora, examining her exotic face with intense affection.

"Terrowin," whispered Allora. "My son."

"Why did Win have to fall in love with a stupid witch?" complained Miranda.

"To stop us from doing what we really don't want to do," I answered.

"Speak for yourself," Miranda said for the third time, seething venomously.

Philippe threw his oldest daughter a cautionary glare. "You seem to have forgotten that your mother, Charlotte, was a skilled sorceress—"

"Which got us into this mess in the first place," Miranda griped, cutting short her father's stern reminder.

"It wasn't Charlotte's fault," I said, raising my voice.

Miranda scowled. "You're going to follow in Terrowin's footsteps, aren't you? Admit it. Aren't you? That's what this really has been all about, isn't it?"

"What are you talking about?" asked Allora.

"This is all about that filthy, vile witch Emeranne."

"You're always rude to her friends. I see how you treat them whenever they come to the Matterhorn. It's not very good for business," I said.

Miranda lashed out at me. "What's that supposed to mean? And who needs their business? As far as I'm concerned, they can go somewhere else."

"That's not for you to decide, Miranda. All customers must be treated with respect," ordered Philippe. Sulking, Miranda retreated.

"Ben, I think you should stalk the Coven this weekend," Allora proposed. I raised my eyebrows, taken aback by her suggestion given the heated discussion. "Just in case…"

"For real?" I asked.

"Yes, for real," she confirmed.

Miranda, of course, objected. "You've got to be joking!"

"Just stalk, Ben. No poaching or…"

"Or destroying. Hey, why not just join those freaks, Bennett?" Miranda seethed, and stomped to the kitchen.

The intense discussion was cut short when the phone started to ring, the panel's tiny squares flashed a fiery red like a spitting fire.

"Let's get back to work, everyone," said Philippe, adding, "this debate is far from over."

The flashbacks visited randomly, not just when I slept, but during the daytime at school and during pizza deliveries. My flashbacks were intense, vivid, and forced me to relive painful experiences.

A period of my life was lost to me forever, the time before I died, silent shadows and intricate puzzles with too many missing pieces and questions with no answers.

Only voices and shapes and sounds of an ocean's *shhhhh shhhhh shhhhh*ing upon a warm, sandy beach as fine as flour, suggestions of ocean and sand and warmth, a plethora of empty memories lost in an endless vortex of nothingness.

The latest episode occurred later that afternoon, the same day I'd revealed my discovery about the sketches. Like a migraine, I felt a flashback coming on, and hoped a peaceful walk near Snow Valley Lake might for once help control its severity, but I knew from experience, I'd never manage. Beneath a warm autumn sun, darkness gathered all around, blocking the friendly blue sky. The flashbacks always went something like,

> sun
> the beach
> sand, waves, wind
> heat
> whispering
> shadows

chills
choked words, soft voices
who are you?
eyes open
glare
blinded
i don't remember
fear
...we do not know...
the debate
...he is dying...
faded words
...his wishes...
who are you?
...he would want...
i don't remember
...no authority...
i don't remember
...to live...
pierced
i
cold
don't
dark
remember
dead

After every flashback, I wrote the fragmented conversations in my journal, pieces of distant voices, like a shattered vase glued back together, except some of the pieces were missing. I'd filled so many journals I'd lost count. I wanted to know who I was before the darkness stifled the inner workings of my mind, before death crushed the shadows of my long lost memory, locked parts of my mind where memories were stored. I was afraid of that darkness, of what I'd find, and yet I wanted to know, wanted to shine a light on the perpetual night that fell inside me so many centuries ago.

Chapter Eight

Big Bear Lake

EMERANNE

Carlton packed his dad's jet-black mini van with little room to spare. He looked at me as though taking measurements. "Ems, you can fit in the back."

I couldn't imagine how anyone could sit on the van's cramped bucket seats, drowning under sleeping bags, tents, deflated air mattresses, backpacks and coolers. Carlton was far more optimistic. Did he really expect me to find a seat under or between all of that stuff?

Carlton's older brother, Cuthbert, drove us to the public campground at the southwest shores of Big Bear Lake. A senior at Snow Valley High, Cuthbert resembled his younger brother, except he was an athletic star: quarterback, long distance runner and triathlete. He'd been Gareth's training partner, until Gareth's accident two summers ago. Cuthbert was a witch. Only he'd renounced witchcraft as long as he was involved with athletics.

"To avoid any unfair advantages," he'd always say with a glimmer in his dark blue eyes.

Gareth's wheelchair was piled on top of nylon sacks stuffed with sleeping bags and crevasses filled with pillows and Carlton's guitar case. I buckled up next to Carlton who, buried under layers of thin foam mattresses, bobbed his head with black headphones over his ears.

During the short drive southeast from Snow Valley, Cuthbert stopped at Grimesby's General Store, owned by Callie Grimesby Laveau's aunt and uncle. The store had been in the same spot, ever since the first Grimesbys emigrated from England generations ago.

I extricated myself from the back seat and went inside the store—one of the few stores that didn't ban me. A shrill bell jingled as I opened the door.

"Well well well. If it isn't Miss Emeranne," beamed Mr. Grimesby, who clapped his hands in delight and raised his bushy eyebrows. He continued to refill a small item, silver in color, on the chipped brown and green countertop. Next to his large hands, swollen and deformed, sat a square tin with a narrow tip protruding from the top. The tin read: Danger. Lighter Fluid. Flammable. Keep Out of Reach of Children.

"Hi Mr Grimesby. How've you been?"

He frowned. "Not so good lately. With the fire and all…"

Of course. The Grimesbys must be devastated. Reminded daily of Violet's murder.

I smiled sympathetically and lowered my eyes. "It must be so…so—"

Mr. Grimesby's melancholy brown eyes looked above my head nostalgically. Then he replaced the tip with a red plastic cap and snapped the lighter shut. "Yes, it is."

"I'm going camping this weekend," I said, hoping to lighten the sullen mood.

"The Kerr boy goin' too?" Mr. Grimesby asked. I nodded to him, then he said, "Nothin' like fresh mountain air, eh?"

"True, Mr Grimesby. How's Mrs Grimesby?"

"Oh the same, giving me a hard time, and here she comes," he laughed with a twinkle in his sad eyes, nodding toward the back of the cramped store. "Delia, Emeranne's here."

Mrs. Grimesby adjusted her hearing aid behind her left ear. "What's that, Roy?"

"I said Emeranne's here, Delia," he said louder, dusting an old soda fountain behind the counter.

"Oh!" she exclaimed, pushing back wisps of hair that escaped the tight bun worn at the nape of her neck. "Heading out for the weekend?"

"Hi Mrs Grimesby! Yes, I'm going camping with friends," I told her.

Mrs. Grimesby tilted her head, watching Cuthbert fill the gas tank. "Feels like rain. Stay warm." She shivered, retied her brown frilly apron around faded jeans and tucked in a ballet pink blouse with pretty fuschia roses. "Is this enough? Do you need any other supplies? Roy, give Emeranne some of those candles back there. Can't sell them...yes, those...dear me...look at these boxes. Damaged during shipping," she said, shaking her head. "Got lanterns, I suppose?"

I'd forgotten half her questions. "Yes, I think so...and flashlights...yeah. Oh, I can't take the candles...I have money," I said, fumbling for my wallet.

"Don't worry, Ems dear...Roy give her some of that bug spray too. And spare batteries, Roy...that should do it," Mrs. Grimesby declared, satisfied. "Special occasion?" she asked, noticing a pile of thick birthday candles on the counter.

"Um, most of my friends turn sixteen this year. We're celebrating together."

"Sixteen already," Mr. Grimesby whispered, lowering his eyes and exposing wrinkles on his heavy eyelids. "How could I forget? Time sure flies," his feeble voice cracked as he pretended to fuss with shelves of batteries, fishing lures and cigarettes behind the counter.

"Happy birthday, Emeranne," said Mrs. Grimesby softly.

Mr. and Mrs. Grimesby traded soothing glances. The doorbell broke the melancholy silence. "Good morning, Roy. Got any of that lighter fluid? You're the only one for miles who still carries the stuff."

"Hey there George, sure."

"Don't need a bag, thanks anyhow." George paid for the small tin of fluid and left, sounding the doorbell again.

Mr. Grimesby packed a paper bag of supplies for me. "Gonna throw in some of these here penny candies."

The jingling doorbell announced a visitor's arrival. "Delivery for…let's see here…a Mr R N Vay…er…Vayl – oh – iss?" The FedEx courier struggled to pronounce the recipient's surname.

"Must be for Ray," muttered Mr. Grimesby.

"You're not him?" inquired the courier.

"Nope. Get his deliveries. He's a boarder, lives above the store," explained Mr. Grimesby, nodding his head toward the ceiling. "A retired janitor. Left early July and visitin' his son overseas."

"Well, I'm not sure I should leave it."

Mrs. Grimesby reached behind the counter and pulled out a stack of unopened mail. "All his," she said, holding a thick pile in front of the FedEx courier's doubtful eyes.

"Oh, well, that's fine then," he said. "Don't want any complaints." He held an electronic device, gave Mr. Grimesby a plastic stick and tapped the rectangular window on the tracking devise. Mr. Grimesby scratched his head. "Just sign here."

"Have a nice day," Mrs. Grimesby called out to him courteously. Mr. Grimesby returned the mail and envelope beneath the counter.

"Before your time, Ems. Ray was the janitor when Jo was in high school and…"

I knew what Mrs. Grimesby didn't say. Violet. When Jo and Violet were in high school. I lowered my eyes so they wouldn't see the tears I felt gathering behind my lids. The doorbell sounded again. It was Cuthbert. "Hey, Mr Grimesby, Mrs Grimesby!"

"Oh, hey there, Cuthbert. You were usin' pump number three, eh? That'll be thirty-five even."

"Come back soon!" Mrs. Grimesby said lovingly. "And be careful out there. Never know what's lurkin' around."

"Don't forget to cast a boundary spell," said Mr. Grimesby.

Mrs. Grimesby reached out for my hand, urging me, "Cast one promptly at the lake."

"Will do," I promised, following Cuthbert out the door.

The campsite was cloaked heavily in a green veil of pine trees and edged with yellow ribbons of mature goldenrods. Dark, gloomy rain clouds reflected off the black van's rear windows, clouds that reminded me of stranded rowboats in a stormy sea.

The spicy scent of pine soothed my lungs, the smooth, *slush*ing sounds of lapping waves curling along the lake's black pepper beaches softly stroked my ears. A few clouds dotted the autumn sky above uneven rows of mixed pine trees, needles in various shades of green, trunks and cones the color of root beer. Threads of rust and crimson and gold wove between plum shadows amidst the tall, sturdy pine stands, creating a stunning lattice effect. A giant mixed herb garden stuffed in terra cotta pots sat on burlap sacks—lavender, mint, sage, thyme, purple-leafed basil and pungent rosemary.

Ardelle, Morgan and Selene arrived shortly afterward. In a clearing nearby, Morgan parked her vintage Citroën with the blue canvas roof. Her white car covered with large royal blue and yellow daisies was recognizable anywhere. Selene waved through a flap-up window, opened the rear-hinged door, and began to unload tents and sleeping blankets.

Selene cast a boundary spell immediately. Morgan and

Ardelle positioned their worn canvas tent to face the postcard lake view. Ardelle fiddled with one of the tent's zippers, her sewing kit nearby. Deftly, she thread a needle from a large spool of thick twine. Morgan arranged food near a designated cooking area with wooden picnic tables and two large grills.

Byron and Leland argued about which pole goes where instead of following instructions sewn on their tent, and debated how close to Gareth and Carlton they wanted their tent to be. Gareth's thunderous snoring was a running joke among the boys.

Selene dropped the hammocks in frustration. "Too many knots," she mumbled.

Ardelle picked them up and unraveled the knots in seconds.

Selene shook her head. "How does she do that?"

"Lots of practice for storm knots," grinned Ardelle. "Though I've never tried the spell."

"Yet," smirked Selene.

When Cuthbert drove away, the black van's red and white brake lights disappeared around a curve of everlasting rows of protective towering pine trees. Their branches cast animated shadows from the early morning sun, like outstretched arms beckoning for refuge.

The sun emerged at last from behind disappearing clouds. The morning passed quickly, filled with volleyball and badminton and lazing around. The glowing sun began to fall behind the jagged and blue horizon.

Byron piled wood in the fire pit and asked Ardelle to start the campfire. She pointed the tips of her fingers at the kindling, and it burst into flames within seconds.

"Sweet," Byron whistled.

Next, Ardelle fired up the grilles. Morgan and Gareth assembled a dozen potatoes in perfect rows of tin foil soldiers. Over the burgeoning fire, pots of macaroni and cheese and chili and scalloped potatoes hung across a suspended metal pole.

"My cooking zip line," Morgan boasted lightheartedly.

Their faces barely visible in the edge of darkness as the last rays of sunlight disappeared behind the pink edged mountain peaks, Leland and Carlton gathered around the roaring campfire, where shimmering firelight illuminated their blue eyes, glistening as together, for added protection, they cast a second impenetrable boundary spell for the evening.

Twilight fell upon Big Bear Lake. Temperatures dipped several degrees. I wrapped myself in a thick woolen blanket, watching the flames dance beneath a brilliant starry night sky. Leland made shish kebobs of marshmallows and distributed long, thin twigs and passed them around.

The unbroken chainsaw moan of a motorboat faded away. Waves tickled the shoreline, blacker than volcanic rock. Twigs popped and sizzled. Logs glowed fiery shades of soft coral, crimson, poppy, watermelon, blazing orange, faded denim.

The wind's path changed. Leaping flames twisted in every direction, creating a bonfire with a distorted, ever-changing profile. My eyes froze upon the bonfire, watching marshmallow flesh transform. Tan, brown, black, pure white skin going dark, its spongy body devoured by wicked flames.

"Ems, your marshmallows are burning," said Ardelle, snapping me out of my reverie.

Quickly, I pulled the smoking twig from the flames. "Oh, uh, thanks." I pinched one of the burnt marshmallows, tore the black outer layer, licked the goo. I'd never imagined anyone burnt like that, their skin, their hair, their eyes, their fingers and toes and arms. Never imagined anything burnt except toast and wood and marshmallows, until I saw Mrs. Kerr. The marshmallow's inner body, bleach white and melted, dripped to the ground. I tossed the stick into the fire. I'd lost my appetite.

I wished an Ice Vision warned me. I wished...

My wandering thoughts were broken when Carlton asked, "Who wants to tell a ghost story?"

"Something blood-curdling," urged Byron, shining a flashlight under his chin, making creepy noises from deep within his throat.

"It was a dark and stormy night," said Selene.

Carlton laughed and removed his guitar from its case. Morgan retrieved hers and joined Carlton, strumming and singing campfire songs. Above the croaking frogs and chirping crickets and birds singing bedtime songs, our voices hummed until Carlton and Morgan silenced their guitars.

Within the indigo forest, someone clapped.

From high above the soaring pine stands, echoing like a speedboat slapping Big Bear Lake, someone was clapping. I squinted my eyes above the trees, but saw nothing except a wall of pitch-black emptiness.

Byron grabbed a giant piece of firewood the size of a battle axe. From beneath the shadows of the black forest emerged a tall figure, his face invisible beyond the uneven peaks of the raging bonfire, growing louder and fiercer and hungrier.

My instincts reassured me: this stranger wasn't hostile, didn't present a threat.

His wasn't the presence I'd sensed.

There was someone else, something dark and malevolent, lurking deep within the forest.

BENNETT

I hated myself for stalking Emcranne to Big Bear Lake and convinced myself it was for the Coven's safety, although Byron was present. I still couldn't figure out why the Den Born hadn't picked up the poachers' scent. It was bad enough Fire Born hunters were fooled by Octavia and Ulric.

Was Miranda right? Did I have deeper feelings for Emeranne Goode? Did I really look at her *that* way? Would I risk the Bassetts' existence? Risk exposing them? Risk retribution from the Varangian Guard?

Besides the inevitable risk, must I intrude upon Emeranne's life, a life somehow inextricably linked with mine? Even though I just met her, there was something familiar about Emeranne Goode. Was hers the face that alluded me, the face missing in centuries of sketches?

Hidden within the thick, dark forest, I knelt away from knives of moonlight cutting through the treetops, wishing,

> *if only I could tell her she was in danger*
> *if only I could keep her safe*
> *if only I were someone or something other than I am*
> *if only…*

Night and day, dusk to dawn, there I remained, transfixed.

watching
listening
stalking
sketching
composing…

> *oh who am I to brighten the mourning indigo nightfall?*
> *who am I to dim the bleeding dawn?*
> *burn, sparkling flowers of night*
> *burn, forests of eternity*
> *burn, ashes of blue*
> *burn, eyes of steel*

Chapter Nine

Legend

EMERANNE

𝒜 tall stranger approached the campfire circle. A stream of light shone toward the fire, blinding me momentarily. Byron laughed.

"Emeranne Goode? That you I hear singing off-key?" The deep voice was familiar.

"River!" I exclaimed, shielding my eyes from his flashlight's glare. "I just saw you—"

"Yeah, yeah, show off," he replied.

Carlton chuckled. "Welcome, River Vale."

River redirected his flashlight and strolled into the edge of a broad circle of orange and yellow light thrown by the campfire's flames.

"Heard you guys singing from across the lake," he joked. "Ems, you still can't carry a tune to save your life."

"Yeah, well, I make up for it in volume." I laughed along with my cousins and friends.

River approached Selene, lovingly kissed her on the lips. "I missed you," he whispered in her ear. "Me too," she said. I sighed, wondering if anyone could love me like that.

River turned and said to us, "What did you think I was? A grizzly bear?"

"Of course," replied Morgan casually.

Seven more shadowy figures emerged from the dark forest's depths. The rest of my cousins appeared, their faces gleaming in the firelight: bronze skin, coal black eyes, and hair in glossy black shades, a contrast from the stark white surrounding their dark pupils—indigo, basalt, blackberry, wrought iron, space galaxy, midnight, ink, soot.

"Is River going on about his crazy grizzly bear stories again?" It was a boy whose voice I recognized as belonging to Lucas Stone, a childhood friend and member of the Serrano tribe.

"Yeah, except the Coven knows my stories aren't crazy," River said.

With my cousins in tow, Luke slowly moved toward the campfire. Some sat on loose logs, others on the ground cross-legged or lay on their stomachs, watching the bonfire rage.

"I felt the presence of the Coven," Storm said. "River suggested we make sure things are fine here."

Morgan and Ardelle served the rest of the birthday cake before Byron devoured it all. "Can't get enough," he smirked.

"Apparently not," Selene replied, holding up the second box, half-empty.

I passed around bags of marshmallows and a pile of twigs. Morgan and Cedar prepared several trays of S'mores. Ardelle waved her hands beneath each aluminum tray to melt the chocolate and marshmallow. Selene distributed the trays and said, "Just make sure Byron doesn't eat all of the S'mores."

"You read my mind," chuckled Byron.

Lost in silent thought, River's eyes searched the indigo sky. Pale moonbows reflected off layers of clouds and swirling puffs of smoke. River swallowed the last morsel of cake then cleared his throat. "This campfire reunion reminds me of the legend my grandfather, Achilles Meadowvale, told me many moons ago, as his grandfather did before him, a legend passed down from one

90

generation to another about the first settlers to arrive in this area, hundreds of years ago. About sharing even in the darkest hours, when all hope seems lost, in a time of sadness, holding back the Ice Vision, shielding the Scent." His dark eyes rested upon Leland. "A time when even friendship was not enough to heal irreparable wounds."

"Is this the story of the Spirit Bears?" Selene asked, smiling warmly at River. "You've only told me bits and pieces."

"Yeah," River answered. "Would you like to hear it?"

"Why not? It's always good to be reminded of what we face," said Carlton.

River inhaled slowly. "Serranos believe our departed ancestors reincarnate as Spirit Bears. Many suns long since risen and set, the Spirit Bear was invoked to protect those whose lives were spared from evil strangers—strangers who savagely murdered members of the Serrano band and a group of settlers from afar, persecuted for their beliefs. Bodies were burned, no life was spared.

"To disrespect Serrano legend dishonors our ancestors, and dishonors the Spirit Bear. The Serrano's Spirit Bear appears as a sacred grizzly bear, indigenous to this region. All bears are similar to library archives, retaining history, folklore, traditional medical knowledge, and mystical powers."

River paused and took a deep breath. "It has always been forbidden for Serranos to wear bear fur, eat bear meat, display a bear head or rug or wear ceremonial necklaces with bear claws, as these are held in extreme reverence. Any who violate the code is exiled forever for breaking traditional tribal law, enraging our ancestor spirits, and bringing down their curse upon the entire band."

Except for the crackling of the bonfire, the cold night was shrouded in silence.

"As for the connection with recent crimes," River continued, "Coop the Scoop was nosing around Moonridge after Ems left, asking the Elders about the old legends."

"Coop the Scoop," I said in a low voice. I hadn't yet shared Cooper's visit with Luke or the Vales, so I filled them in. "And that's how I met him."

"He's bold," frowned Luke.

"No kidding," River agreed. "Untrustworthy, too, sneaking into school without permission."

"Ems, that reminds me," Byron said. "What did Bennett Bassett talk to you about?"

"You mean yesterday, at lunch?" I asked. Byron nodded. "Oh, nothing really. Just small talk. But…there was a moment when he—"

"Yes?" Morgan prompted.

"He had this look in his eyes, like for a moment when he looked at the sketches—"

"What? He saw the sketches?" Gareth exclaimed.

"Just for a moment, then I covered them up with the envelope. How could he know the faces from the fire? It was probably nothing, just a feeling I had…"

"Maybe," considered Carlton.

"Or maybe not," Leland said.

"It was just for a second, but there was this look on his face, as if he recognized them. That's crazy, right?"

A long pause followed. Carlton broke the silence. "We can't be too careful."

River's soot-dark eyes narrowed. "I agree with Carlton. Letting your guard down, even for a moment, can be fatal. Don't forget that members of colonies whose ancestral blood traced back to witches were always in mortal danger. So too were those of mixed Serrano bloodlines, members of Serrano families who married the original persecuted settlers."

"Let me get this straight," Carlton said. "In the case of mixed blood, Serrano and witch, what would happen?"

River pondered a moment. "Serrano blood would probably activate the Scent, though it wouldn't necessarily be as effective as full protection."

"So," Carlton began, "Serrano blood activated the Scent. Full Serrano blood." River nodded. "Mixed blood may or may not activate the Scent." River blinked his eyes once as he nodded his head again.

"Would a mixed blood have Ice Born and Den Born powers?" Morgan asked.

"Rare, but possible," River said.

"*We* provide impenetrable protection from witch hunters," said Brooke Vale.

"Even though a mixed blood witch has some shielding powers," clarified Storm.

Morgan turned to look at me. "Like Ems."

"Like Ems," repeated River. "Is she the only one in this Coven who traces Serrano and witch blood?"

Carlton turned to Byron. "Don't you have Ice Born blood on your mother's side?"

"Yeah, Mom's aunt is Abigail Wolcott."

"Ice Born, correct?"

Byron nodded. "Mom's never developed any powers."

"I see," said Carlton.

"I wonder if Ems will develop both abilities?" Byron mused.

"Time will tell," Carlton said.

"Yeah, I guess so," I said quietly. "Except my dad has Serrano blood, but he never developed Den Born powers."

"Maybe because the powers passed from his mother, Rosemary, weren't potent enough to trigger a shift," suggested Luke. "His dad didn't have Ice Born powers, did he, Ems?"

"My grandfather wasn't either a witch or Serrano."

Leland stared into the fire. "Why did our powers fail?"

"If I knew the answer, Leland, your mother would still be with us," River said. "I can't tell you how sorry I am—we all are. Charlsie was a special woman."

"We haven't been presented with any Ice Visions of witch hunters during our lifetime, as far as I know," Morgan said, "though my sketches might serve as visions." Morgan updated the Den Born.

"Snakes of fire?" Meadow Vale asked. "River told me bedtime stories about them."

Morgan nodded.

"Good," said Meadow. "Very good."

"Any theories?" asked River.

"About our failed powers?" I asked.

"Yeah," River replied.

"Like I told you last week, we're working on it," explained Selene. "Scientifically rather than supernaturally."

Their eyes, large and dark as Ben's gemstone, Cedar and Woods Vale together asked, "Supernatural research? Like what?"

River grinned, raised his eyebrows, turned to his younger siblings and started to say, "Research meaning…"

"Astral travel," Carlton said with a smile. "In addition to scientific trials."

"Experimenting to determine the basis for a witch hunter's immortality," Selene explained.

Carlton elaborated. "We were analysing old samples of *argentum vivum* in the school lab, transforming crushed cinnabar into liquid mercury, and thinking about doing something with the obsidian, until we almost got caught."

"Wallis Bassett walked into the science lab when Carlton and I were examining the living silver," said Selene. "We still don't know exactly what it does, and we're following various hypotheses, one being that it's linked to immortality."

"Bassett…Bassett…I've heard that name before," said River. He put the tips of his calloused fingers together and closed his eyes to reflect for a long, long moment.

"Maybe from me?" Selene asked.

"Maybe," River said. "And from one of the Serrano Elders."

"The Bassetts own the Matterhorn," said Ardelle.

"Bennett Basset moved to Snow Valley at the beginning of summer," added Morgan.

River stood up. "There are three things we don't allow on our territory," he said forcefully. "Box-checkers. Plastic shamans. And filthy bloodhounds."

"River," I began, "are you saying, are you suggesting—?"

"I don't think that family appears to be what they truly are." River leveled a cautionary glare at the entire Coven. "Even if the Den Born *haven't* detected anything."

"Neither have the Ice Born," I reminded him. "And I just remembered something about Ben. You know the ring he wears? He told me it's a rare gem, volcanic, a snowflake obsidian."

"Interesting," said Carlton.

"Guess just about everyone's under suspicion," shrugged Leland.

"Except for us," Morgan added.

"Except for us," Leland agreed.

"And there's one more thing," Carlton said. "About my astral travels." Everyone stopped talking and fixed their eyes on Carlton. "I copied a passage written by this Delacroix guy. I have the copy somewhere," he said, checking various pockets in his khaki cargo pants. Locating a wrinkled square of paper, he unfolded it, skimming it with his eyes. "I didn't have much time. Sometimes I can't read my own handwriting."

"Yeah, neither can I," joked Byron. "Whenever I borrow your class notes, I need you to translate."

Carlton grinned. "Here it is." He held his flashlight above the paper, cleared his throat, and slowly read:

> near a mountain cliff there stands
> caressing the black sun
> the clockwork moon
> the choking stars
> an enchanted tower
> high above the magical valley
> an enchanted tower
> a tower on fire
> on fire
> fire
> the spirits cry out
> pleading, bleeding, needing
> air and earth and water
> a pine needle bed
> pierces naked flesh
> a flowing river weeps
> red tears on tender skin
> branded with orange iron
> held beneath silver stains
> on a lifeless navy sky

No one made a sound. Minutes passed until Carlton spoke again. "Veurçon Aramis Delacroix, *La Morte de la Sorcière*, eleventh century translation from the Old French."

Meadow gulped. "How did you get hold of this?"

"The same way I got the living silver and volcanic rock. The power of persuasion," Carlton said, wiping his knuckles on his chest.

"Nice," complimented Luke.

Leland spoke up. "What does it mean?"

"No idea," admitted Carlton. "Unless…"

"What?" I urged.

"Unless it's some kind of manifesto," Carlton said.

"Like in the old witch hunter manuals," Selene suggested.

More moments of silent reflection passed, interrupted by the rustle of branches. Twigs snapped, fallen leaves hissed, and the metallic wind whistled ominously. I turned my head, certain two silver lights flashed in the woods. I looked up. Moonbeams struck swaying branches.

River glanced at me, then motioned to his siblings. "Cedar. Woods. It's past your bedtime. Mom'll be furious. According to the moon's position, it's almost midnight. The witching hour," he said, twitching his dark eyebrows lightheartedly.

"We'll keep tabs on you, don't worry," reassured Storm.

River kissed Selene. Then the Vales glided silently toward the dark woods.

"Bye Ems," said Luke, as he and River sank into the black ocean of trees.

The bonfire had burned down to blinking embers and ashes. I nearly nodded off from the fire's bittersweet scent, the relaxing music, the warm safety of my Coven. Frosty night air bit the tip of my nose. The smell of fire permeated the air, unusually thick with smoke. It was a cold night, cold enough for wood stoves and fireplaces, judging by the smoke sliding down the mountains and hovering over Big Bear Lake.

"Selene," Leland said softly, "I think it's time to consult the Tarot cards."

Selene sat cross-legged and draped her black shawl on the damp grass in front of her sandals. She inhaled deeply for several minutes, then her raspy voice interrupted the deathly stillness. "First, we must cast a Tarot circle." Her lilac eyes softened like hyacinth petals above lanterns glowing brighter than a jar of fireflies at night. "Ancient Spirits of the Tarot, within our protective circle we ask for guidance, and will be eternally grateful for your gracious assistance this evening," she whispered breathlessly.

"The Coven seated before you has not received an Ice Vision. Likewise, the Scent was ineffective in detecting enemies within our midst. Do you have a message? As always, we thank you, Ancient Spirits, for eternal assistance and guidance."

Selene whipped out a deck of Tarot cards from beneath her black shawl, placed the deck in her right hand and, with her left thumb, gently pulled several cards from the top of the deck into her left palm, pushing the cards back beneath the deck in her right hand. She shuffled slowly for quite some time, rocking back and forth, side to side, in a circular motion. Suddenly, she stopped moving. Eyes wide open, lips pressed together tightly, she split the deck into three piles.

Still in a trance, Selene waved her hands above each pile. "One by one, tap each pile," she instructed us. After each person had a turn, she placed both palms on each deck for a few more minutes, piled all three decks together, and spread all of the cards on her sleeping bag in a semi-circular fan design.

"Who wants to pick one card?" she asked.

After a nervous pause, Leland volunteered. "In memory of my mom."

Selene's eyes shone like amethysts in the firelight. "And now, let us begin."

Inhaling deeply, Selene picked up the card, looked at it intensely, and raised the left-hand tips of her dark nails to her mouth. Decisively, she set the card down and slowly turned it over.

"Oh! The Fool," she proclaimed reverentially.

"Great," moaned Leland. "As if I need a reminder how I feel, how I failed Mom."

98

"We all did," Carlton said sympathetically.

"No no—The Fool is a powerful card in the traditional Tarot deck," Selene said.

"Because?" prompted Byron.

"Because numerically, The Fool's number, zero, symbolizes a beginning. He's not a fool to be made fun of. He's innocent—so much so that he embarks on a journey without fear or anticipation of dangerous obstacles," she said to us.

I bit my lip. "What does The Fool's journey consist of?"

"The journey is always both outward and inward, transformational from without and within," Selene said.

"Why is The Fool's number zero?" Morgan asked.

"Like I said, zero is associated with a beginning, normally interpreted as a journey of some sort. The Fool is seen as an outsider, apart from the rest of the Tarot deck. And among all the other cards, zero is thought to stand in the middle of both positive and negative energies. It's a position of considerable power."

I studied The Fool closely. He stood beneath a white sun. Black rays circled the sun. The Fool carried a stick on his right shoulder with a limp white sack dangling from its end. Jagged white-peaked mountains were visible behind The Fool, who stood precariously, in mid-stride, at a cliff's edge, his head tilted upward. A large brown bear stood by his side, appearing to warn The Fool.

"The Fool seems free-spirited, standing on the cliff's edge like that," I said.

Selene nodded. "True, Ems."

Carlton sighed. "Selene, give us a bottom line. What does this card mean?"

One index finger on her lips, Selene raised her violet eyes skyward, then lowered her head to say, "Some sort of journey.

The Fool trusts his or her instincts, even if those instincts seemed foolish to others. The Fool never gives up."

"The notion of change and a new beginning stand out," observed Morgan.

"The Fool walks forward confidently, without a care in the world," suggested Ardelle. "As if he doesn't mind heading toward the unknown."

Selene nodded her head. "There has always been more to The Fool than meets the eye," she said. "The white sack is empty, waiting to be filled with adventures."

"Anything else, Selene?" Leland asked.

"The Fool is a chameleon, able to replace any card in the deck," she said.

"A chameleon," repeated Carlton faintly. "I think we need to remember that."

Chapter Ten

Vital Signs

EMERANNE

The drive back to Snow Valley went quickly on Sunday afternoon. A soft, gentle rain turned heavy, tap tap tapping the windshield. After dropping Gareth off, the black van climbed the mountain road's steep incline. Thunder rumbled and lightning flashed. Heavy rain poured, hammering on the roof of the van, further punctuating this dreary, downcast day. In the overcast sky above, an expansive swath of bruised clouds spread above the forest's jagged silhouette, like a garden of ripe eggplants.

A low level of clouds obscured the tree line, hiding tree tips behind layers of mist. Most pines edging Snow Valley Mountain Road were shrouded in fog. I could barely see the log cabin when Cuthbert pulled into the driveway.

Selene's Tarot reading altered the Dream that came later that night.

The forest floor disappeared. Side by side, the girl and boy lay near a cliff's edge. I felt I was there, in the Dream, on the ledge with them, desperately begging them to step away from the ledge—but neither moved. I urged them, first the girl, then the boy, pulled their arms until I was out of breath. I stopped to rest, leaned forward, rested my hands on my shaking thighs. My breath escaped from nostrils that seemed like dew-covered cobwebs. When I looked forward, white puffs of smoke wrapped around me. It wasn't my breath. I turned, glanced over my shoulder. A raging fire burned behind me.

I woke up in the middle of the night and barely slept afterward.

Monday marked the beginning of Emergency Awareness Week and the Flu Shot Clinic. Every year, Snow Valley High students received basic first aid training—administering cardiopulmonary resuscitation and taking vital signs: pulse rate, temperature, respiratory rate and blood pressure. It was practical to administer flu shots during the same week, while the nurses were at the school teaching first aid classes.

A lifeless dummy laid on a table between a paramedic and Callie Laveau, Selene's aunt. Partnered with Selene, her Aunt Callie walked over to hug me.

"How is everything with you, Ems? And Jack?" she asked me.

"We're fine, thanks." I smiled.

She held my hand tenderly. "You know, if you ever need anything, anything at all, Gavin and I are here for you, okay?"

"Thanks, I appreciate that." I knew she meant it, knew I could depend on her and Gavin.

The paramedic conducting the training shushed the class politely and introduced himself. "Hello everyone. My name is Matthew and I'm here with Registered Nurse Callisto Laveau from Snow Valley General. Today, we're going to demonstrate life-saving techniques.

"Now, if you ever come across an accident victim, always check first for responsiveness," he said, "by tapping or shaking the victim gently, like this."

Matthew demonstrated on the dummy, instructing students do the same, using mannequins on the floor. Steps ahead, Selene rolled a mannequin toward her and pretended to open the airway. She tilted the head backward and checked for normal breathing by watching for chest movement. The same three boys from science class snorted and giggled whenever Matthew said *breast movement* or *cheek*. Aunt Callie shot them a stern look.

"So let's assume you don't detect breathing," Matthew continued. "What now? This is where CPR comes in. We'll go step by step together. Place both hands, one on top of the other, in the center of the dummy's chest, and press down at a rate of one hundred times per minute."

Three boys giggled hysterically until Aunt Callie stood over them and their mannequins. The boys went silent, their faces fire engine red from suppressed laughter.

Selene administered compressions on her dummy's chest while I counted compressions. One, two, three, four, five…thirty…thirty-one…fifty-nine, sixty…eighty-eight, eighty-nine, ninety…ninety-nine, one hundred.

"That's great," encouraged Matthew. "Now, reassess your victim after two minutes. If the victim isn't responsive, continue CPR until the victim starts to breathe, or first responders like me arrive. As soon as you've finished, switch with your partner. And when you're done with the mannequin, you'll practice on your partner."

The Flu Shot Clinic was set up in the gymnasium, where Principal Lipschitz directed students, according to homeroom class, over the PA system. When my class was called to the clinic, restless, I stood in line, wishing to get the injection over quickly. I hate needles. Knots traveled from my stomach to my throat. I assumed I was turning as pale as today's wintry cloud cover.

Morgan knew my aversion to needles. "Ems, you okay?" I nodded unconvincingly. "It'll be fast, just a pin prick," she said reassuringly, but any possibility of reassurance disappeared rapidly. A visiting nurse sat at the table at the head of my line.

Great, I thought dejectedly. "Who's that?" I asked, jerking my head toward the new nurse.

"No idea," Selene replied.

Aunt Callie tended to the other line. She knew how much I hated needles, and took extra care to distract me while the long, thin needle pierced my arm. I raised my chin, inhaled deeply, and closed my eyes.

As the line moved closer and closer to the nurse and the big, menacing syringes in her gloved hand, I watched her swab arms, jab jab jab one after the other, barely pausing long enough to breathe between shots. Her face was covered with a hospital mask, so I couldn't see her mouth. Only her eyes, lined heavily in a deep charcoal, were visible.

"Pleeze to come up," she said, her voice a husky foreign sound, and motioned to me. I extended the time as much as possible, walking slowly toward her. "Pleeze to hurry," she urged. Before I knew it, she had swabbed and jabbed and slapped a bandage on my arm.

"Ouch," I mumbled and rubbed my arm. The nurse was already stabbing Selene, who complained under her breath, "Not nearly as gentle Aunt Callie."

In the evening, when I removed the bandage, I rubbed my arm in front of my bathroom mirror, noticing the injection area was swollen and bruised. I went downstairs and made an ice pack to relieve the swelling, cursing that brusque tyrant of a nurse under my breath.

Ben and Wallis were absent from art class all that week. In fact, the entire Bassett family missed Emergency Awareness Week *and* the Flu Shot Clinic.

BENNETT

All through Emergency Awareness Week, I remained indoors with my cousins, out of sight, avoiding the risk of being spotted in town. The Matterhorn was closed. Whenever a school event might compromise our secret, it was always time for a relative's funeral or some other excuse. Allora notified Principal Lipschitz about the death of a grandparent. Seems the Bassetts have lost many relatives over the centuries. But no one except the Bassetts lived long enough to know that crucial piece of information.

It wasn't advisable for Fire Born to have vital signs taken, risk the chance that students other than my cousins partnered with me might search for—and not find—a pulse or a heartbeat. Nor was it advisable for us to get an injection other than living silver, a substance that would ooze from the tiny puncture a flu shot would make. None of us had normal vital signs or veins, and our hearts didn't beat like a mortal's: seven beats per minute instead of the average of seventy.

At times, I imagined a regular heartbeat, the feeling of dark red blood pumping through my heart, sensed the red liquid pulsing through my veins. Then I'd stab my arm, inject living silver, remembering that was what filled my veins instead of blood, remembering I wasn't human, wasn't at all like Emeranne, with a heart, a pulse, red blood, and a mortal life.

Days, I reclined on the lower bunk in the small bedroom Henry and I shared, a simple room with one desk, one chair and bunk beds. I'd sketch, or scribble in my journal. Today, I thumbed through Mary Shelley's *Frankenstein* for an English assignment. I knew the novel word for word, could recite passages—as if Mary had written about me. Actually, she did, but that detail needn't be revealed to the world. Oh, the stories I told her about immortal monsters!

But I left out one crucial fact: that immortal monsters were real. And I was one.

Venefici Venator Immortalis

Immortal witch hunter, perpetually relocated to the home where a new generation of a coven emerged, with a new assignment, to still their mortal pulses, silence their mortal hearts. Then I fled, to begin the cycle yet again.

I was—I am—a monster created to destroy witches and their covens, to wipe the scourge of witches from the face of the earth, to implement the letter and spirit of the *Malleus Maleficarum*, the ancient guide urging hunters *to destroyeth witches and their heresy.*

As if the tome *Invectives Against the Sect of Waldensians* weren't enough! Through clenched teeth, I fought to suppress my abhorrence of my eternal assignment, my implacable rage toward the first one who conceived such reprehensible acts of murder and destruction.

Frustrated and furious, I slammed *Frankenstein* shut and threw it against the wall, tearing the faded blue and white striped wallpaper at one of the seams.

I didn't need to read about another monster, I already knew what it was like to be one.

Still, this was—is—my life, such as it is. Owning that painful knowledge, I got up, walked into the bathroom I shared with my cousins, rifled through a drawer to retrieve—carefully—a syringe, and measured into it the serum necessary to prolong my angry, pitiful existence. It was a weekly ritual, unless I'd exerted more energy than normal, exceeding the protection provided by my usual dose.

Concentrated in several rows on the inside of my left arm, tiny scars stood at attention, like soldiers waiting for another recruit to join their ranks. Without swabbing alcohol or worrying about hurting myself, I positioned and launched the syringe filled with the silvery substance, like a harpoon or a deadly spear, toward my arm, cutting myself without flinching.

Centuries of memories flooded my thoughts, filling my chest, the tips of my fingers. Memories harvested through all the years since my death and conversion. I don't recall anything of my life before death, before that moment of immortality; some do, some don't. I was one of the unlucky ones.

Or maybe I didn't *want* to know my past: where I'd lived, what my parents were like, what they did for a living, how my father laughed, how my mother cried, did she hold me in her arms at night, rocking me to sleep.

Memories lost forever.

But I have to admit my curiosity drove me. I'd searched and searched for answers about my past, a past gone from the moment I died, the moment I became someone else. Something else. Often, when I closed my eyes, I'd recall one particular event not from that ancient, unremembered life, but from countless searches I'd undertaken to find it.

In the first century after my conversion, I lived in Sicily and worked for a village blacksmith, who couldn't understand how I could withstand hours and hours hammering the anvil near the fire. One day, I went to the market for supplies. An old strega—a wise woman, or witch—walked up to me as I waited for the merchant. Wordlessly, she motioned. *Follow me*, her curled index finger said to me. Her face was obscured by the hood of her cape, tattered and threadbare. I followed her down a winding, narrow alley. The strega limped and stepped carefully on the cobblestone alley, never looking over her shoulder, certain I followed. She stopped in front of an archway with a wooden door, as wrinkled and weathered as she, pulled out a large, heavy key, and unlocked the door. With great effort, she pushed the door open, turned her head and motioned to me again. *This way*, commanded her gray eyes, barely visible through sagging eyelids.

Through another stone archway and up a flight of wide stone steps, I followed her through a second wooden door, as old as the first. Inside, she sat at a small table in what appeared to be a kitchen, dark and scented by bundles of herbs hung upside down, drying near an unlit fireplace. Glass jars sat on rows and rows of crooked, wooden shelves—jars filled with clear liquid, marinated blobs, dried flower petals, crushed powders, shriveled items in all shapes and sizes and colors.

"Sit," she spoke at last and spread a deck of tarot cards in a fan on the table. "Choose one," she commanded. I didn't dare disobey.

The old woman turned the card over with one trembling hand. "Ah, the Two of Cups," she whispered. The candles in her dimly lit kitchen flickered.

"And?"

"You will search for your True Love. Many many years. And when you find her, you must make a difficult choice. Eternity, or death. Live forever, or die with her. There will be strife, there will be much pain and agony, there will be sorrow and loss, there will be separation and reunion. Until then, you will not leave this earthly world for the next." I didn't respond. What could I say?

Her gnarled hands reached out for mine, turned one hand over, traced a long fingernail down my palm, a satisfied look on her face. I withdrew my hand quickly.

"You do not believe me." She shook her head slowly and clicked her tongue. "Ah, but I know what you are."

"You're not afraid of me?"

"No. You would not seek me out to kill me."

"I didn't seek you out."

"Ah, but you did. You have questions. I have answers. The cards do not lie. Your destiny was sketched on your palm before you were born."

108

I hesitated, then asked, "Do you really believe all this?" I waved the hand she read, palm up, over the kitchen table. "True love? Soul mates?"

"You doubt me."

I nodded.

"It matters not whether I believe. The Tarot, palmistry, these are vehicles for the Spirits to communicate. I do not choose what to say, I am told what to say. Over this I have no control."

"And this, this person, my True Love, how will I know her?"

"You will know," she assured me.

"But how?"

"You will know," she repeated. "Here." She pushed a piece of parchment and one of charcoal into my hand. "Now you must sketch."

"Sketch what?"

"Sketch *her.* The one you seek."

"How?"

"With your heart," she replied, raising one hand and holding the palm against her chest.

I laughed. "I don't have one anymore."

"Oh, but you do. The physical heart may be very different than it once was, but its shadow remains constant. The heart's shadow remembers."

"The heart's shadow remembers." I repeated her words and felt them engraved on my very nonhuman heart.

"Now leave," she ordered, pointing to her apartment door. "Go sketch and sketch, again and again, until at last you see her face."

Hesitantly, I got up to leave, turning my back on the strega, still seated at the table. When I turned to ask her more questions, she was gone.

Later that night, I sketched and wrote poetry in my leather journal in front of the livingroom fireplace in my family's isolated log cabin, hugging the black shores of Snow Valley Lake. The pile of logs crackled and spit as they burned. I bit the tip of my pencil.

Now you sketch, the strega had instructed, *again and again, until at last you see her face.*

How many times I'd closed my eyes, hoping to see her face, etching her eyes, her lips, the tip of her nose, I couldn't say. I imagined a pale sunlight filtering through her long hair, twisted in my longing fingers. I imagined a gentle breeze capturing her presence, hers and only hers, floating on rippling, sunlit waves, pushing it toward me, filling my lungs with a perfume bottle of her foreverness. I imagined her face, the curve of her lips, the timid smile that ignited her eyes, eyes that were always as green as a moonlit forest, haunted and mysterious.

You will know, the old woman had assured me.

You will know...

"You haven't heard a word I've said for the past ten minutes!" Miranda shrieked.

"Uh, what?" I said, startled.

"Hel-lo-o. Emeranne Goode? Her Coven? Your obsession with that pathetic witch? The one everyone voted you follow to Big Bear Lake? Everyone except me, of course."

"Of course," Giselle repeated.

"Since when was it a Fire Born's task to keep witches safe? The Varangian Guard will destroy all of us, and Delacroix will hand out trophies to all of you for doing exactly what you're *not* supposed to," she scoffed.

"The Coven was safe, and the Vales showed up just as I reported as soon as I returned home from Big Bear Lake."

"And Moe Stone's son, Luke," reminded Wallis.

"Oh, woopdeedo. Maybe you should be their body guard, protecting them and especially that Goode witch," challenged Miranda.

"What do you care about Emeranne?" I said to her curtly.

"Because if you have feelings for her, and I'm pretty sure you do, you'll get us in trouble. Just like Terrowin." Her words slashed into me as though her tongue were a dagger.

"Almost, dear, almost," corrected Allora.

"Whatever," she said, unconvinced. "Same difference."

"Mind your own business," I said, raising my voice louder than I'd intended.

She shot back. "It *is* my business!"

Allora sighed. "Miranda, dearest, it's only natural to develop feelings for…"

"For a witch? Let me remind you, Allora, the only feeling a Fire Born is supposed to have for *any* witch is elation, every time a coven is annihilated!"

"In this case, the young, the innocent Snow Valley Coven," Giselle pointed out sheepishly.

"Innocent? Don't make me sick," huffed Miranda. She stuck her finger down her throat and made gagging noises.

"Feelings for humans are only natural," I said defensively.

"No they're not! Not for Fire Born," Miranda argued. "In case you've forgotten, we're not exactly human any longer."

Wallis stood up. "Truce."

"Miranda," replied Allora, softening her voice, "you're not the only one who had a life before death and conversion. We can't change the past. What's done is done. You're no longer living in fifteenth century France. Now, you must exist for today, and today alone."

111

"Oh, how very prophetic," Miranda said, curling her lip, a flash of malice in her eyes.

"Miranda," warned Philippe, raising his authoritative voice, "that's quite enough."

"We still haven't resolved the problem at hand," I reminded them.

"Octavia and Ulric," Giselle said under her breath. "I always knew—"

Henry cut in. "They'd screw up one day?"

"They're certainly reckless," said Allora.

"They?" Miranda exclaimed. "And we're not?"

"That's not what I meant, Miranda," replied Allora. Miranda huffed.

"What now?" pressed Wallis.

I clenched my teeth. "Find Octavia and Ulric before any others die. Stop these senseless massacres—"

Philippe spoke up. "To end centuries of slaughter."

"End the witch hunt?" Miranda gasped. "That'll be a guaranteed second death sentence. *Our* death sentence. Are you out of your mind?"

"No, Miranda, I'm most certainly not," replied Philippe in his singular voice, rich and low. "Ben has retained more of his humanity—more, it appears, than any of the rest of us care to admit."

"Besides my son, Terrowin," reminded Allora.

Philippe nodded and turned to me. Sincere emotion from his ashen eyes sunk into mine. "Bennett, you have been many things to Allora and Terrowin and to my family," he said, acknowledging his four children. "With Sir Terence and Allora and Terrowin, you saved my family, gave us this immortal existence, although," he said with sad eyes, "Charlotte didn't survive the conversion."

"And I regret her death every day," said Allora, choking back tears.

I put my hand on Allora's tiny arm, whispering softly, "Me too."

"Ha!" cackled Miranda. "I bet you do."

"Miranda, that's truly quite enough!" ordered Philippe yet again. He turned to Allora. "It wasn't your fault. You weren't the one who betrayed my family. Had us arrested, tried for witchcraft. Imagine, my own brother!"

"Wait 'til I get my hands on him, my uncle!" spewed Henry, clenching his fists and pounding them together.

Allora drew a shallow breath. "Miranda, would you rather have had a short life over immortality?"

"It would have been better if we'd all died with Mother in that putrid, squalid dungeon," moaned Miranda.

"Do you really mean that?" Allora asked.

Miranda crossed her arms and clenched her teeth. "Yes."

"You don't like being what you are, yet you have no doubts about killing witches?"

"Well, maybe at first, but not any more."

"I don't understand," said Allora.

"I think I do." I tried to supply an explanation. "There are times when I question whether or not I'm glad you and Sir Terence saved me on the beach, where you said I'd washed ashore after the shipwreck," I admitted. "But that doesn't mean I'm not grateful."

"A short life would have been better than this, I don't know what to call it, this...this curse," replied Miranda aggressively.

Philippe redirected the conversation. "We can't change the past, as Allora has correctly pointed out. And I wanted to add that after Bennett helped us, all of us," he said, staring directly at Miranda, "to escape from prison, during the worst witch trials Europe ever experienced, Bennett obtained new identities for us, led us to safety. Out of all of us, Bennett was always the most compassionate, continuously experiencing such heart-wrenching agony every time we carried out assignments. Questioning why, why must he be, feel like, like—"

"A monster," I mumbled softly.

"But you're no such thing. We, none of us are, for that matter. And, above all else, Bennett, you and you alone have struggled the most with your immortal existence and the gruesome tasks you've been ordered, under threat of elimination, to undertake time and time again. And yet you've remained loyal and obedient."

"Wow, such a glowing review," Miranda laughed icily. "You'd think you haven't any other children who've been just as loyal and obedient."

"Miranda, what your father has tried to say doesn't renounce anyone's loyalty or obedience. Rather, it goes to what Ben has expressed outwardly, longer than any of us. That we all must retain something, some feeling deep down inside, from before we were immortal, before the conversion. When we still knew and expressed kindness, compassion, and respect for life." Allora, threw a sympathetic glance to Miranda. "If, darling, that is what you meant to say?"

"Yes, my love," Philippe answered Allora softly. "And yet, Miranda, despite loyalty and obedience and memories of life before death and immortality, you object more than any of us to the possibility of an alternate way, a better way, one we can all live with, so to speak."

"Terrowin made a choice," whispered Allora sweetly, ignoring Miranda. "Ben, too, has always questioned what we've been created to do. As did Sir Terence."

"Yes. And Sir Terence paid dearly for his doubts," agreed Philippe, shaking his dazzling white hair.

"What, then, have we resolved this evening?" I asked impatiently.

"That we're still so, so screwed." Henry smiled, sad and remote.

"Find Octavia and Ulric," said Wallis.

"And then freeze or boil the crap out of them," Henry said harshly.

"Or," Philippe suggested, "demand answers. Why they've come here, without any assignment. How it was possible to elude our unfailing detection of other witch hunters."

"Yes," nodded Giselle. "That's really troubling."

"And," Wallis added, "Who sent them to kill Charlsie. And why."

"We need to know," I said, "before any more witches in the Snow Valley Coven die."

"Before any more witches in the Snow Valley Coven die," Philippe repeated. "Shall we vote?" Everyone nodded.

Philippe cleared his throat. "Be it resolved that Bennett, of unknown origin, and the Bassetts, originally of the House of Valois-Faubourg, currently resident in Snow Valley, shall make every effort to locate, incarcerate and through nonviolent persuasion," Philippe emphasized as Henry pounded one fist on the table, "question Octavia and Ulric. And refrain from harming or allowing harm to the Snow Valley Coven in any way. All in favor, say Yea. If not, say Nay," he said, counting voices. "That's six Yeas, one Nay."

Only Miranda did not vote in favor of Philippe's plan, crossing her arms upon her chest, huffing and sneering. With one fist in the air, counting to three with her fingers, clenching her jaw and grinding her teeth, Miranda declared defiantly, "Assimilate. Infiltrate. Eliminate."

Chapter Eleven

Pulse

EMERANNE

The following week, school returned to normal for me and the rest of the Coven.

In geography class, Mr. DelMonaco handed out a thick stack of papers, the sight of which made students shuffle uncomfortably. "As you've already been informed, we'll be studying volcanoes in this class and in Mrs Yin's science class," he explained.

Carlton yawned as Mr. DelMonaco gave a boring, tedious lecture on volcanoes, or what he called ruptures in the planet's crust. The usual trio of boys snickered and snorted and made childish faces whenever Mr. DelMonaco used the words *escaped gases* and *eruptions*. The teacher grabbed my attention when he reviewed various types of volcanic rocks produced from lava, including cinnabar and obsidian.

Wasn't Ben's ring set with a snowflake obsidian? I'd guessed the stone was rare, I just didn't know how rare it was. The thought was still rolling around in my head when we got to science class.

"Open your textbooks to page forty-seven," instructed Mrs. Yin. "There you will find instructions for creating a classic chemical volcano and a mercury beating heart. Class will be divided into two. This half," she said, pointing to my section, "will recreate the heart. The other side, the volcano." She waved in the direction of Byron and Carlton, who sat at one of the black-topped lab desks at the back of the class.

Reading what I guessed was *Sports Illustrated* hidden in his notebook, Byron reclined against the wall where he rested his broad shoulders and interlaced his fingers behind his head. His feet were on the desk and his ankles crossed. He continued to recline and read until Mrs. Yin ordered him to remove his feet from the table and sit up straight.

"This is not your livingroom, Mr Walker."

I dragged my textbook out of my backpack, buried beneath my parka, which I'd draped over the bench, and turned to Chapter Three. When the class quieted down, Mrs. Yin squeaked chalk on the blackboard. When finished, she stepped away and pointed to a list of ingredients and a complicated formula next to the words ammonium dichromate: $(NH4)2Cr2O7$. She handed out masks, gloves and glasses, and opened all of the windows after distributing a deep rectangular aluminum tray filled half way with golden sand. The rest of the materials and equipment required for the volcano experiment were inside the trays: twenty grams of ammonium dichromate (that looked like orange crystals resembling tiny candied fruit), one round bottom flask, a porcelain filtering funnel, and Bunsen burner.

"Remember to use proper ventilation for any experiment. Since we do not have individual vents at our lab tables, I have opened the windows for your safety," she explained, waving one hand toward the long row of high windows. "Now, class, you can watch me first before we conduct the volcano experiment together, step by step. There are three main steps in this experiment. First, pour the ammonium dichromate into a large flask, like so, making sure to use gloves and wear a mask in this process. Ammonium dichromate is toxic and carcinogenic, which means it will irritate the skin and mucous membranes, and could cause cancer. It might look like a harmless powder, but it is acidic. Some call it Vesuvian Fire because it is used to make these experimental volcanoes and is also used in pyrotechnics.

"Next, cap the flask with a filtration funnel, like this, the second step," she explained, as she capped the flask with the funnel. "This will prevent most of the chromium oxide from escaping. As ammonium dichromate decomposes, it produces green chromium oxide ash. You will see this occur in a few minutes, as soon as I apply heat to the flask's bottom with the Bunsen burner, the third step in this process," she said, her eyes as wide as a child's on Christmas morning.

The same three boys from geography class giggled. "She said *bottom* and *bunsen*."

After that, Mrs. Yin demonstrated the mercury beating heart. This experiment required students to recreate an electrochemical reaction, making the silvery-white mercury beat like a human heart.

"I trust Mr. DelMonaco reviewed volcanic rock this morning and one of those rocks is cinnabar. To produce liquid mercury, crushed volcanic cinnabar ore must be roasted in rotary furnaces. During this smelting process, pure mercury separates from sulfur, evaporating. Quicksilver, or liquid mercury, was collected and stored in iron flasks. Samples are being passed around."

"Thank you," said Selene removing a flask from a metal container and passed it on to the next student.

Mrs. Yin elaborated. "Mercury, the only metal that remains liquid at room temperature, has a high boiling point. Six hundred and seventy-four degrees Fahrenheit to be precise. And its freezing point is somewhere around minus three hundred Fahrenheit or so. Very difficult to destroy." After an extended pause, Mrs. Yin turned the student's attention to the experiment.

"For the mercury beating heart, pay attention carefully. First, place a drop of mercury in your Petri dish, like this. Then, cover the drop with sulfuric acid, like so. Third, add hydrogen peroxide as an oxidizer. I'm almost done, ready to start the beating heart."

Selene and I turned our heads and cast the same look at Byron and Carlton. They nodded. The experiment required mercury. *Living silver.*

"The fourth step is crucial. With the tip of an iron nail, approach the drop of mercury very slowly. Do not touch the mercury! As soon as the nail is close to the mercury, the heart will start to beat for fifteen or twenty seconds. The mercury heart will stop beating after half a minute. Imagine the heart pumping blood through veins, although blood of course does not look like liquid mercury. The pulse on your wrist, your neck, cannot exist without the heart working, beating, pumping blood, that wondrous muscle preserving your life. Now, you try."

Mrs. Yin's voice faded in the background. I hastily scribbled a note in our secret code, based on my birthday, and slid the note toward Selene.

KGZVNZCZGKHZ
YJTJPOCDIFWZIDNVCPIOZM

Selene unfolded the note, deciphered it silently, nodded ever so slightly. Extra-vigilant today, Mrs. Yin caught me the minute I gave the note to Selene.

"Ms Goode!" Mrs. Yin's voice was as shrill as a football referee's whistle and twice as loud. "You are not to pass any notes in class! Give it to me this instant, Ms Laveau. I am surprised you'd get involved with Ms Goode's monkey business."

Selene handed Mrs. Yin the note with her head hung low, hiding a grin behind her mask. "What is the meaning of this?" she shrieked louder. "Explain yourself, Ms Goode."

"Um…you can ask Selene. She asked for a scrap piece of paper. The scribbling means nothing, Mrs Yin. It's just random doodling," I said contritely, batting my eyelashes.

Mrs. Yin searched my masked face and turned to Selene, who nodded. "It's true, Mrs Yin. I asked Emeranne for paper… just like she said."

Mrs. Yin's face appeared as red as the multi-hued cinnabar ore, having chastised me for passing nothing but a meaningless scrap piece of paper. Or so she thought. She returned the note to me. I thrust it inside my parka's puffy pocket.

"The good old Caesar shift. Works every time," Selene whispered.

I looked at her with grateful eyes through the scratched lenses of my oversized safety glasses. Selene scribbled in her notebook and turned to me, her eyebrows furrowed.

"As for your note, I translated the first line, *please help me*, and the second, *do you think Ben is a hunter*. The first part, you mean science class?" I nodded. "Of course, I'm happy to help, Ems, you can count on me. But the second part, why do you think Ben is a killer? Because of River's comments at the campground?"

Unable to answer Selene at that moment, I simply nodded slightly.

Selene loved science experiments and enthusiastically completed the silver heart. As her lab partner, I didn't object. Globs of quicksilver pumped on one side of the room and, on the other, orange ammonium dichromate decomposed into sparks. Carlton's volcano, by far the most impressive, spewed colorful streaks of light and glowing sparks that looked like a thousand fireflies dancing in the air.

When the buzzer sounded, Selene turned to me and said, "It's a mystery to me, Ems. I wouldn't draw conclusions about Ben or his family. Not yet."

120

The day of Snow Valley High's Homecoming dawned radiant and sparkling blue. All week, alumni arrived from near and far, crowding the little town of Snow Valley. Lively tailgate parties started days before the annual football game against Big Bear High Grizzlies. Given that Snow Valley High didn't have its own stadium, football games were played at Hastings Field off Snow Valley Lake Road.

The bleachers were almost full when Morgan pulled into the stadium parking lot. Morgan, Ardelle, Selene and I volunteered to decorate the outdoor bleachers in purple and silver, the school colors, draping banners, huge rosettes, and flags all around the stadium. The Big Bear Grizzlies' fans hung black and gold banners. We'd painted our faces with silver stars and wore purple felt pointed hats and purple woolen scarves, Ardelle's unmistakable imprint radiated on each hand-made accessory.

Ben and his cousins sat in the bleachers, a few rows up on the opposite side of the stairs that cut through the benches where I sat. Ben exchanged polite waves and nods to students and parents, recognizing many who frequented the Matterhorn.

The Grizzlies' mascot, clad in a faux fur grizzly bear costume, mock wrestled with Snow Valley's silver bearded wizard on the field. The wizard waved his wand at the bear mascot who raised his paws and collapsed, much to the screaming delight of the Wizards' boisterous fans. Marching bands played mash-ups of pop tunes. Cheerleaders took turns making complicated pyramids to entertain fans.

Dad arrived minutes before the coin toss, squeezing his way apologetically to sit with me. He was greeted enthusiastically, with warm pats on the back of his worn out school jacket. The Wizards won the toss and opted to receive. After kick off, the Wizards caught the ball on their own thirty-yard line, failing to advance. Play after play, the Grizzlies' defense blitzed constantly.

Dad hollered, urging the offense forward and encouraging Cuthbert Cameron to throw the ball long. Finally, the Wizards managed a first down, but their offense struggled against the Grizzlies' defense. Cuthbert was sacked twice, by the nose guard and outside linebacker. The Wizards were forced to punt on fourth and twenty-five.

From the sidelines, Cuthbert removed his purple and silver helmet, slammed it on the grass, barely missing the Gatorade dispenser. Coach Lombardi did the same with his AT&T headset when, on second down, the Grizzlies were on the scoreboard with a touchdown. And another. And another.

Over and over again, Cuthbert darted giant defensive ends and humungous linebackers, pushing the Wizards' helpless offensive line to the limit. The game didn't get any better for the Wizards, although the defense managed to contain the Grizzlies to a three-point field goal.

After the special teams left the bright kelly green field, Cuthbert huddled and as soon as his offense was set on the line of scrimmage, pumped the ball, turned left, right and left again, avoiding sack after sack, until he could no longer prevent the inevitable.

With a few seconds left before halftime, Cuthbert collapsed on the field.

The entire crowd gasped.

"There's no back-up quarterback," groaned Dad. "Rodgers tore his ACL during last week's practice."

Morgan threw me a look, the one that always said the same thing: time for a miracle.

By halftime, a twenty-four to zero score didn't sit well with Snow Valley High's fans, disgruntled at their team's poor performance. Henry Bassett raced up the bleacher stairs and threw his hands above his head and appeared to be in a heated argument.

All at once, Ardelle, Morgan and I held our breath.

"Did you have—?" I said.

"An Ice Vision!" squealed Ardelle in disbelief.

"*Shhh!*" Morgan ordered. "Careful! We can't be overheard!"

I stood up. "Let's get out of here."

Ardelle, Morgan, Selene and I shuffled past my dad, who looked at us suspiciously.

"I know what you're thinking, Dad," I said to him, "but we're leaving to get ready for Homecoming Dance. You know how much time it takes girls to get ready, right?"

"Yeah," he murmured. "As long as it's only the dance you're concerned about," he warned, following us down the stairs to the sidelines where Cuthbert was being driven off the field, stretched out on the back of a golf cart. He gave the cheering crowd two thumbs up.

We left the stadium in Morgan's car and drove away to save the game.

Chapter Twelve

Trance

EMERANNE

I stared into the fieldstone fireplace where water simmered within a deep, wrought iron pot hanging from a large hook imbedded above the hearth. Morgan sprinkled a special herb mixture in the pot. Scents of incense, sandalwood, and others I didn't recognize filled the livingroom.

The Coven's breathing slowed. A thick blanket of mist surrounded us. Sound receded, leaving a sense of detachment and deep concentration. The fireplace was out of focus. Together, the Coven broke through the mists.

The Ice Vision presented the third quarter kick off.

Shock flashed across Morgan's face. "Do you see? See what I—?"

"Ben? Ben Bassett?" said an uncertain Ardelle.

"Jogging on the field," I confirmed.

"He's so private, always sketching and scribbling in his notebook," remarked Morgan.

"I didn't know he played football," Selene said.

"Byron and Leland are on the field too!" Ardelle reported excitedly, pushing her horn-rimmed glasses up her freckled nose. "Do you see them?"

"Yes!" I said.

"And I see, I see the football snapped to Ben," said Morgan.

"Oh no, Ben was sacked, pushed back to the Wizards' fifteen-yard line," Ardelle said.

"Second down and fifteen. Ben took the snap," continued Morgan.

"Wait a sec, did the announcer say something about an off-tackle rush? Faked handoff to a tight end? Rushing the ball, gaining, what's that? Five yards! Ben slid safely," I gasped.

Morgan raised her eyes to the ceiling. "Focus on the Ice Vision. And, Selene, it's time—"

"To consult the Spirit Board," she said. "I'm on it."

Anxiously, Ardelle encouraged us. "Visualize Byron breaking tackles and darting and bouncing around the defense like a pinball past linebackers and defensive ends and cornerbacks and safeties," until, at last, she took a slow intake of breath and calmly exhaled.

"The huddle breaks. Offense takes its formation at the line of scrimmage," I said intensely, imitating a television sports announcer, until I heard Dad's voice. Pistol, was all he said, whatever that meant. I went on. "From the pocket, Ben yells KILL KILL KILL." I shouted out loud as I heard Ben's voice in the Ice Vision.

"The offense shifted, catching the defense off guard," huffed Ardelle, as if she herself was in the game. In a way, she was. We all were.

All except for Selene, who announced, "A message from the Spirit Board."

I prompted Selene. "And?"

"Double double toil and trouble…"

"Fire burn and cauldron bubble," completed Ardelle in a low voice.

Morgan raised her eyebrows. "Macbeth. Again?"

"A good sign," Selene concluded, wearing a mischievous grin.

The Coven plunged into a deep trance, deeper, deeper... blue sky yellow sunlight stroked purple silver black gold jerseys green white gridiron brown football...snapped pumped brown purple silver flash...down the field...black gold smothered purple silver...purple silver faked handoff...spin...brown into purple silver smoking cannonball shot out of the pocket...faster faster faster...five ten fifteen twenty yards...come on, Byron, come on...I shared Ice Vision images with Ardelle, Morgan, and Selene...run all the way all the way down the field don't stop... thirty, thirty-five...run bounce spin evade black gold...running running moving moving spinning spinning purple silver flickered dissolved black gold...eighty yards end zone.

Selene cheered. "Did you see—"

"Touchdown!" Ardelle said.

I saw the Wizards score a two-point conversion from a perfectly executed pass to Leland. Saw an onside kick. Saw a special teams' player recover a fumble at the Grizzlies' twenty-eight yard line. Saw him run into the end zone.

"Another touchdown!" I shouted.

"Because the Grizzlies fumbled again," laughed Morgan. "Who thought of that?"

Ardelle curled the fingers on one hand and polished her nails on her shirt.

"I knew it was you!" I chuckled. "Good one, Ardelle!"

"Well, I do watch Monday Night Football with my dad on occasion," she grinned, "and picked up a thing or two."

Morgan concentrated. "Ben completed a brilliant reverse hand off to Byron, rushing for a third touchdown."

"What's the score?" asked Selene.

"Twenty-four to twenty-two," I replied, scanning the scoreboard high above the field.

"Twenty-three," corrected Morgan. "Ben gambled and scored another two-point conversion."

"It's late in the fourth quarter," Selene said in a serious tone. "Enough time for one last play." I nodded, joined hands with Selene, to my left, and Morgan to my right with Ardelle holding hands tightly between Morgan and Selene who chanted along with the Coven.

If only the Grizzly quarterback fumbled or was intercepted, I wished silently.

Black gold first down fourth quarter...quarterback long throw purple silver brown flash. A pick six! Wizard fans screamed and cheered wildly.

Ardelle's eyes widened in disbelief. "Henry intercepted the ball!"

Catch the ball catch the ball catch the ball, I mumbled over and over again...*deafening black gold roars...ball snapped...left right fall back pocket...faked handoff*...I closed my eyes, hoping for a miracle pass to Leland...*catch the ball...Leland catch it*...closer...close enough for a field goal...

The announcer's voice hoarse—football snapped—black gold pumped football purple silver glued to black gold pressure brown on blue a Hail Mary pass Hail Mary Hail Mary Hail Mary the announcer screamed over and over and over and...

When the curtain of mist drew closed, the Coven floated within, as though the mists were summoned to carry us back to reality. However, heavy fog did not recede from me. I floated away from Coven. Three sets of eyes, sea foam green and hazel and amethyst, held mine, then disappeared.

silence
relief
collapse
blackout

"Ems," a fearful voice said to me, shaking me and raising her voice, "Ems, you okay?"

Light as a feather, my body floated. My voice struggled to say *I'm fine I'm fine I'm fine.*

Ardelle's pleas reached my ears. "Ems!"

"Rest for a while, Ems," Morgan said, gentle and troubled.

A cool liquid watered my aching throat, trickled down my face, dropped on my neck.

...apples moonlight glowing eyes fire...

Darkness had fallen in Snow Valley by the time I woke up.

"Feel better?" Morgan asked maternally.

I nodded, searching for my voice.

"Seems the Ice Vision drained you the most," said Selene.

"I'll draw a bath with my healing oils and herbs," said Morgan. "By the way, the Wizards won, the final score, twenty-six to twenty-four."

"A field goal," added Selene.

I gestured with my eyes, unable to find my voice.

Except for Selene, we got ready for the Homecoming Dance. Reluctantly, I agreed to wear a dress for the first time in my life. Ardelle had sewn outfits based on Morgan's designs, conforming to the dance's nineteen eighties theme, staying clear of Miami Vice pastels, Risky Business black wayfarers, Flashdance leggings, Boy George makeup, Madonna lace.

Instead, Carlton's favorite group, the B52s, inspired our costumes.

"I forgot my sunglasses. Whoa, those dresses are bright," remarked Selene. "Where'd you get the material?"

"Big Bear Vintique," boasted Ardelle, adding, "for a steal!"

Morgan raised one eyebrow. "I bargained for a pile of used clothes. And the boots, too."

"Are you sure you can't convince River to come to the dance?" Ardelle coaxed.

Selene shook her head. "Not on your life and besides, I have nothing to wear."

"River's driving up Snow Valley Mountain Road," Morgan announced as she stretched her neck by the dormer window.

"Well, gotta go. Bye. Have a nice time. Catch you later." Selene laughed, dashing out my bedroom door.

I pulled on black vinyl boots, a yellow sleeveless dress dropping straight down from my armpits, past my hips, above my knees. Morgan gave me a huge beehive wig in shades of black and gold. Her dress was hot pink and Ardelle's, a shocking lime green. Their boots, neon blue and traffic cone orange. Morgan's beehive, a creamy whipped blonde. Ardelle's, a bright fiery red, brighter than her naturally auburn hair.

I had trouble getting into Morgan's low car, barely able to fit my beehive inside. Together, we drove to the dance, our towering wigs sticking out of the Citroën's open roof, the practical solution, apart from removing our wigs. Morgan picked up Gareth, squeezing his wheelchair into the tiny vehicle for the drive to Snow Valley High.

Tonight, the gymnasium's bleachers and folding accordion divider were pushed back. Framed movie posters hung from the hand-crafted wooden walls—*Sixteen Candles*, *The Breakfast Club* and *St. Elmo's Fire*—and eighties pop music throbbed from the student deejay's elaborate sound system.

Most students stared at our bright outfits as soon as we arrived. Morgan ignored them, stretched her model-like legs as if she were on a catwalk, purchased tall glasses of pink lemonade, and delivered one tray of drinks to a discreet corner where I huddled with my friends, sipping and swaying to the music.

Dapper in an electric blue suit with a narrow multicolored tie in neon colors that coordinated with our dresses, Gareth laughed hysterically with Morgan, who'd wheeled him to the dance floor, swinging her arms like windmills to New Order and OMD and Depeche Mode.

Understandably, Carlton skipped the dance to stay with Cuthbert at the hospital.

"Too bad," I chuckled and waved my hand from the tip of my head to my boots. "After all, this was his idea!"

Fortunately, Cuthbert's prognosis for a full recovery was positive.

When girls screamed and boys cheered, I knew the victorious football team had arrived. Their voices echoed off the folded bleachers. Hovering around the large group of hysterical girls, Byron and Leland looked terribly uncomfortable in their swanky suits. And flanked by Kandida and Alba Kanz in their cheerleaders' uniforms, looking more uncomfortable than Byron and Leland, Bennett Bassett walked into the gym, dressed in a black tuxedo with a burgundy vest and white shirt, dark hat and a dramatic coal black cape lined in white draped over his broad shoulders. A disfigured white mask molded perfectly to Ben's face, hiding his face except for two holes for eyes and nostrils. At first, I wasn't sure who he was supposed to be. But when I glanced back and forth to one of the posters hanging on the gymnasium wall, I figured out his costume.

Ben Bassett was the Phantom of the Opera.

Morgan and I stepped out of the gymnasium, her beehive hair towering over mine. We strolled to the bathroom and adjusted our cone head wigs in front of the narrow mirrors.

"Ben looks so handsome, doesn't he?" she said.

I applied cherry flavored lip gloss, and shrugged. "Whatever."

Morgan examined me with narrowed eyes and mumbled, "Hmmm."

We walked out of the bathroom toward our discreet corner. When my eyes adjusted to the faded light, our group had grown. I sighed, relieved. Just Byron and Leland. However, I hadn't spotted someone else crouched down on one knee, waving white-gloved hands, recreating a pass from the miracle game, talking to Gareth.

Phantom Ben of the Opera. Unexpectedly, butterflies flapped in my stomach.

"Hi Emeranne, Morgan," he said with a tip of his hat.

My tall gold and cobalt hairdo glided toward Ben, who swung his cape, ran white-gloved fingers through his hair, straightened the scarf thing around his neck.

Transfixed, I stared as Ben slid his gloved palm down his burgundy vest.

"You look nice," he said to me, his voice deep and low. "And tall," he added while drawing a line from his fedora to my beehive.

Morgan nudged me. "Uh…th-thanks," I mumbled. "So…so do you. Look nice."

I dropped my eyes and felt my face burning. In a softer voice, he said, "I like your outfits, so very original, in my opinion. Most girls are Madonna before she hit it big. A bit too messy for me."

I scanned the gym. My eyes found Ben's cousins, all wearing ornate masks. Henry wore a blue and silver brocade vest under a long-tailed jacket. Giselle and Wallis wore long white gloves covering toned arms and elaborate ball gowns in glistening fabrics framing perfect figures.

"Oh, I almost forgot…congratulations. I didn't know you played on the football team."

"I don't. But Henry begged me to play after Cuthbert was hurt," he said. "I saw you leave at half time. I guess you couldn't bear to see the massacre?"

"Oh, you know what girls are like," I stammered. "Took us ages to get ready."

The music slowed down and I mouthed the words. Ben gave me a warm glance, and motioned one white glove toward the dance floor. "How about a dance?"

Me? I pointed to myself.

Ben nodded and held out one gloved hand. He took mine gently in his as he guided me to the middle of the dance floor. All eyes were glued on us when he locked me in a warm embrace and pulled me close, touched my cheek gently and rocked me around in small circular movements. His eyes never left mine. When his hand moved from my right hip to the small of my back, my heart pounded. He smiled and held my hand close to his chest, beneath The Phantom's signature mask, dancing in a magical world where no one else seemed to exist.

Moments into the song, he pulled away from me and ever so slightly lifted my chin toward his mask. I almost thought he was going to kiss me right there in the middle of the dance floor. But he didn't.

Still, Ben's touch created shockwaves of chills inside. Not the kind of chills from a cold, blustery wind or drops of freezing rain down your back or jumping into Big Bear Lake on a warm, summer day or wearing a wet snow suit after a sunny winter afternoon of lying face up on slowly melting snow, sweeping snow angels.

These chills were different. Chills I'd only experienced near Ben, whose expressive silver eyes evoked worry through his mask. "Are you cold?"

"No." I lied.

Ben didn't believe me. He removed his left hand from my back and draped me in his cape, pulling me closer, closer toward him. Closer to his mouth, his broad chest, his suit of armor.

Closer and closer and closer.

Ben sighed a sigh that matched the beating of my heart.

I exhaled, closed my eyes, imagining his warm soft lips on mine. Imagining how I'd run my fingers through his dark curly hair. How I'd place my hand on his chest, how he'd lift my chin, just before I imagined he'd kiss me.

Ben's sweet breath would brush my neck, his lips on my forehead, on my cheek, on my neck. His lips. My lips. Pressed together. Again and again and again…

I wished I could dance within Ben's strong, protective arms, dance to an everlasting playlist compiled just for us. Dreamily, I drifted away, lost in thought, until someone pinched my left shoulder. I turned my head, glanced over my shoulder where one long, black fingernail protruded out of a black lace fingerless glove, the finger poking me until my shoulder hurt.

Another tapping sound, a pointy black leather ankle boot over ripped black fishnet stockings, stomping impatiently. I followed the stockings upward, past the full, pale pink puffy crinoline, past a racy black lace bustier, past countless strands of hearts and crosses dangling from her neck, past the purple-black lipstick and one faux beauty mark painted above curled, snarling lips. Up to glaring blue eyes shaking with rage, tossing long heart-shaped pendant earrings framed by blonde, messy curls tied back with a big black bowed ribbon.

"I'm cutting in," announced Kandida curtly. "You've had more than your share." And just like that, Kandida Kanz squeezed my arm, tore it away from Ben and forcefully shoved me away. "It's my turn, freak."

I rocked back on the heels of my boots from the force of Kandida's shove.

Ben glared at Kandida. "The song isn't over yet."

"Oh, but I think it is," she snarled back.

Ben adjusted his mask and searched my face. I found my footing and glued my heels to the floor, unable to react one way or the other.

"Emeranne, I'm so, so sorry," he said sweetly.

"You're not the one who needs to apologize," I said curtly. "Not like I'll get one," I mumbled, adding something about Kandida getting what she'll deserve.

"What's that supposed to mean? Should I be scared? Shaking in my ankle boots?" Kandida hissed. "Why don't you take your oversized hairdo and your pathetic bumblebee self and go back to that stinking hive of loser friends over there before you sting anyone else."

I didn't move and Ben didn't let me go either.

"Hell-o-o? Didn't you hear a word I said?"

"Oh, I heard you loud and clear, Kandida Kanz. You remind me of around two thousand three hundred and seventy-seven girls I've met, and not in a good way."

Kandida's face froze. "Excuse me? Is that supposed to be funny?"

"No, actually, it's supposed to be the truth," he said with a mischievous smile on his face.

"Oh, ha! Ha ha ha ha ha! You really *are* funny, Ben. Now, let's get serious. Are you coming to my party tonight? After the dance? She's not invited, but you are and Henry and the rest of your cousins," cooed the wannabe Madonna.

I let go of Ben and walked away.

"What did that ghastly girl do now?" Morgan fumed, leaning over Gareth's chair. Byron threw his huge arms around me.

"Oh, you can imagine. Kandida tried to cut in. Ben resisted but I wasn't going to stand there and let her talk down to me like that. Let's leave," I said to my friends, "before I do something I'll regret."

Kandida's shrieks of laughter followed me all the way across the gymnasium door.

BENNETT

The first snowfall blanketed lawns and clung to drooping pine boughs as though snowflakes were puffs of icing sugar, dusting edible ornaments thrust upon mounds of fluffy layer cakes. Winter reliably arrived early in Snow Valley.

Miranda's words had really stung. *Stupid witch*, she snapped. *Your obsession with that pathetic witch…will get us all in trouble.* Miranda's words echoed in my mind. Was she right? Was I obsessed with Emeranne? I didn't think so. Well, maybe a little bit. I don't know.

I was more obsessed with finding *her*, the one, whoever that may be.

You will know, the strega had said to me.

As the snow fell heavier and heavier, and the road accumulated more and more layers, I thought about the centuries that had passed, wishing hoping believing the visions of her, the dreams of her, the belief I'd held onto wasn't merely an illusion. A hopeless delusion, as Miranda would have me believe.

"Give it up, Bennett." I'd heard Miranda say that for centuries, whenever she examined my sketches, drawings of a girl I'd never met. To me, this girl was real, alive—flesh hair eyes lips shoulders arms hands chest. Real too, was my composition, made while driving, editing it as though I wrote in my journal:

> ~~how many lifetimes~~ no, that's not accurate
> I haven't had a lifetime since, well, since…

only eternal after lifetimes…

try this instead… *how many sunsets*
~~*would you wait*~~ *would your eyes endure*
to be with the one you ~~*adore worship*~~
think think think… ~~*dream about*~~ no
love
love only *love* just *love*
one sunset?
is one enough?
you blink
and that first sunset
is over…

My poem had to wait. I braked and parked my Silverado on the side of the road minutes after I left the school's icy parking lot. Walking on Snow Valley Mountain Road to who knows where, in the middle of a snowstorm, Emeranne turned her hood away, avoiding me, and fixed her eyes on the snow-covered ground, shielding her face from being slapped by piercing snowflakes amidst a howling blizzard.

I reached over and opened the passenger door. A blast of ice pellets blew inside the truck.

"Are you insane? Get in!"

Emeranne lifted her chin. She hesitated, and seemed to assess the weather, then climbed inside the warm truck.

"In case you haven't noticed, the weather is bad, like snowstorm bad."

"It's not that bad. Normal weather for Snow Valley," she shrugged indifferently.

I covered my nose with my hands, thumbs resting below my jaw, tips of my fingers pressed together. After exhaling a few warm breaths into my palms, I put my gloves on, turned to her and asked, more sharply than I'd intended, "Did you really intend to walk home in this weather?"

She bit her lip pensively. "I didn't think—"

"Obviously, you didn't. Next time, ask me for a ride. Agreed?"

Emeranne hesitated for a long, long moment. "Agreed."

I drove north on Snow Valley Mountain Road, omitting to ask where she lived. I already knew, having followed her home from Big Bear Lake, at a safe distance. Emeranne pushed back her parka's hood. Flyaway strands of her smooth black hair stood up from the top of her head, tickled her ears, stuck to the sides of her face, held by static electricity.

Swatting at a few strands of hair, she exhaled. "It's one three three one."

A slight grin formed around my mouth. "Interesting address," I mumbled quietly, almost to myself. "You were going to walk home? Really?"

"It's not that far. I do it all the time. Well, usually on my bike," she asserted.

"In case you haven't noticed, it's not exactly mountain bike weather any more. No more walking home in snowstorms." Emeranne nodded silently. "You left the dance so quickly and I didn't get a chance to—"

"My friends wanted to leave," she interrupted curtly.

"That was rude what Kandida said to you. She really pissed me off."

Her green eyes shone though her voice remained neutral. "Just her usual antics."

"I gave Kandida quite an earful," I told her reassuringly.

Her icy voice layered with doubt, Emeranne revised my comment and said, "You mean, you gave her an earful during her party."

I laughed and tossed my head back. "Are you serious? I wouldn't attend any Kanz party! They'd never top Studio 54. Now that was a party."

"Huh?" she asked, confused.

"Oh never mind," I grinned. "Right after you left, I told Kandida she was rude, and some other stuff I'd rather not repeat."

Emeranne raised her eyebrows in surprise. "Really?"

"Yeah, really."

"Bet that went over well."

"Yeah, Kandida threatened she'd have Daddy downgrade the Matterhorn's A rating."

"She didn't!"

"Yeah, she did. Can you believe it?"

"Yeah, knowing Kandida. Don't be surprised if she follows through."

"As spoiled as the twins are, Mayor Kanz knows better than to mess with Allora. She may be petite but she's tough as nails," I added, leaving out the *you don't know how tough she can be* part. Instead I changed the subject. "Since Homecoming you've been so elusive. I didn't see you at the last football game."

"Oh, I've been busy."

"The Wizards won the championship in case you're wondering."

"I heard."

"Were you avoiding me?"

She crossed her arms. "No."

I didn't believe her but didn't argue the point. I turned up the music and hummed contentedly. My truck climbed at a snail's pace, the roads increasingly slippery—plow trucks with sand and salt hadn't touched Snow Valley Mountain Road. The windshield repelled thousands of huge snowflakes, the road ahead barely visible. As the snow tires dug in, thick layers of ice and snow were sliced efficiently.

"How are your art class projects coming along?"

"Oh, pretty good," she said, further remarking, "though I'm not as good an artist as Morgan. Or you."

"Your sketches looked better than pretty good to me, you know the ones I mean? The two on the picnic table. Were they drawings of anyone in particular?"

Emeranne's face turned white and she swallowed a few times. "Oh, um, no, those weren't mine, they're Morgan's," she stuttered uncomfortably. "Drop me off on the right, up here, near the mailbox," she said abruptly, pointing to the side of the road.

"I don't think so," I replied. She didn't realize I referred to both of her comments. The sketch detail was better kept to myself.

I turned into the driveway, certain I heard her heartbeat pick up. She got out of the truck quickly and said a quick *thanks* then shot me a look of surprise as I opened my own door and followed her toward the house.

A snow shovel sat on the porch. Without another word, and before Emeranne could object, I cleared the front walkway. Keys jingled and a click sounded from the porch. I put the shovel back in place and looked into Emeranne's dark eyes, mysterious and secretive and serene all at once. Reflecting the pine forest deep within. Snowflakes landed on her long, curly eyelashes.

"Thanks again for the ride, Ben. And for cleaning the pathway…my dad'll be happy."

"No problem. Anytime." Emeranne opened the door to go inside. I wanted to prolong the rare chance I've had to chat with her, so I asked, "You don't drive yet, do you?"

"No. I'm supposed to start Driver's Ed soon. But I'm not all that keen, to be honest."

"I can teach you how to drive if you'd like," I offered.

Her face lit up, then darkened slightly. "I wouldn't wish that on you."

"You don't want to drive?"

"Not really. I prefer my bike," she admitted.

"Well, if you change your mind, the offer is open," I said, and whispered, "this was nice. Spending a bit of time with you." I was taking a chance, but I couldn't help myself, wanting to see her reaction.

Her face transformed from a pale shade of pink to a hint of red. "Sure, um, and thanks again. I'd only be half way home right now."

I waved one index finger, scolding her. "Never try that again. Ever." Emeranne offered her best look of repentance. "Are you going to the Halloween fundraiser?" I blurted.

Snow Valley Town Council proposed using the high school's gym for trick or treating, given that the Lookout Murder remained unsolved. During a heated Council public forum, parents voiced objection to traditional door-to-door trick or treating, worried about potential dangers with a killer on the loose. Others wanted the event cancelled altogether. Mayor Kanz struck a compromise that narrowly passed, ensuring kids wouldn't miss out on Halloween and the school could raise much-needed funds for local charities. The school site offered a secure alternative.

"Yeah. I guess so. What about you? Going as the Phantom again?"

"Yes I'm going. And no, not as the Phantom. That was so eighties," I joked.

"Yeah. Eighteen eighties," she laughed, wiping a cluster of snowflakes from her eyelashes.

"Believe me, it's an overrated era," I said.

"What?"

"Oh, nothing." I smiled silently and extended my hands to catch snowflakes in the palms of my gloves.

"Every snowflake is different," she said to me, moving her gaze from my eyes to my gloves.

"Do you like being as different as a snowflake?"

Emeranne thought for a moment. "Yes," she replied eventually. "More interesting."

I smiled and adjusted my snow-encrusted trapper's hat. "I'll be late for my shift."

"Oh," she said to me, sounding disappointed. "Um, drive safely."

"I will," I promised. "Before I forget, here's my cell number. You don't have an excuse to walk home ever again."

"Here's mine," she said. "And I will."

"See you tomorrow," I said.

Neither of us seemed to know what to do next, our boots frozen on the porch, so she made the first move and pushed open the front door. In doing so, she ran into me. Inadvertently, I half-hugged her as she stumbled into my arms.

I tipped my head, touching her forehead lightly, hearing her hold her breath.

"Bye, Emeranne," I said, lowering my voice and parting my lips and closing my eyes for a moment, to feel her exhale, her soft thin breath brushing my face. After an extended, silent minute, I let her go gently and walked to my vehicle.

"Bye, Ben," I heard her say quietly behind me. I turned my back and hesitated, watched her wave from the threshold as though in a trance until I got in and drove my Silverado to the Matterhorn.

While delivering pizzas that same evening, I continued the poem, whispering each word to myself, reciting what I'd composed so far, working out the next words, asking questions I'd feared to ask, fearing the answers wouldn't be what I longed to hear. Words streamed in front of my eyes. I imagined her eyes sparkled brighter than icicles in the midday sun.

> *how many sunsets*
> *would your eyes endure*
> *to be with the one you love?*
> *one sunset?*
> *is one enough?*
> *you blink*
> *and that first sunset*
> *is over*

More words came to me, inspired by snowflakes dusting Emeranne's curving eyelashes and blushing lips and whispering eyes. I'd never thought about any specific girl whenever I wrote poetry. Never, not in all those centuries. Never, that is, until tonight. Emeranne was the first girl I ever thought of while composing. With that emotion, I added,

> *how many sunsets*
> *can you endure*
> *to wait for the one you love?*

I didn't have any answers to my own questions.

I knew only one thing for certain: I longed to find out the answers.

You will know, I heard the old Italian woman say to me as I drove through the soft snow. *You will know.*

Chapter Thirteen

The Hunter's Moon

EMERANNE

On the morning of Tuesday, October thirty-first, the aroma of coffee told me Dad was already up. Stretching my arms high above my shoulders, I sat up and yawned, showered and changed. I hadn't had any nightmares since the day Ben drove me home. I didn't think there was any connection, only a coincidence. And then, I reminded myself: Snow Valley didn't have coincidences.

Downstairs, Dad prepared blueberry pancakes dripping with maple syrup. Matt and Geneva sniffed the air eagerly, raised their snowshoe paws, and rested one paw each on my thighs, wagging their tails. Dad's face beamed, looking more and more like Grizzly Adams, sporting his bushy winter beard and wearing a red plaid flannel shirt. "Happy sweet sixteen, Ems."

Matt and Geneva barked enthusiastically.

"Thanks, Dad," I said appreciatively, cutting generous portions of pancake for Matt and Geneva, their foreheads wrinkled in anticipation.

"Just wanted to make your day extra special," he said and lowered his voice and looked away for a moment. "And here's...here's something handed down from Jo's side of the family. Maerlynn said Jo'd probably want you to have it for your sixteenth. But if you don't want…"

I had to rescue him from this torture. "Sure I'll take it off your hands." I winked and took the small package wrapped in burgundy tissue paper. Even though Jo's mom, Gran Maerlynn, lived in nearby Crestridge, we weren't close and hardly saw one another, too painful for Dad, too many memories.

"Ems, I'm sorry, but I gotta go. See ya tonight."

As soon as Dad left with the dogs, I nervously unwrapped the burgundy paper to find a beautiful oval stone—the same deep color as the tissue paper—set in a silver pendant shaped like a crescent moon. The stone itself was the size of a large walnut. A sudden sensation like a lightning bolt shot up my arm when I held the stone in my hand. The stone sparked and turned flaming red with orange and gold highlights. Startled, I gasped, and dropped the stone. The necklace hit the kitchen floor and the pendant turned blood red.

Hesitantly, I picked up the pendant and put it around my neck. The stone wasn't broken, and had stopped glowing. I wondered if it was just my imagination. I wore the necklace to school beneath my hoodie.

Classes were a blur that morning, consisting of adorning the gym with decorations. The gym was now chock-full of spiders and cobwebs and floating ghosts. I stopped by my locker to drop off textbooks I didn't need for the afternoon. When I opened my locker door, a note fell out. I looked around, wondering at first if a student dropped the note accidentally, but when I picked it up, the folded paper had my name on it. I didn't recognize the writing. I read the note.

> *and of love*
> *what does the heart say?*
> *it beats its silent wings*
> *before it flies away*

Either this was a joke or a mistake. Yet, my name was on the unsigned note. I rushed to the cafeteria where my friends waited at our usual table.

"Happy birthday Ems," said Ardelle, her smile brightening the entire room.

"Yeah, happy—"

I cut Byron off. "Thanks. Look, someone left this in my locker." I passed the note around. "And I don't want to be teased. It's my birthday."

"No signature," remarked Leland.

"Curious," said Carlton.

"A secret admirer." Byron's mischievous grin annoyed me.

"I said no teasing."

Morgan looked at the note again. "Do you recognize the writing?"

"No."

"Must be someone really shy," suggested Ardelle.

"Guess I may never know," I said and put the note into my backpack.

Selene saw my necklace, and with a quick intake of breath commented, "A bloodstone. I've only heard about bloodstones in legends but haven't seen one in person. You know, Ems, bloodstones are extremely rare and magical." Ardelle and Morgan nodded.

I recounted what happened when I held the bloodstone in my hand.

"Interesting," was all Selene offered.

The Blood Moon shone high on the night of my sixteenth birthday. It had risen slowly in the clear evening sky. As it rose, the full moon seemed to overflow from the crimson sky onto the valley below. Reddish tones cast strands of light, transforming the calm white landscape to an ominous blood orange hue and spilling inside the gym through windows high above.

Dad called it the Hunter's Moon, immense and round and bright, so much so that it assisted hunters to track and kill their unfortunate prey. I preferred to call it October's Blood Moon. Selene said it was a transformational period. A magical time. A time when the glowing Blood Moon reinforced intricately woven charms.

In the early evening, we returned to set up our booth. Morgan and Ardelle distributed our costumes, and we changed in the locker room, buzzing with excited girls changing into costumes and jostling for mirror space to apply their Halloween makeup. Morgan was Snow White, just stepped off the movie screen. Her ivory cheeks were rosy with blush and eclipsed by full lips, the perfect shade of crimson. She wore a chin length black wig with a red ribbon tied at the top of her head. Her royal blue dress had a full yellow skirt and puffy capped blue sleeves with yellow pleats. A tall white collar stood stiffly behind her neck, draped by a long red cape, flowing off Morgan's tall, slender body. Tan shoes with red bows were fitted on white tights. The only thing missing were tiny blue and white birds to hold up the bottom of her dress. Or was that Cinderella? I always mixed up fairy tales.

Morgan's costume, coupled with a plastic toy pickaxe in her hand, suggested a dwarf was my most likely character. After all, the dwarfs were miners.

"Ardelle and I felt younger kids would love Snow White, rather than something scarier, like vampires or ghosts or zombies," she explained thoughtfully. "We've planned bobbing for apples, cotton candy and a Dunk the Dwarf tank."

"And Carlton was okay with this?" Carlton usually had the last word on such ventures.

"As long as he was Doc," said Morgan.

146

"Always a catch with Carlton, huh? Wait a second. Where did you find a dunk tank?"

"When Selene told River about the Halloween fundraiser, he asked Luke for ideas. Luke had worked at Big Bear City's midway last summer. It was either that or one of those horrid shooting games, you know what I mean, with revolving tin ducks and toy guns. And we all hate guns and hunting. Not child appropriate, either, in my view."

"Really? Luke Stone?" I had no idea he worked at the midway.

"Yes. And he's coming to the fundraiser tonight. Luke and the Vales are bringing kids from the Moonridge reservation. They don't really have Halloween in that area, according to Selene..." Morgan's voice faded.

I knew what she didn't say regarding the reservation's poverty and persistent unemployment. "That's nice, though I didn't think Luke would see me in a dwarf costume," I said to her as I pointed to a lime green tunic with huge gold buttons.

"Ems, you can wear mine if you'd prefer," she offered generously. "And this is the very last costume. You'd insisted it didn't matter what you wore...the guys agreed you wouldn't want to wear a beard. I'll switch costumes, I mean, you're the birthday girl, after all!"

Reluctantly, Morgan pulled out a skin-toned headpiece from a box of accessories.

"Dopey?"

"Yes. But if you don't want..."

"Oh no, Morgan, I think it's perfect, actually," I laughed. "I'm not really the Snow White type."

The oversized tunic easily slipped over my head and spilled to the floor and lay at my feet in a huge puddle. A patch on the right elbow, in a darker shade of green, was sloppily stitched with thick brown thread, a nod to Dopey's amateur sewing skills.

147

Inside the tunic, a tag was sewn in silvery black thread: *A Curst Original*.

I held up the tag. "Hey Morgan, what's this?"

"Ardelle and I finally chose a name for our future clothing company. Our names combined: Curry and Hurst. What do you think, Ems?"

"It's perfect."

Morgan handed me a black cloth belt with a large, square buckle. I pushed back the tunic's extra-long sleeves to drape the belt around my waist.

"The tunic is supposed to be too big, too long," Morgan explained. "That's how Dopey's outfit is always portrayed in animation."

"Dopey's shoes look like giant potatoes. If I get hungry I can bake them in tin foil."

Morgan laughed. "I never thought of that! His shoes do resemble potatoes. Everything about Dopey is larger than life."

"Um…including his ears, apparently," I discovered, slipping huge cloth ears over my own. "And a big red nose," I added, adjusting a soft foam ball on the tip of my nose. "I wonder what Kandida and Alba will say when they see my costume. I can hardly wait," I moaned, wiggling my big ears with my fingers in front of the mirror.

"Who cares? You look great, honestly. It's for fun, for the kids, and fundraising, right?"

"What did you say? I can't hear you. My ears aren't big enough! The things we do for charity," I sighed, adjusting my bald wig and tucking stray strands of my long hair under the rubber edges. I placed a large, floppy pointed purple cap on my head.

Selene arrived and sneezed. "Guess who I am?"

We laughed together as Morgan put blush all over my face and stroked sparkly silver shadow across my eyelids. And she kissed the top of my bald head. Just like a perfect Snow White.

148

"Dopey played with diamonds Doc discarded in the mine. He put them on his eyes," Morgan explained. I shrugged. We returned to the gym.

Selene overstuffed plastic loot bags with candies. I ran the hose to the dunk tank after Morgan filled Snow White's glass coffin. Morgan added shiny, red apples, which floated on the calm surface. Moon beams reflected swirling patterns on the gym's hard court, the clear water in the glass-like coffin, and dunk tank, as though blood drops stained the floor and disturbed the calm water.

The rest of the dwarfs arrived, all white haired and matching beards and whistling. Carlton smirked and adjusted round, clear glasses. "Ready?" We nodded.

The Kanz twins sneered and snickered, their large white bows on their blonde wigs bounced as they threw mean looks our way, shaking tall, curled shepherd's staffs. Their booth displayed pieces of plywood cut in the shapes of two sheep. A hole was missing where sheep faces should be. Photos With Little Bo Peeps: Ten Dollars their booth sign said.

"They've lost their sheep and don't know where to find them," said Morgan.

"They've lost more than their sheep," suggested Leland, sporting a yellowish-brown tunic, walking sheepishly behind Bryon, hands clasped behind his back, eyes upturned slightly and shoulders raised toward the spooky ceiling.

"You got that right, Bashful," grumbled Byron.

Yawning and wearing long eyelashes attached to fabric eyelids strung around his head like a mask, Gareth wheeled toward the cottage. He pretended to fall asleep and slouched in his tan tunic. "Puh…puh…past your bedtime, Sleepy?" inquired Selene between fake sneezes.

"Long day in the mine," said Gareth with a huge yawn.

I began to whistle again, until I heard someone finish the dwarfs' familiar tune and tap my shoulder. I spun around on my potato shoes, nearly colliding with a chest as firm as a suit of armor. I lifted my chin and gulped.

It was Ben Bassett. In full costume. There he was, standing tall, in front of me.

Dr. Frankenstein's monster.

A perfect monster in every way. His towering height. Black, ill-fitting suit. Intricately painted slate makeup with profound black shadows under sickly, yellow-toned contacts. Hollowed cheeks. Thin low-lighted lines snaked down and around his neck where two bolts stuck out of both sides. Even his large exposed hands were painted and his head was fitted with a flat black wig. Numerous cracks were drawn on his forehead, nose and chin, giving his face a marbled effect. And there were stitches. Many, many stitches.

"Hey Emeranne. Or should I say, hmmm, by the looks of it, yes, bald head, big ears, red nose, but no antlers. So, not Rudolph, right? You must be Dopey."

I nodded. He grinned a huge monster grin, pointing to himself. "So, what do you think?" I didn't answer. "Emeranne?"

"I'm in character. Dopey doesn't speak," I said.

Ben laughed. He held out his arms, Frankenstein straight, and turned me around for a better look. I spilled water from the garden hose, and he took it from me. "Let's avoid a flood," he said to me, laughing.

He finished filling the tank. "Dunk the Dwarf? Are you sure about this? It's rather cold outdoors."

But I'm Ice Born, a fact I kept to myself. I looked directly into Ben's eyes and said, "I'm planning on hiding behind the cottage's façade. When I'm not giving out candies, that is."

"I see. You have it all figured out," he teased, patting my bald rubber head.

I left out the inside joke. The ducking of witches was popular centuries ago. An accused witch was forced to sit on a ducking stool that looked like a big wooden paddle, dipped into a pond or other body of water. "Yes, I do. By the way, where is your booth?"

"Back there," he pointed. "The haunted house."

I craned my neck to look over his shoulder. As soon as I saw the haunted mansion, my face froze.

"It was Miranda's idea. And Miranda gets what Miranda wants," he said to me.

Henry was Ben's monster clone and, gathered in front of a haunted mansion where loud, screeching organ music played, the rest of his cousins were dressed as witches. Their pale skin, painted bright green, more vivid than a traffic light, was covered with warts on large hooked noses, on protruding chins, on exposed foreheads. Hair long, black and stringy, spilled from beneath tall black pointed hats. Wallis stirred a huge smoking iron cauldron and waved a long, thin wand. Miranda stroked a plush toy black cat cradled in her arms. Giselle carried a corn broom and fed a feathered toy raven perched on her shoulder. Curly black nails dangled from spearmint green fingers. Miranda put the fake cat on a crooked stool. Together, they dropped their brooms and wands, grasped green hands and encircled the cauldron, cackling vivaciously.

I tilted my bald wig in the haunted mansion's direction. "Do me a favor. Ask your creepy cousins over there not to scare too many kids, okay?"

"Okay, but I'm not making any promises," he laughed and patted Dopey's bald rubber head. "And I think Jacob and Wilhelm Grimm would approve."

"Huh?"

"Oh, never mind." He grinned, as though there was more to what he'd said. I don't know why, it was just a feeling I had.

Ben lurched toward the haunted house, walking with lock-kneed stiffness, arms outstretched. The Kanz twins stared at him as he staggered in front of their display. I stood in front of the Dwarfs' cottage, watching Ben's back as he staggered away.

Unexpectedly he looked over his shoulder, gave me a huge monster wink and said, "I'd stay away from the Vampire Blood Brew and Spider Venom." Ben sliced the air with one of his outstretched arms and pointed to a booth run by the three boys who always giggled in class.

I gave him a thumbs up and a smile.

"Ems," a distant voice said. "Ems!"

"Huh?"

"Ems, the doors are about to open!" exclaimed Ardelle "Ready?"

"I guess," I replied, still in a daze.

Struggling to make an announcement on the crackling PA, Principal Lipschitz adjusted his pince-nez and yanked his goatee nervously. He blew into the microphone, causing the speakers to let out a piercing screech.

Within minutes, the gym crawled with screaming children in elaborate Halloween costumes: princesses, knights, fairies, ballerinas, superheroes, cowboys, ghosts, zombies, witches, wizards, werewolves. And vampires. Lots of vampires. In contrast, a few girls and boys dressed in modest, home made costumes walked by. This small, shy group seemed unsure what to do. River and Luke urged them forward, and waved.

"Trick or treat," they said politely, then a sweet, "thank you," when I gave them each an overflowing loot bag, placing each one carefully in plastic bags from Moonridge Valu-Mart. Their faces beamed, as though Christmas had come early.

"Thanks, Ems," said River.

Luke laughed. "See you around, Dopey."

A boy dressed as a baseball player walked up to Carlton next to the Dunk the Dwarf sign. Swiftly, the boy handed Carlton a bill, picked up the baseball and threw it in the air. He continued to throw and catch the ball. Carlton leaned down to hear what the boy whispered in his ear. Slowly, Carlton raised his plastic pickaxe and waved it in the air, inviting Snow White and the rest

152

of the dwarfs to the dunk tank. I sighed, put down the loot bags and walked over to the tank. "This kid wants a chance to dunk Snow White and the Seven Dwarfs. One by one," smirked Carlton.

Morgan grinned. "Oh does he, Carlton?"

Byron narrowed his eyes. "I'm sure I recognize that kid."

The boy didn't stop tossing the baseball in the air while he walked to an invisible mound and, like a seasoned baseball pitcher, took his stance. He brought his arms together and placed the ball in his glove. Looking over his left shoulder mechanically, he checked for a phantom runner on a non-existent first base.

Leland thought for a moment then said, "Isn't he Roberto Rodriguez, that pitching phenom in the Little League?"

"Yeah, that's who he is," Byron answered.

"Morgan, are you thinking what I'm thinking?" Selene asked.

"Whatever are you suggesting, Selene?" replied Morgan, batting her dark Snow White eyelashes.

"Lemme go first," grumbled Byron. "And again, for Gareth." He fist bumped Gareth and climbed the tank's ladder. "Let's see what kinda phenom he's gonna be tonight."

Selene hid her head from the growing crowd and snorted. Ardelle looked around. "Are you sure it's safe?"

"Yeah, why not? I could use a laugh," Leland said.

"Wait a sec, we didn't ask Ems if she's in," blurted Ardelle.

One eyebrow raised, I adjusted Dopey's tunic and smirked. "Do you even need to ask?"

I summoned my powers. I had to be so, so discreet.

Barely moving my lips, I recited, *"double double toil and trouble. Fire burn and cauldron bubble."*

The majority of the crowd took one side, chanting, "Bo-bby! Bo-bby! Bo-bby!"

When Little League Bobby wound up and released the ball, I followed the baseball's trajectory. It swerved and missed the target. The crowd moaned and grumbled and *aaahhh*ed, urging

Bobby to throw the second pitch, one that swirled in the air and landed with a loud slap in the tank. Somehow the ball spun around and around within the water, now bubbling furiously.

"C'mon, kid, show me your best stuff," taunted Byron. "Two balls zero strikes."

"Bo-bby! Bo-bby! Bo-bby!"

Fuming, Bobby didn't hesitate to release the third ball that somehow flew above the Dwarfs' cottage and landed on a target that cracked and shattered as loud as a lightning bolt. The next ball barely made it a foot or two until it dropped, short of the tank.

Carlton pointed to the ladder. "Walk!" Bobby tried again, but Byron escaped a thorough soaking in the dunk tank, only sprayed a few times when the ball splashed water into the air.

Bobby stared down each dwarf before winding up as the swelling crowd continued to chant his name.

"Bo-bby! Bo-bby! Bo-bby!"

Leland took his place on the stool. Bobby released four balls at lightning speed. The last ball hit the metal disc with a deafening clang. Leland dropped into the tank.

Long after Bobby's parents ran out of cash to purchase more baseballs, the pitches continued to fly. The crowd paid for Bobby's dunk tank game that turned into a spectacle.

"I'll pay fifty dollars to dunk the dwarf!" one parent yelled.

"I'll pay one hundred!" another offered, as if an auction was under way.

"And I'll pay one fifty," a third parent roared.

The offers continued. Money poured into my team's coffers. Carlton collected cash and checks from parents who balanced checkbooks on their thigh or on their child's back. All money raised would be donated to various local community services programs.

Over and over and over again, Bobby wound up, pitched, missed, stomped one running shoe, threw his glove to the floor.

154

There weren't any balls left. Some disappeared in the tank, water bubbling and steaming slightly. Others disappeared around the gym. When it was my turn, I narrowed my eyes and stared directly at Bobby.

"Hit me with your best shot," I said under my breath. Bobby dropped the ball before he had a chance to release it. I suppressed a laugh.

Disgusted, he pointed two fingers into his eyes and then gestured toward Snow White.

Morgan stepped toward the dunk tank. Little girls screamed. One of the many Cinderellas waved cotton candy in her hand, sniffling, "No Mommy! No! Not Snow White!"

Fortunately for the sobbing girls, Morgan didn't have to ascend the ladder.

Carlton shouted the news. "Sorry, kid, but we're all of out baseballs," over objections, groans and boos and hisses from the angry spectators, who dispersed when it was clear Snow White wasn't going to be dunked. When the crowd thinned, a man with a scruffy face and a cigar stub wedged between his teeth, wearing a crumpled hat and a wrinkled trench coat that hung from his drooping shoulders, stared at the dunk tank and wore a mischievous grin. He stroked his moustache.

Cooper Kozalski. What was he doing here?

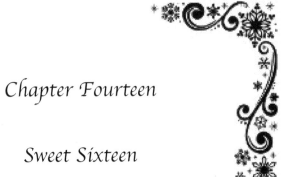

Chapter Fourteen

Sweet Sixteen

EMERANNE

Though Leland was the only dwarf dunked, we were all soaking wet. Most of the baseballs landed in the water, and sent jets of water into the air. Morgan distributed beach towels. I wrapped mine around my shoulders.

Ardelle huffed. "Lucky Snow White," Ardelle huffed. "She stays dry *and* gets the prince!"

"Don't forget, she was poisoned by the evil witch," reminded Morgan. "Not so lucky."

"Witches like that one give you all a bad name," grumbled Byron. "I would've taken care of her, as if she were a *you know what.*"

"Spoken like a true Den Born," Gareth said, fist bumping Byron's huge clenched hand.

Carlton announced that our final haul from the dunk tank exceeded the sum of all other fundraising booths. "Wish me luck for I'm on my way to break the news to Principal Lipschitz," he sighed dramatically, executing a perfect pirouette.

Byron licked his lips. "That means we won pizza from the Matterhorn."

"I can't wait!" Ardelle gushed. "Pizza *and* birthday cake!"

Morgan's face froze. "*Shhhh*, Ardelle, it's a surprise!"

156

"Don't worry," I reassured Ardelle, "Dad told me something was up tonight. *Please, Emeranne, clean your room before your birthday.* That's about the only thing he asks me to do around the house, *clean your room once in a while,* so I knew there was going to be company."

"Ems, we've seen your room a million times," Selene laughed. "I'd have thought your dad would give up by now!"

"It's not like we're having the party in my bedroom," I said.

"We ordered your favorite cake," Ardelle said. "*Custom* made."

"Ardelle!" Morgan chided with a half smile on her face. She raised her arms. "I give up."

"Good to know," I said. "I'll save room for dessert."

"See?" Ardelle turned to Morgan. "Ems is grateful to know about her birthday cake."

Morgan raised her chin and gazed at the ceiling. I thought I heard her say, "I surrender."

"Let's clean up and get out of here," Selene said. "After all, we have a birthday to celebrate."

Together, students and teachers pitched in on the massive cleanup. The cavernous room echoed with the sounds of chairs being moved, dragged, and stacked on the gymnasium floor, its hardwood littered with empty paper cups, chocolate bar wrappers, cotton candy cones, and lollipop sticks chewed into bits. Vampire Blood Brew and Spider Venom stained the floor, and there was water. Water everywhere.

The Dwarfs' cottage disassembled, glass coffin and dunk tank emptied, Morgan collected the wet wigs in a large plastic bag. "You can give me the costumes later," she called to four of her seven dwarfs, who were heading for the boy's changing room.

I packed unused apples and mopped the floor around the dunk tank and glass coffin, then, overloaded with empty candy bags and potato chip boxes, I made my way to the recycling bins set up inside the gym for the Halloween event. Finished with crushing the boxes with my Dopey potato shoes, I threw the cardboard into the blue recycling box. When I turned around, Coop the Scoop was breathing down my neck.

"Hey kid," he seethed. "Real lucky with that dunk tank, aren't ya?"

"Sure, real lucky," I replied.

"Made lots of dough, didn't ya?"

"*For charity.*"

"That so, huh?"

Unwilling to give him the dignity of a response, I turned to walk away, but Coop was persistent. He caught up to me.

"So tell me somethin'. Was the tank rigged?" I ignored him, but he kept pushing. "Maybe the bullseye tightened?"

"Are you writing something for your fictional column in the *Standard*, or just looking for free candy?" I demanded. "Because you may as well know I'm all out of loot bags."

"Now, kid, don't get all huffy with me." He chomped his cigar stub nervously. "That remark is aimed below the belt."

"Really? Like the lies you wrote about me?"

The reporter shrugged. "Gotta do my job, kid."

"Yeah, I *bet* you do." I was fuming.

Morgan rushed across the gym floor toward me. "Oh there you are, Ems. We're leaving now," she said, guiding me by the elbow and casting narrowed eyes at the scruffy man in the raincoat. Once out of earshot, she asked me, "What did that vile man want?"

Ardelle looked worried. "I wish he'd leave you alone."

"He's asking for it," Selene said.

I sighed. "And he's not giving up, is he?"

"Whatever he's looking for, he's going to look for a very long time," Morgan promised grimly.

We made our way out of the gymnasium. Ardelle and Selene joined us in the parking lot minutes later. Waiting for Morgan to unlock the car door, I gazed at the full moon, blood red except for a pale circle of light in the centre, like a small sun within the moon.

Cars formed a line in front of the high school, where parents waited for their children. I noticed a few of the kids had to be supported by teachers and friends. *Spider Venom* and *Vampire Brew*, I mumbled and shook my head. Silently, I thanked Ben for the warning.

At that instant, my eyes fell on Ben's Silverado. The Bassetts were loading the truck's bed with boxes and pieces of their haunted mansion. The boxes looked as if they were on fire, reflecting the light from the evening's Blood Moon. Miranda caught me watching them load. She stood behind the truck with her arms crossed, glaring furiously. Nearby, her siblings stood expressionless, and Ben stared at me suspiciously. For just a few seconds, I could have sworn his eyes turned orange. Must be the blood moon reflected in his gray eyes, I convinced myself, though I didn't think the art class color wheel would support my conclusion.

Morgan's car keys jingled like sleigh bells. Her hand trembled, fumbling for the ignition. "The moon is so dark, I can hardly see a thing," she said. Ardelle threw sparkling light in the car, the key found the ignition, and the tiny Citroën sputtered to life.

The cold air stung my face, and red-tinted vapors swirled from my nostrils in the frosty night air. Morgan stared straight ahead, driving into the blood-red moonlit sky. Her Citroën struggled up Snow Valley Mountain Road, slipping and sliding on newly fallen layers of snow. Huge, wet flakes thwacked the foggy windshield, dissolving on impact. The howling wind picked up, blowing snowflakes into the frosted windshield, obstructing Morgan's view. She wiped the windshield until the glass resembled a finger painting.

The crimson Blood Moon fighting through gathering snow clouds. The windshield, misted and smudged, was dappled with melted blobs resembling drops of blood. Swiftly passing clouds reflected the moon's sinister shade of red. Morgan turned the wipers and heater on to their highest settings; cold air blasted through the vents. The ancient heater always took ages to warm the car.

An irritating clicking noise distracted me from the streaking wipers and cold air and bleak road. Searching for the sound's origin, I glanced at the dashboard, barely able to see my reflection in the Citroën's side mirror, caked with snow and frost.

What little I saw in a tiny bare patch wasn't encouraging. I rubbed my eyes. What I could see of my reflection had to be a mistake. My face was streaked with silver makeup. My lips were a medium shade of blue, and my hair was a bird's nest wet and twisted after the rain. I towel dried strands of hair that had escaped Dopey's bald wig, which wasn't exactly a swim cap, and certainly not waterproof.

At that moment, I realized the clicking noise was chattering teeth. Three sets to be exact. Snow White was so lucky—I'd eat a poisoned apple, too, just to avoid that frigid tank, though my Ice Born telekinetic power spared most of us from a dunking, but we still got soaked.

"Sorry I can't throw a bit of fire around, it's not exactly safe, and my dad would kill me," Ardelle apologized.

"Too bad," I groaned. "But could you put your hands on us for a while?"

"Sure." Ardelle turned around and leaned over the seat, taking my hands in hers. Selene reached out a few minutes later and Ardelle did the same for her. "Better?"

"Much," I replied.

Selene held her palms to her face and sighed, "*Ahhhhh.*"

I squinted out at the dark road ahead, focusing on two glowing red lights fanned out across the gently falling snow driven by escalating winds into our headlights. Morgan pulled into my snow-covered driveway. The Citroën's headlights found two tread lines stamped in the snow, burning beneath the moon's red light. She parked behind Dad's truck, cut the headlights.

"Run inside, Ems," she said. "We'll be along in a minute." Ardelle turned around in her seat and winked.

Dad took one look at me, wrapped in a towel, and furrowed his eyebrows. "What the devil?"

"Thanks to the dunk tank." I waved my hand toward the top of tangled, knotted hair. I'd piled it high after towel drying as much as I could, but I was still wet, and cold, clear down to my toes.

Geneva whimpered and Matt buried his big furry head between my right thigh and hand.

"A *what?*"

"Dunk tank," I repeated. "A fundraiser for charity."

Dad looked puzzled. "Yeah, well, you guys better not catch pneumonia!"

"Don't forget we're Ice Born." I liked teasing Dad.

"Doesn't mean you've gotta be splashed all over, even if it *is* for charity."

"I'm going to finish drying my hair." I grinned at him, and took two steps at a time on the way to my room.

"I'll get a fire started," he mumbled, then raised his voice. "I bet the rest are as wet and cold as you are."

"Not Morgan, she was Snow White," I shouted down to him. "Oh, and Ardelle's outside, too. She'll start the fire if you want." I stepped into my bedroom and closed the door. Soon, Ardelle and Selene joined me. We scrubbed the dwarf makeup from our faces, and took turns with the hair dryer.

Morgan walked into my bedroom with a few backpacks. "Our change of clothes," she said.

As I changed into a worn forest green pullover, headlights reflected on my bedroom curtains. I peeked out and saw the Cameron's black van. "The guys are here," I announced.

"So when's the pizza coming?" I heard Byron say as I took the last step down to the main floor where my friends were gathered in the livingroom, seated around the fire. Some were on the sofa, others on the carpet with Matt and Geneva.

Gareth laughed. "Byron, are you always hungry?"

"Always," he answered. "Gotta prepare for hibernation."

"Except you don't hibernate," said Selene.

"Yeah, well, it's in the Den Born blood," he replied. "And no one answered my question."

"The pizza will arrive when it arrives," Carlton proclaimed.

"That's not an answer," said Byron, suppressing a grin.

"But it is a universal truth," Carlton replied earnestly.

Byron didn't bother arguing the point, knowing any debate with Carlton was pointless. I know too, because I couldn't understand him most of the time. *Genius*, I'd heard the teachers say about Carlton.

Dad helped Morgan and Ardelle pass around cans of Coke.

Matt growled, Geneva barked, and both ran to the front door. A few seconds later, the doorbell rang.

"Pizza's here!" Byron leapt up from the rug to follow the dogs. "Gotta love the early warning system," he said, patting Matt and Geneva playfully, then opened the door. "Hey Ben."

I froze. Of course, the Matterhorn donated the pizza. "Hey," I heard Ben reply.

BENNETT

I stood on the porch with a stack of red and white insulated pizza delivery bags marked with the Matterhorn logo, each full of steaming pizza boxes. Two huge Bernese Mountain dogs sniffed the air, wagging their furry tails.

Emeranne called them, "Matt, Geneva, come!"

Obediently, the dogs retreated into the house, but looked back a few times, foreheads wrinkled and eyes wide.

"Didn't recognize you without your makeup," Byron said. "Cool costume, by the way."

"Thanks. You too."

"Here, lemme take that heavy load off your hands," Bryon said, his voice deep and ravenous.

"There's more in my truck," I told him.

"Hey Gareth, wanna gimme a hand over here?" I heard Bryon say. "Coming," Gareth replied just as I closed the front door behind me. By the time I got back, Gareth sat in the foyer behind a man I knew to be Emeranne's dad, who stood at the front door and held it open for me. "C'mon in," he said. "Pretty cold out there tonight."

"Yeah, sure is," I answered. Mr. Goode took the second stack of pizzas from me, and put them on Gareth's lap. He wheeled away just as Byron returned with the insulated bags.

"Thanks," I said and took the bags from him.

"Gotta have respect for these things," he said, tilting his head to the bags, "cuz of what they carry inside. Precious cargo."

I laughed out loud. "Oh, I almost forgot—there's one more box." I'm sure I heard Byron lick his lips. *A bear's muzzle*, I thought. Allora had given me a pastry box, tied with string, like a present. I hadn't asked her what was in it. Occasionally, she accepted special orders for French pastries: Croissant, Éclair, Macaron, Petit Four, Profiteroles.

I stepped back into the house and realized there were gift bags and wrapped boxes in the foyer where Byron waited. "I'll take that off your hands," he said hungrily.

"Byron, you better not open that box!" It was Morgan's voice. Byron mumbled under his breath, "Always on my case …"

I turned to Byron. "Congratulations, by the way. That tank was a hit, so to speak."

"Yeah, well, not so much a hit for that kid, what's his name…"

"Bobby," I heard another voice say.

"Bobby Rodriguez? The Little League wunderkid?" Mr. Goode whistled. "How did you guys manage to make money?" Byron shot him a cautionary glance. "Oh, er, yeah," Mr. Goode laughed nervously, pressed his thumb and index finger together to draw a line across his lips, then under his breath to me, "they didn't cheat, not really, but sometimes those old tanks can get a bit, how can I say, rusty in certain places?"

"Gotcha," I said to him, though I'd already guessed the tank was in perfect working order. "Didn't hear a thing," I reassured him.

"Oh, hey, where are my manners? Don't think we ever met formally, did we now?" I shook my head. "Jack Goode, nice to meet ya," he said as he held out his hand to me.

I took off my glove. "Ben Bassett. Nice to meet you."

"Why don't you come in? The gang's all here drying by the fire."

Coven, you mean. "Uh, that's nice of you, but I'm working."

Jack put his strong palm on my shoulder and patted cordially. "C'mon, it's a week night and most kids are stuffed with sugar right about now. Their poor folks! I remember Ems' chocolate highs. Sure you can't take a short break?"

"Looks like a celebration. Are you sure I'm not intruding?"

"Heck no! The more the merrier!" Jack exclaimed.

"Yeah, c'mon in Ben," I heard Bryon's voice boom.

"It's Ems' sixteenth birthday." Jack beamed.

I hesitated. "You're right, the parlor isn't busy tonight. This was my only delivery so far. I'll just text my aunt," I said and sent her a quick message. "With coven won't be long text when u need me."

164

I removed my boots and walked into a tiny livingroom crammed with the Coven. One large pizza box balanced on his massive thighs, Den Born Byron was already half way through an entire pepperoni and mushroom pie.

My eyes found Ems immediately, seated on a padded footstool next to the fire, beside a worn recliner where Jack sat. "Hey, happy birthday," I said to her.

"Hey, Ben, thanks," she replied, averting her eyes.

"Hungry?" Ardelle offered me a slice. "Or are you sick of pizza?"

"Yeah, I get that a lot, but no."

"If Byron delivered pizza for the Matterhorn, your family would go bankrupt," warned Gareth.

"You got that right," Bryon howled through strands of cheese and pieces of pepperoni. "The smell of pizza would drive me nuts."

"The smell of *any* food drives you nuts," Jack said.

"True," Byron agreed unapologetically, licking his thick fingers one by one. "Next!"

Selene handed Bryon another pizza box. She turned to me. "I know him well by now, he doesn't have to ask."

I raised my eyebrows. "Like you can read his mind, huh?" Selene blushed at my comment and smiled nervously.

Morgan quickly changed the subject. "More Coke anyone?" She headed to the kitchen.

"Who makes the pizza?" Ardelle asked me.

"My Aunt Allora," I replied.

Selene's violet eyes opened wide. "Hope you don't mind me asking, but how long have you lived with your aunt and uncle and cousins?"

"On and off most of my life. I have another uncle in France that I spend a lot of time with."

"So, your parents…" Selene began to say.

"I don't remember them at all."

"I'm so sorry," she said quietly. "I don't remember mine, either."

I knew a bit about Selene's life but didn't let on. "Sorry to hear that," I said instead.

Sensing the conversation had taken a serious turn, Gareth changed the subject. "Allora's pizza is the best ever."

"You got that right," Byron said with his mouth full.

"My favorite is the one without pepperoni or anything else," Emeranne said, "just cheese and sauce and basil."

"That's the Pizza Margherita," I told her. "Aunt Allora's specialty."

"I could eat this every day," she admitted.

"Me too," Byron echoed, his mouth still full.

"What a surprise," laughed Emeranne. Matt and Geneva nuzzled my hand. "They like you," she said.

"No, they like pizza," I said.

"Enough begging, you two," Jack said to the dogs. "People'll think I don't feed you."

"I doubt it," I chuckled. Matt and Geneva whimpered and licked my hand.

"Oh no, you're in trouble," Gareth warned me. "They'll never leave you alone now. Believe me, I know."

"Is your aunt the only one who makes pizza?" Ardelle asked me.

"Yeah, mostly. Giselle helps in the kitchen. Miranda manages and helps Wallis wait tables. Henry and I take turns delivering and pitching in with whatever else needs doing."

"What about your uncle?" Carlton inquired.

"He takes care of accounts, orders supplies—business things."

"Where did Allora get the recipe?" Carlton asked.

"From an old friend," I said.

"Nice friend," Bryon said. "Send her my regards."

"His. And he's dead," I replied flatly.

166

"Oh, sorry, didn't mean—"

"No need to apologize. He died a long time ago."

"Sorry," Bryon repeated.

"His name was Raffaele Esposito, the best pizza maker in Naples, Italy. He invented the pizza you like," I said directly to Emeranne, "Pizza Margherita, in honor of visiting Queen Margherita. She wanted a pizza in the colors of the Italian flag."

"That's really interesting, Ben," Morgan said, having just returned with more cans of Coke. "I caught a few words here and there. When did you say he died?"

"I didn't. It was way before your time, around ninety-eight or ninety-nine," I offered.

Morgan arched one eyebrow. "It wasn't that long ago."

"I meant eighteen ninety-eight or ninety-nine, sorry I didn't specify."

No one said a word. Even the dogs went silent.

"Good one, Ben!" Bryon howled. "You nearly got us there!"

With a straight face, I looked at Byron. "Who said I was joking?"

An extended, awkward silence followed, interrupted by Byron's booming voice. "You're good, I have to admit."

If Emeranne and the Coven knew the truth, knew I wasn't joking...I couldn't think about the possibility. Yet at times, I just couldn't help myself; I needed to make light of my existence and all of the history I've witnessed. I'd experienced so much in the past seven centuries, so much I wish I could discuss with friends, with people I cared about, and who cared about me—but it was out of the question. Emeranne and her friends would only see the monster in me. The only people who understood me and still looked on me as anything other than a monster were themselves as monstrous in their existence as I.

I looked around the warm livingroom. The Coven was a close-knit group. No one needed to speak, because they understood one another. That much, at least, I had in common with them, given my relationship with the Bassetts.

My gaze fell upon Leland Kerr, who barely said a word, chewed mechanically and sipped Coke as if in a daze. Thinking of his murdered mother, I felt my anger surge. *The poachers*, I fumed to myself. *They're going to have a rude awakening.*

"Where's the cake?" Byron asked.

Ardelle giggled. "Finished already, Byron?" He stretched out and patted his stomach. "First course," he exhaled. Ardelle left the room and returned with Emeranne's favorite dessert: a St. Honoré cake that resembled a giant cream puff with whipped cream and custard.

Byron licked his lips and reached out, one hand extended toward the cake.

Ardelle put the cake down in front of Emeranne, who slid to the floor from the footstool and sat in front of the rough wooden plank coffee table supported by short, thick posts. Ardelle slapped Byron's hand. "Ouch," he yelped, faking pain.

Morgan narrowed her eyes at Ardelle, and tilted her head a few times toward the mantle above the fireplace, until Ardelle picked up the box of matches from mantle, removed one, struck it against the box and lit sixteen sparklers arranged in a spiral.

"And one more for good luck. Happy birthday, Ems!" said Ardelle. Wordlessly, together we watched the sparklers fade away.

"Did you know that birthday parties were uncommon before the eighteen thirties in America?" I said, as the last sparkler fizzled out.

Carlton raised his eyebrows and pressed his fingertips together. "You're full of interesting trivia," he observed. "Why aren't you a member of the debating club?"

"Too busy working after school," I replied.

"In case you change your mind, the club meets once a week, Wednesdays at four o'clock."

168

"Were there birthday wishes before the eighteen thirties?" Ardelle asked.

"Wishes have always existed," I remarked. "But they don't always come true."

"Well I beg to differ," Ardelle replied as she removed the burned out sparklers and gave Emeranne a knife. "Make a wish, Ems, and let's see if it comes true!"

Emeranne waved the knife in my direction. "So tell me, Ben, in what century was cutting the birthday cake introduced?" The Coven laughed.

I raised my hands. "No idea. But I do know this cake was named for Saint Honoré, the patron saint of bakers and pastry chefs."

"Of course you do," Emeranne mumbled. "I suppose you met him too," she challenged from a safe distance, the knife pointed at me.

"Whoa, Ems," Gareth said, "careful with that knife!"

Emeranne lowered the knife, touched the top of the cake with the blade, closed her eyes, and sliced through whipped cream, custard and pastry.

"No," I answered eventually. "As a matter of fact, I didn't."

"Well, too bad, 'cause you could have thanked him for his cake," she grinned, running her index finger along the blade's side. "It's delish." She licked her index finger and hummed happily.

"Leave some for us," Byron said.

"Don't worry, Byron, there's enough for everyone," assured Jack, who took a plateful from Morgan. Selene finished cutting the cake and passed pieces around the room.

"Just a small piece for me," whispered Leland.

I realized then that from now on special occasions would be difficult for Leland Kerr. Birthdays, holidays, spent without Charlsie Kerr. There would be a lot of difficult firsts for him.

Ardelle clapped her hands. "Time for presents!"

One by one, Emeranne unwrapped presents and emptied gift bags.

"From me." Ardelle squealed delightedly when Emeranne held up a cream colored wool hoodie. "A special pattern," she winked.

There were more presents. An astrology book from Carlton, a Forty-Niner's winter hat from Byron, a loose tea blend from Selene, bath oil from Morgan, a free mountain bike tune up from Leland, a gift certificate for dry cleaning from Gareth. A Black Watch plaid flannel shirt from her dad. "The girls picked it out," he explained, blushing. "Said you'd like it. Something about hippies."

"Hipsters." Ardelle giggled.

Emeranne put the shirt on, tags and all, over her pullover. The forest green pullover and plaid shirt synched perfectly with her eyes, dark and mysterious.

"Thanks everyone," she said warmly. "This was the best birthday ever!"

"Um, sorry, I didn't bring a gift, didn't know it was—"

Emeranne cut me off. "Don't worry about it. You brought the pizza and cake."

"You *won* the pizza, and your friends *bought* the cake," I said to her. "That's not a gift."

"Don't worry about it," she repeated. "It was nice having you here."

"Ems, show Ben the bloodstone," urged Ardelle. "From your—"

"Oh, I doubt he's interested in jewelry," Emeranne interrupted nervously.

"Actually, I'd love to see it."

Reluctantly, Emeranne pulled out a necklace from under her forest green pullover, which reflected the secrets of the dark forest. As soon as I saw the stone, I suppressed a gasp.

I'd seen the stone in that setting once before. But where?

170

At that moment, I heard the tri-tone sound indicating a text message. "Excuse me," I apologized. The text was from Miranda. The message was short, just three words. But she made her point loud and clear.

"Assimilate, infiltrate, eliminate."

"Uh, sorry, I have deliveries. Thanks for everything," I said. Jack got up. "Don't worry, I can see myself out."

I rushed out the door to my truck that glowed beneath the Blood Moon floating in the aubergine sky and peeking through pale snow clouds tinted pink and red.

And still, I remain forever a monster, I sighed dejectedly as I drove away.

So many times I'd wished I were human, celebrating birthdays, growing older, like Emeranne. Sure, I had the Bassetts, but a part of me deep inside wanted more, wanted my own family, someone to share the rest of my life with. Yeah, right. I had to face reality. Who'd ever want me? No mortal, that wasn't possible. A witch hunter like Octavia? Not going to happen. She'd never accept my choice to walk away from my existence. And I couldn't accept someone like her, who wouldn't.

On my way back to the Matterhorn, the poem gushed out, like a tidal wave smashing through a levy.

how many sunsets
would your eyes endure
to be with the one you love?
one sunset?
is one enough?
you blink
and that first sunset
is over
how many sunsets
can you endure
to wait for the one you love?

two?

are two enough?

so you hope or *wait…*

I preferred the flow of *so you wait*

so you wait

but she's gone or *not there*

I'll try *but she's gone*

she appears in your dreams…

My nightmares have always been dominated by a world of blue soaking my lungs, pushing me farther and deeper into an endless watery grave. *My* grave. And then, a bright light shines above, scattering the darkness, pulling me up, higher and higher, faster and faster, until my head breaks the surface of the waves and I am carried by a strong current, deposited on a beach of sand as fine as flour. It cushions my broken and bruised body. An intense heat sears my skin until shadows shroud my face. Always the the same voices speak to me.

*…we do not know his wishes…*they always say to me.

you were dying…

unruly mobs

we did what we thought was best…

pyres

what we thought was best…

fires

thought was best…

recalling

was best

witch

what

hunts

is
centuries
your
ago
name

Chapter Fifteen

Storm Knots

EMERANNE

Shortly after Ben left, Dad suggested the party break up early.

"Snow's getting worse out there." He shrugged on his winter jacket with the rest of my friends, except for Morgan and Selene. "Don't bother calling Cuthbert," Dad told Carlton. "The mountain road is real slippery tonight."

The cold north wind whistled outdoors, endless scales of pattering notes. Snow flurries dove onto the windows, painting each pane with swirling frosted silhouettes, like flames.

I retrieved bedding for Selene from the linen closet and helped her make the daybed. The wrought iron frame just fit under the slanted roof's lowest point. Strings of lights flickered around thick wooden trusses.

"Thanks, Ems," Selene said, tossing a point blanket on the bed.

From beneath my duvet, came Morgan's muffled voice, "Good night."

Morgan and Selene breathed rhythmically in sleep. Neither woke from my tossing and turning overnight.

The Dream returned.

Summer turned to autumn, the air crisp and leaves inhaled their final breath before floating and dancing until each settled on top damp layers of pine needles. I found the faceless boy as before, his face obscured and his body rigid. A single red leaf fell upon each eye, then burst into crimson and russet flames.

In the middle of the night, I woke, wondering what this dream meant and why it wouldn't let me go, persistent as Coop the Scoop.

When I woke again, the sun shone through the skylights on the peaked roof. I rubbed my eyes and focused on one wall where a Smokey the Bear poster hung beside three framed prints of fireflies, butterflies, and dragonflies. I bolted out of bed. My clock read ten-thirty! I'd slept in, and missed school. Why didn't Dad wake me up? Or Morgan? Or Selene?

Morgan chuckled from the rocking chair. "Relax, Ems. It's a snow day."

She held Mom's old guitar on her lap—another belonging left behind seven years ago—and strummed a few chords.

"Earlier this morning, your dad told me school was canceled. Hungry? I thought I'd make French toast."

"Yeah, starving."

I leaned forward, wrapped my arms around bent legs and rested my forehead on my knees.

"Is Ems awake yet?" Selene called from the bathroom door.

"Yes," Morgan told her. "Let's eat."

I hesitated before following Morgan and Selene downstairs to the kitchen. "I wonder," I said.

"Wonder what, Ems?" Selene asked.

"I wonder what Mom left behind in her studio?"

"I've always wondered too, Ems, but didn't want to ask," Morgan said.

"I don't have the key," I said.

While Morgan prepared French toast, the conversation continued. "Doesn't your dad have the key?" Selene asked.

"No," I said.

"Do you want to look for the key?" Morgan asked.

"Yes. No. I don't know."

"It's your decision, Ems," Morgan said. She changed the subject. "How's River doing, by the way?"

"He's still frustrated," answered Selene, her voice strained. "The Elders meet regularly in the Spirit Lodge, but haven't found solutions."

"Because the Scent failed the Den Born," I said.

Selene closed her eyes and sighed. "Yes. Carlton and River text back and forth about it every day."

"Any updates on your research with the liquid mercury?" I poured maple syrup generously, soaking the toast in it like a body on quicksand.

"Carlton needs more time for his astral travels. He's getting close, but hasn't yet broken the formula, not since we last talked at Big Bear Lake," answered Selene.

Morgan pressed further. "What formula?"

Selene inhaled slowly and paused before elaborating. "Based on Carlton's numerous astral travels of late, he's stumbled upon clues on how immortal witch hunters survive."

"And?" I urged between mouthfuls.

"Carlton may have discovered how the conversion process worked," she replied.

"Worked?" Morgan asked.

"Worked in the beginning before modern science. The first few times Carlton astral travelled in search of answers, he uncovered documentation in France's National Library, dating back to the Medieval Ages."

"And?" I prompted, transfixed.

"A witch hunter's manual," she said candidly.

"The *Malleus Maleficarum*?" I asked with surprise.

"But Carlton wrote a monograph on the *Malleus* a few years ago, didn't he?" said a puzzled Morgan. "I thought he'd exhausted that avenue."

"No, not the *Malleus*. Another manual for medieval witch hunters, a manual predating the *Malleus* by twenty-six years," replied Selene.

"What?" Morgan and I echoed.

"*Invectives Against the Sect of Waldensians*," she said. "The Waldensians were considered heretics because their rituals and beliefs clashed with prevailing attitudes. Waldensian became a code word for witch. Carlton, under the guise of an Oxford University Medieval Studies expert, Professor S Holmes—"

Morgan chuckled. "You're kidding!"

Laughing, Selene struggled to get the words out. "No, I'm not!"

I grinned. "Leave it to Carlton."

"Esteemed Professor Holmes, complete with pipe and tweed coat and deerstalker hat, walked into the rare books section of the library and examined a translation from Latin to Medieval French. Then he traveled back to that era. And guess what he discovered?"

Morgan and I couldn't say a word, though our mouths were wide open.

"Carlton found out about a rudimentary concoction, ingested as a tincture, used in the conversion process of a person on the brink of death. Conversion into an—"

"An immortal witch hunter," I said under my breath.

"Carlton suspected there had to be a serum connected with immortality. This serum consists mostly of liquid mercury— living mercury—but we haven't been able to identify the other properties."

"He obtained a sample?" I asked in disbelief.

Selene's violet eyes shimmered. "Disguised as one of the inquisitors during the witch hunts of that era. Using a syringe,

Carlton extracted a sample from a witch hunter's arm while she slept."

Morgan frowned. "She?"

"Yeah. Females worked undercover, pretending to be wise women, healers who were accused of witchcraft. The hunters betrayed true wise women who were captured and tortured until they confessed to having committed crimes, though they were innocent. These inquisitors showed their appreciation by giving the witch hunters the privilege of carrying out the executions."

"So he met...met..." stammered Morgan as she cleared the harvest table and filled the dishwasher.

Selene nodded. "Witch hunters in the flesh. One in particular, who went by the name of Delacroix, was, in Carlton's words, *utterly ruthless.*"

I covered my mouth with one hand.

"Delacroix...Delacroix. Carlton read a translated passage written by Delacroix at Big Bear Lake, didn't he?" Morgan asked.

"Since then," said Selene, "we've been experimenting, trying to isolate the properties. It's taken up a lot of our time. Carlton's frustrated, but hopeful."

I was confused. "But mercury is poisonous. Isn't that what Mrs Yin said?"

"Sure. But what if it's transformed into another property so powerful it could transform a person into—?"

"Into a monster," said Morgan through clenched teeth.

"Based on his research, Carlton theorized the serum's been updated, modernized, easier to use," continued Selene.

"Such as?" I asked.

"Such as a needle, an injection of some sort, or maybe a transfusion."

"And injections could leave scars," I said, placing my elbows on my knees and tilting my head in my hands.

"What's wrong, Ems?" Selene asked, placing her hand on my curved back.

"Ben," I whispered. "Ben has scars. I saw them. In art class. Scars on the inside of his left arm."

"Are you sure?" Selene asked. I nodded. "Maybe it's from something else, maybe he has diabetes?" she suggested.

"Could, could that be why, why I can't...we can't—?" I stammered.

"Are you suggesting the Bassetts are—" cut in Morgan.

Selene closed her lilac eyes, shook her head, and finished the sentence. "Witch hunters."

"It's possible. But their faces didn't emerge from the fire, Ems," Morgan said. "Ice Visions never presented the Bassetts as anything other than what we know them to be."

"Just a quiet family running a pizza parlor," said Selene.

I crossed my arms across my chest. "Or Mrs Kerr's killers."

"Let's not jump to conclusions, Ems," Morgan said. "People haven't stopped talking about Mrs Kerr's murder. Mom was in Angie's Beauty Salon yesterday. That's all anyone talked about, she told me. If they only knew..."

"Well they don't," I said, and changed the subject. "I made up my mind. Let's go upstairs. I wanna look for the key and see what's behind the studio door. I've never been interested before—"

"Before Mrs Kerr's murder," sighed Selene.

"Good idea, Ems," encouraged Morgan, trundling upstairs.

"If your mom left a key, where would she hide the key?" Selene asked.

"No idea."

Morgan turned to Selene. "Why don't you use the Spirit Board for clues?"

"Great idea!" Selene rummaged around in the linen closet. "I don't think I need the Spirit Board."

"Why not?" I asked.

"I found a key!"

"What?" Morgan said.

"I've rummaged around that closet a thousand times. Why haven't I ever found it?" I said.

"I'm not sure, but it doesn't matter, does it?" Selene said.

"Let's try it," I said.

Selene held out her hand. "Here, Ems."

"No, you do it," I said. "I'll hold the Spirit Board."

Selene slid the key in the lock and twisted left and right. I held my breath. The key didn't turn. I exhaled. "Wrong key," I said.

"It's been locked for years. Let me try a few more—" The key turned. Click. "The door is unlocked!"

Slowly, Selene opened the door. She paused and looked over her shoulder. "Ready, Ems?" I nodded. My heart raced.

I already knew Mom's studio would be dark. Both dormer windows faced the backyard. From my treehouse, I stared at the drawn curtains, hoping light would spill from the windows. This went of for months after Mom left, until one day I gave up.

A flood of memories drowned my mind. Mom sketching at her drafting table. Mom cutting fabric. Mom stitching lining inside a fancy hat. Mom looking up from her work when I peeked inside the studio. Mom smiling at me.

"Ems? Are you okay?"

"Yes, fine." I lied. Morgan held my hand and led me farther inside the studio.

Selene drew open the curtains. Layers of dust were disturbed. She laughed and coughed at the same time.

"What's so funny?" I asked.

"Jo's studio isn't as dusty as your bedroom."

"I don't like to dust. So what?"

Morgan smiled. "Let's look around."

The studio was exactly as I remembered. A small sofa sat against one wall. Like laundry on a clothes line, Mom's sketches were clipped on rows of wire Dad installed above the sofa. Bookshelves lined another wall. The shelves matched the peaked roof's slant. I ran my fingertips across book spines. The bottom and middle shelves held books on millinery, fashion design, pattern making, textiles, and vintage hats. Sketch pads and fashion magazines were piled neatly on other shelves. Everything was in its place, untouched for years, just like Pompeii I'd studied in freshman history class. Mom's studio was frozen in time.

Morgan flipped through pages of sketch pads, whistling at Jo's designs. "She's really talented, Ems, just like you."

"Hope the *whole* apple doesn't fall far from the tree," I moaned. "But you're a way better artist."

Morgan raised her eyebrows, about to say something, but changed her mind. My eyes wandered up the shelves. "Selene, can you give me a boost?" I placed my left foot in Selene's interlaced fingers for a leg up, swung my right foot up, leveraged on a middle shelf and leaned forward, and clutched one dusty book. I blew dust off the cover. Morgan and Selene coughed below me. Gently, I tossed each book down, one by one. "There, that's the last one." I brushed dust off my palms. "Plus my old Etch A Sketch. Want it, Morgan?"

"Sure. Until I can afford one of those fancy tablets, I'll use it to doodle."

"Just don't shake it until you're done," I told her. She grinned back.

When I landed on the studio's wooden floor, one of the floorboards dislodged. Selene lifted the loose plank. "Look!" she exclaimed.

Beneath the floor, several books lay hidden. Mom's studio floor was covered with dust bunnies. Streams of sunlight filtering through the curtains and caught fleeing dust motes, escaping from every corner of the studio.

Why were the books were in perfect condition?

Morgan reached for the books. "Ouch!"

"What's wrong?" I asked.

"I don't know," Morgan said. "My hand feels like it was stung by a bee."

"Ah," smiled Selene. "She used the *Mellifera* boundary spell. Aunt Callie taught me how to cast it."

"How do you *uncast* it?" Morgan asked.

"Do you have honey?" Selene asked.

"Yeah, I'll get the jar from the kitchen cupboard."

When I returned, Selene was waving her hand above the books and chanting. "Open the honey jar," she said.

I opened the jar. A blinding bolt of golden light shot out from beneath the floorboards and into the jar.

"Like bees to honey," Selene said.

"Or bears," I said.

This time, when Morgan reached for one of the books, she wasn't stung. "Hmmm, let's see. *Three Books of Occult Philosophy* by Henry Cornelius Agrippa, and *A History of Magic.* Eliphas Levi."

"Why would Jo hide books?" Selene wondered. "And cast the *Mellifera* spell?"

I shook my head. "Dad knew she was a witch."

Selene picked up three more books from beneath the floor. "*Forgotten Folklore, Myths and Legends From Faraway Places* edited by Hannah and Draga. "Aren't they Jo's grandparents?" I nodded.

Selene thumbed through the first book. "The First Coven," she said. She skimmed the pages, lost for several moments.

Morgan assembled Mom's books on the sofa and chose a leather-bound book with no title or author. "Let's look at this one," she said, untying the cord wrapped around the book and opening the cover.

Several faded handwritten pages spilled out. Selene caught her breath. "Oh," was all she said.

Morgan carefully picked up the fragile pages, one at a time, handling each carefully. "This one is an intricate drawing. Look," she said, holding up the page with a double-ringed circle divided into dozens of tiny boxes. Selene raised one thin eyebrow penciled a shade of charcoal. Each box enclosed a single, unusual symbol. Three hexagons contained within the innermost ring included a star within another circle, traced around a crescent moon and sun.

"Oh," Selene repeated and held up her right wrist. "A pentacle, just like my tattoo."

"A magical symbol," agreed Morgan. "And ancient, older than time itself, mistakenly associated with devil worship."

"True. During the Spanish Inquisition, this ancient healing symbol was linked with heretics and Satan."

"According to rumors," I reminded them, "I'm involved in a devil-worshipping cult."

Selene shook her head and sighed. "Imagine living centuries ago?"

"No," Morgan said.

"Pentacles represented Venus, Goddess of Love," continued Selene. "Archaeologists found pentagrams on pottery as early as thirty-five hundred BC in Egypt, Greece and Rome. In witchcraft, pentagrams were considered amulets, alongside other magical tools like knives, chalices, swords and wands. And were featured prominently on Tarot cards."

Morgan drew a long, patient breath. "Each of the star's five points represents The Spirit, unifying four elements," she explained and held up her hand, counting with her fingers. "Fire. Water. Earth. Air. Four elements essential to life."

I turned my attention to three strange words on the celestial drawings.

"Sig…sigill…" I struggled.

"*Sigillum Secretum Mysteriorum*," enunciated Morgan. Selene's violet eyes widened.

"Huh?" I asked, further perplexed, looking back and forth from Morgan to Selene.

"*Sigillum Secretum Mysteriorum*," repeated Morgan. "A secret magical diagram. It literally means a mysterious secret seal. This must be Jo's personal copy ..."

"Except," I interjected, "this isn't Mom's writing. Look at her drawings."

"And the initials," added Selene, reading out loud, "VG."

"Violet Grimesby." My voice quivered. Selene's eyes narrowed.

"This *Sigillum* would have given Violet virtually unlimited powers," explained Morgan.

"What for?" I probed, gazing down at the hexagon.

"Witches often used a *Sigillum* to write, read or interpret messages written in code with various symbols," said Morgan.

"Alchemical symbols, astrological signs, hieroglyphs in Greek and Latin," continued Selene. "Maybe this is why the *Sigillum* was hidden."

"In ancient times, each witch developed his or her own personal *Sigillum*," elaborated Morgan, "to read or create coded messages."

"You mean like our own personal code? The Caesar Shift?"

"Precisely," replied Morgan. "Except this one has limitless magical implications."

I shook my head. "What's Violet's copy doing here? Under the floorboards?"

"Jo left those memories behind," said Selene in her raspy voice, solemn and low.

"Maybe Mom hid the journal after Violet's death," I suggested.

"Guess we'll never know," Selene said. "Unless—"

"Don't even think it," I snapped rather harshly. "Sorry, Selene, I just can't—"

"I know, Ems," she said softly. "I shouldn't have brought it up."

"I never want to see Mom *ever* again," I declared.

Morgan smiled soothingly. She carefully handled another fragile-looking piece of parchment. "*Scalam Veneficae*," she said. "The Witch's Ladder."

A blissful expression deepened the warm butterscotch glow of Selene's face, emphasizing her lovely violet eyes. "From Jo's *grimoire*."

Morgan nodded. "A witch's personal book of spells. My grandmother kept one, and a Book of Shadows handed down for generations. Modern witches don't keep them anymore. A shame, really, that these traditions are disappearing."

Selene picked up a smaller leather-bound book and opened the front cover. "This is in Jo's handwriting," she said, flipping a few pages at a time. "I found something else." Selene withdrew an old, folded photograph, unfolded it and held it up. "Ems, is that your mom?"

I looked at the photo and recognized a younger version of my absent mother.

Selene read the back of the photo. "Me with Violet. First day at SVHS."

The familiar main building was in the background. Two teenaged girls smiled for the camera. A crease divided the two girls where the photo had been folded between them, years ago. The first girl, petite, blond, tanned, wore a sleeveless, knee length dress and a pretty straw hat. The other, taller than Mom with long, thick, wavy black hair, and fair skin. She wore a dress, shawl, and laced ankle boots, black from head to chunky heel.

Selene replaced the photo, randomly turned several of the journal's pages carefully, and read a passage.

"*Last night I dreamed Violet and I floated on air, high above Jack and Vince. Neither could see us from where they played on the football field.*"

"Who's Vince?" Morgan asked.

"Dad's older brother. He played football at Snow Valley High."

185

"Right. I forgot," apologized Morgan. "He dated Violet?" I nodded. "Bet he took her death really hard." I nodded again.

"Where's Vince now?" Selene asked.

"He lives in San Francisco and works for the Forty-Niners."

Selene's expression changed. She turned more pages. "Seems to be Jo's personal journal. I don't want to read further, Ems, it's too invasive."

"I'm a little uncomfortable, too," I admitted, uncertain I wanted to read about Mom's awkward teenage years, or anything about her at all for that matter.

The studio door swung open. I held my breath. Was Dad home? I exhaled. "Ardelle!"

"So this is what Jo's studio looks like!" Ardelle's brown wool cap laden with snow clung to her thick red hair, and a crocheted scarf with multicolored squares in shades of tangerine, lilac, chocolate brown and vintage avocado draped her shoulders. She removed her foggy horn-rimmed glasses and her outerwear, huffing, "What did I miss?"

"We found some of Jo's books, including her *grimoire*, a journal, and old magic books," explained Morgan.

"Wow," exhaled Ardelle, unbuttoning an ankle length ivory wool coat, motioning her head toward me, causing her thick red hair to move forward, catching the light.

Selene updated Ardelle on Carlton's astral travels, his discoveries, and the old texts hidden beneath the floorboards.

"I agree with Morgan," she said. "It's too soon to make conclusions about Ben and his family."

"What does your dad think, Ardelle? He's so close to the Lookout Murder investigation."

Ardelle paused for a moment to catch her breath. "Yes, because of the fire. Byron's dad keeps mine up to date. Dad never mentioned the lighter and hankie, you know, evidence Cooper Kozalski said he'd obtained from *sources close to the investigation*," she replied, making quote signs with her fingers. "Dad said Coop the Scoop lied—"

I cut Ardelle off. "I know all about his lies."

"Yeah, well, Ice Visions haven't warned about Coop the Scoop or his seedy meetings with so-called sources."

Selene broke her silence. "We can guess what that slime bag was up to."

"No good," seethed Morgan.

"Strange," I mused. "Maybe Ice Visions only warn about things we can change, but not those we can't."

Morgan paused, then said, "No one was warned about Mrs Kerr's death, so maybe we *couldn't* have prevented it."

"I can't figure any of this out," I said.

"My dad questioned Philippe and Allora Bassett," Ardelle said. "They couldn't help. He concluded they're being honest and cooperative and didn't object to an interview at the Matterhorn. So there's been no progress, not a single new lead."

"I don't get it," Morgan said, "how Mrs Kerr's murder has gone unsolved this long. How not a single member of the Coven, young or old, has any answers."

"Don't forget Violet Grimesby's murder, as well, two decades ago, and still unsolved," reminded Selene. "I'd like to consult the Spirit Board again, if you're up for it, and this time channel the power of your pendant."

"The bloodstone?" I asked, surprised. Selene nodded. "It's on my desk."

"Let's go back to your bedroom, Ems. Ardelle, would you mind helping me carry these books?" Morgan asked.

"Not at all," Ardelle said.

"Ems, I'll lock the door and put the key in the linen closet." A few minutes later, Selene joined us in my bedroom. She picked up the bloodstone on my desk. With the curtains drawn, the only light came from thin rays of daylight spilling down from the skylights. Dust particles swirled like snow squalls through the room's air. After the usual preparations and incantations, Selene placed her steady hands above the planchette, moving firmly, easily, from one letter to the next.

When the planchette stopped, she whispered, "*Fair is foul and foul is fair.*"

"*Hover through the fog and filthy air,*" completed Morgan.

"I think it means that nothing is as it appears to be," said Selene.

I bit my lip and frowned. Altering the somber mood that descended upon my bedroom, Ardelle, eagerly pouring over various journals, particularly noting one loose page in Morgan's hand, could hardly contain her excitement. "What's that one?"

"*Scalam Veneficae.* Storm Knots."

"Witch's Ladder!" Ardelle shrieked. "At last! I've been practicing for ages and ages—"

"Really? I hadn't noticed," chuckled Selene.

A new spell only meant one thing: new trouble.

Morgan scattered dried herbs and sprinkled essential oils on several beeswax candles. Selene struck a match and lit the wicks. Ardelle expertly knotted a long piece of twine. Holding hands in a sacred circle, we chanted together. Ardelle inhaled deeply, closed her eyes, and recited the invocation, untying the first knot, then the second knot. Ardelle's fingers worked skillfully until the third knot was undone.

Swiftly, the wind picked up outside, screaming above the forest. In unison, we chanted to close the circle. Snow appeared above our heads inside the bedroom, in the middle of the sacred circle. The snow swirled, pushing a gentle breath from a summer breeze to become a tornado raging indoors. The snow formed a funnel, twisting faster and faster until the funnel turned into a bright light. The twisting funnel exploded into a million tiny lights.

We ran to the windows and drew back the curtains to survey the situation outdoors. The swirling funnel of tiny lights reappeared, exploding once again. Tiny lights turned into snowflakes, floating aimlessly in the air, rising and falling on whispering breezes. Flurries increased until white-out conditions prevailed. A crying wind sobbed relentlessly.

"It's storming," I said.

"It most certainly is," said Ardelle.

"What have we done? Can't we undo it? Stop it? Oh, this is so bad!"

The developing blizzard brought strong winds and dumped more snow, until the green tips of pine trees disappeared. Boughs struggled to hold round mounds of snow resembling ice hammocks on a beach.

The phone rang. I ran downstairs, into the kitchen, and answered the phone.

"Ems?" It was Dad. "Wanna let you know it's storming real bad over here in Moonridge. Was meeting with Moe Stone and a few other rangers when all of a sudden a storm came outta nowhere," he panted. "Probably gonna hit Snow Valley soon."

My stomach turned into a labyrinth of knots. "Yeah, uh, it's snowing already."

"This is gonna be one of the worst storms in over a decade," he advised. "Don't go anywhere. The girls still there?"

"Yeah. Ardelle too."

"Make sure the girls check in with their folks," he said. "Sure hope you weren't messin' around with the weather, Ems."

"I, uh, I don't know what you're talking about, Dad," I said innocently.

"Bet you don't," he mumbled. "Gotta go, Ems. No more monkey business if you know what I mean." Dad hung up the phone, crackling with static, until it cut off. I pressed the old rotary phone's cradle, clicking it several times and held the receiver back to my ear. No dial tone.

The storm raged all morning. Power lines blew down, cutting off electricity. Over three feet of snow piled high outdoors, burying roads, crippling the town. Ardelle, as usual, lit logs in the fireplace. Selene warmed milk for hot chocolate. Morgan stabbed leftover chicken wrapped in tin foil with a poker like a large shish kebob, holding the long iron above the fire.

We played board games all day. In the middle of a tense game of Snakes and Ladders, the phone rang. It was my dad. Telephone service was restored, electricity not.

I hung up the phone. "I feel so bad for the problems we caused."

"The problems we *may* have caused," corrected Ardelle.

Selene shook her head. "Have faith in your powers. You conjured a storm."

"Can't you stop it, Ardelle?"

"No. We called up a storm and it has to play itself out."

"I'm never going to do it again," I declared. "Never. Ever."

"Don't say that, Ems. Never know when a good snowstorm will come in handy," said Ardelle.

"But we caused essential services to be cut off," I said.

Grinning, Morgan raised one index finger. "Allegedly."

By late evening, electricity was restored. Given the impassable state of the roads, my friends stayed overnight. Schools in Snow Valley County were closed until further notice. Consecutive storms proved too much for Snow Valley High's old pipes, bursting and flooding the main building.

For the rest of the night, the string hung at my bedroom window, where it swung wildly, then more gently until it stopped abruptly. So did the storm. That's when I was certain the storm spell worked. The Coven had never experimented with such a strong spell before.

The blizzard had ended, but there was no way to reverse considerable damage from the snowstorm. Snow Valley High remained closed for the rest of the week, while the buried village cleaned up. Snow plows worked overtime, blowing the town's allocated snow removal budget.

I wasn't sure if I wanted to experiment again, but as Ardelle reminded us, the storm knot spell could come in handy sooner or later.

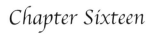

Chapter Sixteen

Hike

EMERANNE

"*T*oday's assignment involves a field trip to take advantage of the beautiful scenery in and around Snow Valley," informed Ms. Beltane. "Such an inspiring region."

I turned to Morgan and Ardelle and gave them the thumbs up. I pictured the three of us hiking to Roars Hack Falls and Hunter's Point Lookout until the memory of Bellavista Lookout drowned my happy thoughts. The Lookout Murder. Could I ever go near that area again?

"I've divided students into pairs for this assignment. I'd like students to work with a partner who is not a best friend, so to speak, because it's important that you break out of your comfort zones." I groaned and bit my lip. "Now, I made a list based on my observations during class. I have posted that list on the back wall. After class, please consult the list and make plans with your partner. With that in mind, let's turn to the study of pointillism."

Ardelle, Morgan and I exchanged glances, while taking notes and making tiny dots on sketch paper. "I hope we're not paired with one of the Kanz twins," I whispered. Morgan stuck her finger down her throat and pretended to gag.

When the buzzer sounded, I walked to the back of the class and stood in line. Fortunately, the Kanz twins were partnered with two of three giggling boys, today drooling all over Kandida and Alba. Morgan turned to me and under her breath she said, "Serves them right." I suppressed a chuckle. Ardelle and Morgan found their names next to girls they knew from Fashion Design Club. They sighed with relief, and waved to their partners.

That left me. I scanned the list and looked for my name alphabetically. I was about to turn around and ask Ms. Beltane if she forgot to add my name, but I didn't have to.

"Emeranne," a deep voice said to me. "Looks like we're partners."

Ben Bassett and I were paired together. I gulped and forced a smile. "Great," was all I said to him.

Frantically, I assembled my friends at home for their opinion. We sat in front of the fireplace and discussed me partnering with Bennett. I trusted them and their instincts and knew we'd always protect one another.

"What's to be nervous about?" Morgan said. "He's never been presented in an Ice Vision."

Selene narrowed her eyes "This is about your dream, isn't it?" I nodded. "We'll keep watch. Leave your bloodstone with me and I'll make a pendulum for scrying."

"Carlton found your map upstairs in your desk drawer, you know, the one of Snow Valley County," Gareth said. "The one we had to draw for Mr DelMonaco's freshman geography class."

I objected strongly. "Not that one, Gareth! It's awful!"

"It has your energy infused in the map, Ems," said Gareth.

"Gareth's right," Carlton said, holding up my map. "I can follow you on the map."

"And Carlton can locate your cell phone," Gareth said, pointing to Carlton's laptop.

I had no idea how Carlton could track me, but I knew him well enough to avoid asking questions.

"It's just a field trip, Ems. What could go wrong?" Selene said encouragingly.

"Know where you're going yet?" Morgan asked. I shook my head slowly.

Ardelle held up my cell phone. "Text us as soon as you know, okay?"

I gave in. "Okay."

The next day in art class, Ben asked if I was available Saturday morning. "The Matterhorn is closed until four o'clock so I won't have to work until late afternoon."

"Sure, no problem," I replied. "Know where you want to go?"

"Do you have a preference?"

"No," I answered. *As long as it's not where Bellavista Lookout used to stand.* I kept that thought to myself.

"Dress warm," he told me. "I'll text you in the morning."

"Okay, see you tomorrow."

"Until tomorrow, Emeranne."

Dad, Geneva and Matt left for work early, that sunny, mild Saturday morning. Actually, Matt would sleep in Dad's office instead of his favorite spot near the livingroom fireplace. I wouldn't be home to dog sit.

I peeked out the brown and beige striped curtains hanging inside the front door window. Snow started to fall and land lightly on the porch. While I waited for Ben's text, the conversation I'd had with my friends raced through my mind.

He's never been presented in an Ice Vision, reminded Morgan.

What about River's warning? *Filthy bloodhounds*, he'd said.

I didn't know who or what to believe any more. I cast my doubts aside as soon as I heard my phone's tri-tone, a text from Ben, that read simply, "Meet me outside at 8."

Delicately falling snow kissed the windshield of Ben's Silverado during the silent ride up the fresh snow covering Roars Hack Falls Road, twisting and turning higher and higher away from Snow Valley Mountain Road. When the flurries stopped, blinding sunlight reflected off freshly fallen snow. The late autumn sunshine warmed my face. Walls of snow framed the road, leftovers from last week's snowstorms. Snowstorms that I'd had a hand in creating.

My cell phone pinged. Ben raised his eyebrows. "Just a text. My friends checking in," I said lightheartedly. "Where're we going, by the way?" I hid my mounting anxiety.

"To a place where I hike whenever I want to be alone."

The Silverado dug into the road. Although there weren't any tracks to follow on the road, Ben's truck didn't get stuck in the deep snow. He drove past Snow Valley Campground, past thick stands of pine trees that thinned out the farther up the mountain the Silverado climbed, until Ben veered the truck left. I assumed he was taking me to Snow Valley Ski Resort for a hot chocolate and ginger cake with whipped cream at the Interlaken Café overlooking the ski trails snaking down the mountain—a nice place to sketch—but Ben drove by the resort.

"I come up here all the time," Ben confessed, He pulled the truck into a parking area where tourists often stopped in the summer to admire the breathtaking view of the mountain valley. The lot was knee-deep in snow, but Ben had no trouble cutting through the drifts. He came to a full stop and parked.

"We'll have to snowshoe the rest of the way," he said. "You don't mind, do you?"

"No. We've got all day."

"Until four o'clock."

Ben didn't seem worried about hiking with me, knowing I'd grown up in Snow Valley, raised by a forest ranger dad who'd strapped me on his back when he'd hiked up the mountain or in a child seat whenever he biked the uneven, rugged trails, until I

195

was old enough to do it myself. Ben pulled four snowshoes from the storage chest in the truck's bed, the chest gleaming in the sunshine, a pattern of sparkling diamonds. "I thought you were about Giselle's size," he said, handing me the smaller pair.

I strapped on the clunky wooden frames as ancient as oversized wooden tennis racquets I'd seen hanging on the walls of Kerr's New and Used Ski and Board. Expertly, he fastened his snowshoes around his large boots and shrugged a heavy backpack over his shoulders. Ben offered to carry my art supplies. "And some food," he'd added. Ben's ashen eyes reflected sunlight trickling through treetops overhead. "Ready?"

I nodded, trundling behind Ben, north through thick pine stands. Beneath the warm sunshine, boughs drooped and dripped under the tremendous weight of accumulated snow. The cold, stormy snap having temporarily retreated, thin ice crusts squeaked incessantly. The more we climbed, the more we sank into deeper layers of ice and snow, crackling and crunching and clinging to our snow shoes, heavier and heavier with each step. Every minute or so, Ben looked over his shoulder. "You okay?" he'd stop and ask. I smiled and nodded every time.

A sudden gust of wind shrieked and howled, nearly blowing my woolen hat off. I held my hat in place and looked up through cracks in the vast forest canopy. Streaks of aqua light and sunrays peeked down, like twinkling lights and golden fireflies. A few snowbirds wheeled in the air, their high-pitched shrills mixing with intermittent sounds of splintering ice crashing down from weary branches grateful for today's thaw. Bare rocks jutted from the mountainside, snow unable to cling to their steep angles, shaken by the howling wind.

Picking up my pace, carefully avoiding falling snow that loosened as it melted on surrounding branches, I managed to keep up with Ben whose breathing was normal, unlike mine. I sensed he slowed down every so often for my benefit. As soon as

I'd caught my breath, he'd continue upward. Higher and higher and higher.

Buried deep beneath snowdrifts, and with no trails to follow, Ben carved a wide path, winding his way through labyrinthine stands of imposing conifers. I felt the air thinning as we climbed further and further above the clouds that encircled the mountains. Fallen trees along our impromptu route created obstacles, piled higher with snow, making it more difficult to step over with heavy snowshoes. He and I got down on all fours, angling our snowshoes awkwardly and crawling over thick horizontal trunks.

I stayed close behind Ben, climbing over more fallen trees draped with mounds of snow, amid veils of sobering shades within an enchanted forest. Where supernatural occurrences surpassed reality. Where anything was possible. Fantasy thrived in this magnificent stand of ancient pine trees, their branches wearing magical cloaks of snowflakes. Here, in this forest of unlimited imagination, I could believe anything. Even the existence of witches and witch hunters, if I hadn't already known they existed.

I managed not to lag behind, concentrating on watching Ben's shoulders turn left and right, thoughtfully moving branches out of my way, constantly looking over his shoulder, smiling his rare, infectious smile that seemed reserved especially for me.

Ben pushed forward. I saw a clearing ahead. We crossed an icy, snow-covered bridge, walked along the frozen banks of the Roars Hack River to the falls, which we'd heard gushing, and saw at last, two breathtakingly beautiful mirror-image cascades. Towering pine trees shrouded the twin falls from the blue skies and sun above.

Ben sat on a rock to watch thousands of gallons of ice-cold water spill down the mountainside. "Let's sit here for a while," he suggested, patting the rock next to him.

I sat down next to him and caught my breath. I dug my snowshoes' heels into the snow and waved them back and forth like windshield wipers going in opposite directions, glad to rest before pushing on. I stood up and walked to the edge of the clearing and sat down again, resting in a rare slice of warm sunshine next to an imposing pine tree.

"I love this spot," I said to Ben, lifting my chin toward the sun.

Roars Hack Falls growled and moaned and hissed nearby. I crouched on the snow and picked through nylon strings, hoping to lighten my snowshoes by removing heavy, clinging snow, knocking it off against the trunk of a tree, and wishing I could do the same with the heavy burden weighing on my mind, my fear that Ben was the faceless boy lying in the forest, whose eyes turned to flames, as they had beneath the Halloween Blood Moon.

I shook my head. *Stop it*, I said to my imagination. *It's not him. Not him. Not him.*

Chapter Seventeen

Bear Paw Lookout

EMERANNE

Ben's deep voice broke the tranquil silence, and the turbulence of my thoughts. "We're almost there," he said.

We had hiked silently, but for the repetitive sounds of snowshoes digging into layers of flakes and ice beneath our boots, for what seemed like hours. The quiet that had fallen between us stretched five minutes into sixty. The sweat running down my back froze like icicles, my heart raced, pumping blood through my veins as fast as cold mountain water tumbling down Roars Hack Falls and into the river, gushing and hissing.

Through the dense forest canopy, past the last thin stand of trees, Ben led me to a familiar place. A place that I'd always loved.

Bear Paw Lookout.

I'd not been back since cutbacks in the National Forest Service's budget forced Dad to abandon responsibility for maintenance on several remote lookouts.

"I know this place," I whispered.

Ben stopped in front of me and smiled and held out his hand. "I hoped you'd like it."

Puddles of playful sunlight illuminated the lookout's windowpanes, brightening their soiled faces, sad and neglected. Shimmering puffs of snow blew off the lookout's slanted roof.

Dad and one of his Forest Service colleagues, Moe Stone, regularly brought me and his son Luke to Bear Paw Lookout when we were kids. Luke and I built forts out of fallen branches in summertime and snow forts in the winter. Lying on our backs, cushioned by freshly fallen snowflakes, we melted away hours and hours of wintry days, making powdery snow angels. Nearby, rotund snowmen and women and girls and boys emerged from the snow, their oversized river rock eyes smiled and pine cone noses sniffled and stick arms waved. Wool scarves draped around their uppermost curves, where their head met ample midsections.

I found myself at a place I'd loved with all of my heart, beating furiously now, in this safe, warm place. Bear Paw Lookout was all that and more to me, even when I fell off the deck from the high timber-framed tower. Luke and I had made cardboard wings with scotch tape and string, believing we could fly. It turned out I couldn't. Instead, I broke my arm.

Ben gently rested one of his thick mittens upon my lower arm. "I hope you don't mind coming here. After what happened at Bellavista Lookout…"

His voice trailed off. I didn't reply for a long, long moment.

I covered my mouth with one mitten, stifling a deep intake of air, and stepped further away from the dark forest, toward the lookout. "It's fine, really."

Ben stood behind me and wrapped his arms around my shoulders and rested his chin on the top of my head, near the very same place where he'd kissed my bald Dopey head.

"It wasn't just a bike helmet you lost that day. I know it was much more."

I froze. Speechless, I dropped to my knees and covered my face with my mittens.

At last, I spoke. "How did you know? Unless…"

His voice laced with stifled panic, Ben said, "It was in the papers."

I pushed myself up and turned to face him and said as calmly as possible, "No one knew about my helmet. Except my dad."

"I, um, I guess he said something to me that night at your birthday party—"

I screamed. "Don't! You! Lie! To me!"

"I'm not. I'm not. Not…"

"You were there," I hissed. "You killed her, didn't you?"

"No."

"Admit I'm right. Admit you've been hiding a secret. Admit it was you."

"No."

"Why? Why did you have to kill her?"

"I didn't! You have to believe me!"

"Why else would you be there? I know it was you!"

"Emeranne, wait. Wait!"

I backed away, while continuing to scream at him. "It's the only reason you were there. Why else would you be up on the mountain?"

"I saw the smoke. And thought…thought…"

"You thought you thought you thought…you thought nothing! Except to kill a woman and set her and the lookout on fire!"

"No no no no," he pleaded again and again and again. "No!"

I screamed louder, so loud that the snowbirds stopped chirping. "It was you!"

"Emeranne please please please believe me. It wasn't me wasn't me wasn't me."

"It's the only way you knew about my bike helmet. Only someone who was there would have known." He didn't say anything else. How could he defend himself? He couldn't. "You hid, didn't you? Watched me? Didn't you?" My shouting carved into the icy air. "Didn't you? Didn't you? Tell me. Tell me to my face. Didn't you?"

Ben fell to his knees and wrapped his arms around my waist. I stood there, shaking. With his head buried in my parka, he whispered, "No."

"That's why you came to Snow Valley, isn't it? To kill Mrs Kerr."

"No, you have to believe me."

"Why should I believe you?"

"Because I wasn't the one who abducted Mrs Kerr."

"So you knew she was abducted? How? And if it wasn't you, then who was it?"

"I can't say, shouldn't tell you."

"You know who did this monstrous thing? And you've said nothing to the police?"

"I can't, Emeranne."

Beware, the faces in the fire warned, *for one of your Coven shall be next...*

"Emeranne? What is it? Is there something you're not telling me?"

I couldn't tell him what the Coven had discovered in the fire or what the sketches he saw that day on the picnic table really meant.

"Nothing," I threw back at him. "Nothing."

But the curious look he returned made me suspect that he didn't believe me.

River was right to be suspicious of the Bassetts, even though the Coven hadn't any Ice Visions, and the Den Born didn't pick up any discernable Scent. But why not?

Ben didn't have to be a witch hunter to have murdered Mrs. Kerr. Maybe he was a copycat killer, having read about Violet Grimesby's murder. After all, her murder remained unsolved and was featured occasionally in the newspapers. Not hard to miss.

Was my short life about to end so quickly? Here on the mountainside? Just like Mrs. Kerr? That's why he brought me here. To kill me then burn another lookout!

But where was River? Byron? Hadn't they picked up on the Scent today? And if not, why not? Why not once again?

Warm rays of sunlight broke through the scattered clouds. I saw my pale shadow on the glimmering snow-covered ground. A fleeting silhouette imbedded in the snowfall's memory, disappearing now in this false spring-like thaw.

Soon I would die, painfully no doubt. I could stop now. Stop, at last. Stop running. Stop worrying. Stop hiding my secret for the rest of my life. The Coven's secret. I couldn't betray them, no matter how much Ben planned to torture me. I sensed my body slow down, knowing it was about to shut down. When I removed my mittens from my face, Ben's mesmerizing silver eyes gazed into mine.

That's when I decided to run. Run for my life. Whatever life I had left.

I ran for my life down the mountain. Stomping on my snowshoes, I picked up my pace, wrapped my arms around tree trunks to my left. Right. Left. And again left. Right. Right. Right. Left. Staggering forward, winding through a never-ending maze of trees, growing thicker now the more I descended.

Ben's voice trailed behind me, his pleas floated to my ears through my thick, woolen hat. I gasped for air and fought through the pain in my stinging lungs and burning legs.

Desperately I fumbled for my cell phone. I'd forgotten to text the Coven. When I reached into a side pocket on my jacket, I couldn't feel the phone. I must have dropped it somewhere on the trail. So much for Carlton's tracking plan, I groaned.

I ran until my legs gave out. I hid behind a stand of pine trees where I ducked to catch my breath, mittens on my shaking thighs, part exhaustion, part fear. I couldn't stop myself from falling forward, planting my face on the snow. *Ouch*, I groaned. My face shattered thin layers of ice that buried the pine straw ground. I rubbed my face and looked up.

Ben dropped his backpack and glided toward me. I couldn't move a muscle.

Dejectedly, I rested my head against the cold, rough bark of a protective tree trunk, its boughs sagging under layers of ice and snow, until the boughs gave up and let the layers drop.

Don't give up, I told myself.

I am Ice Born, I reminded myself. *I am Ice Born.*

A tree falls. A tree falls. A tree falls, I mumbled.

And just like that. *Thwack!* A massive pine tree fell, noiselessly for the most part, except for stirring up clouds of snow as boughs on neighboring pines were grazed on the tree's descent.

I removed Giselle's snowshoes and stumbled away, following the riverbank downward, occasionally glancing frantically over my shoulder.

Another tree fell. With one foot Ben rolled it aside. My powers couldn't stop him.

But I didn't give up. Something drove me. Something from deep, deep inside. Again, I concentrated. When I opened my eyes, Ben stood inches away, shaking his head.

"Emeranne." His deep voice bounced off the emptiness of the crowded forest. "Don't you know your powers don't work on our kind?"

Ben touched me with one mitten and gently stroked my arm and placed his other mitten on my frozen cheek. His touch sent fear and death and joy and life into my thumping heart. Nothing but the gushing sound of Roars Hack Falls was perceptible. Ominous, crashing water. "Please, Ben, if you don't mind, I'd appreciate it tremendously if you'd make it painless. And quick." I waited for his reaction. A subtle movement or sign. But he didn't flinch. Didn't react. Motionless, his smoldering eyes weren't those of a killer.

His were smiling, protective, compassionate.

And Ben did the last thing I expected him to do.

He moved his mitten from my arm and held it out toward my hand. I scowled and stepped backward slowly, not taking my eyes off his. "I'd never hurt you, Emeranne. Had I wanted to kill you, I'd have done so the first time I saw you in class." His voice was sincere and contrite.

"How can I trust you, Ben?"

"You shouldn't, I wouldn't if I were in your shoes. I don't know what to do, how to make you believe me," he admitted.

The hair on the back of my neck rose. I didn't believe him. But then he moved forward and put his arms around me, hugging me tightly. When he let go, I collapsed. Ben sat down next to me on the frigid snow. "Why would I hurt you?" he expressed earnestly. "I'd never dream of hurting you, even if my own existence was jeopardized. It's time you knew the truth about me, all of my secrets. And you can share whatever you wish, or not. Your secrets are safe with me until the end of time."

I shifted my position on the ground. My snow pants started to stiffen uncomfortably. I considered his offer. To tell me his secrets. But what could I say to him without putting the Coven in harm's way?

"I didn't kill Mrs Kerr. Please, Emeranne, please believe me," he implored.

In fact, I hadn't actually witnessed Ben anywhere near Bellavista Lookout. And yet, a loud voice warned me I was in mortal danger. "You say that so sincerely. I want to believe you…" My voice trailed off, disillusioned.

Effortlessly, Ben rose from the ground, crusted with ice shavings, lifted me, and swept me up in his muscular arms. I struggled to break free, but my efforts were futile.

I was locked in his ironclad embrace.

I tried to scream, but my vocal chords strangled any sound I'd struggled to make. And who would hear me? Here, high up the mountainside with no one around? It was hopeless. Instead, I only managed to mumble one question. "What now?"

"Go to Bear Paw Lookout where we can talk in private. And don't forget, we still have the art assignment to do, although I realize that's not exactly high on the agenda at the moment."

"You think?" I shrugged. What choice did I have? Carefully, Ben loosened his grip and let me slide slowly to the ground.

Ben held out Giselle's snowshoes. "Look what I found." I put on the snowshoes and followed Ben who retraced my tracks until Bear Paw Lookout's windowpanes were visible again. This time, I was sure the panes of worn glass cried. A frosty chill punctuated the autumn air. Veils of transparent mist drifted over the mountains. I lifted my chin, asking myself what I was doing here, perched near a perilous cliff.

A metaphor for my life, forever hanging in the balance, hanging on the edge of a dangerous cliff. A bitter wind found gaps in my scarf and seeped around my neck. I repositioned my scarf, unable to block out the heartless slashes like claws extending from the whipping wind.

Seemed fitting, I mused, that I should return to a place where I'd fallen in my past. I surveyed the lookout's exterior, in a sad state of disrepair.

Momentarily, the beauty of this area merged with the biting breath from an angry wintry breeze. The snow around the lookout was icier, opalescent and glistening. I fought tears and focused on the shadows of my snowshoes floating upon the ice. If I hadn't heard Ben's inadvertent admission, that he was present when Mrs. Kerr had died, this day would have been a perfect day to sketch the breathtaking scenery. Well, so much for perfection. It's highly overrated, I realized.

I stared at the high tower behind the rocky outcrop. Its two-story ladder extended beneath the small cabin above.

Ben sighed. "I wish we could've come here in the evening, when the fading sun sets, the westward view is amazing from the lookout's balcony. Layers of red and orange, purple and navy, asleep above black contours of rugged landscape."

"Yes, it is," I agreed, unable to find fault in his observations, although I'd have felt more insecure in the dark.

"Let's go inside," he suggested tenderly, reaching out to touch one mitten.

Instinctively, I withdrew my mitten and screamed. "Don't touch me! Haven't you done enough already? How do I know you won't lure me up there only to…to…kill me and then…then set a fire? Just like I found…found—"

I couldn't finish my sentence. Couldn't say it. Say her name, the witch I'd found at Bellavista Lookout. Between heaves of sobs and snivels, I caught my breath. Waves of dizziness overcame my impulsive outburst. Ben motioned for me to sit down. I obeyed, unwilling to teeter near the cliff's edge.

Ben reached out again and caressed my face and wiped tears from my cheeks. He spoke soothingly, spoke words I wanted to believe were true, spoke what I wanted to hear.

"I've never killed anyone in Snow Valley."

"In Snow Valley," I repeated. "But you have elsewhere."

Yes was what his smoke filled eyes spoke to mine. As though a fire had burned deep inside and only ashes remained.

I stopped sobbing momentarily, searching Ben's downcast face beneath the hood of his jacket. I wanted to reach out and lift his hood. Wanted to see the world through those incredibly hypnotic eyes. Wanted to confront the mysteries that Ben presented. To dive into his beautiful eyes and discover his secrets. "Not, not here…?"

"Never here," he said flatly.

"So, you're saying…you have…have…"

He nodded. "Emeranne, let's go inside and I'll start a fire," he offered, clarifying when he saw me shudder, "in the fireplace."

As if I couldn't give in to those silvery eyes, peeking out from under wispy eyelashes. As if I could remain angry with Ben. As if I couldn't listen to what he had to say. As if.

Ben was silent for quite some time. He just stood there, deep in thought, his sad graphite eyes focused upon the surrounding valley. A million questions invaded my mind. Without second-guessing myself, I stood up, dusted snow off my behind, turned around and walked to Bear Paw Lookout's tall ladder, zigging and zagging upward.

"Well, what are you waiting for?" I said to him.

Ben raised his eyebrows and smiled. Cautiously, I scaled the twisting ladder to a square opening under the deck and pulled myself up on the snow-covered planks. Within seconds, Ben ascended. "Wait here one minute." He disappeared and left me alone with my thoughts about today's events until he returned, interrupting my wandering mind.

The deck gleamed with ice crusts. Despite the snowfall, a well-worn path was visible and led to the cabin's single red door.

"I come here all the time, to think, be alone, write, sketch. I find solace here, high above the clouds, surrounded by the beauty of nature."

"I felt the same way, when I used to come here. That no one could hurt me. No one, other than myself, apparently," I joked.

"This is one of the few places where I can be myself," Ben said.

"I fell. I thought I was an angel. With paper wings."

Ben lowered his eyes. He opened a torn screen door, then the faded red one.

"You'll never fall again. Not here or anywhere else, as long as I'm around. I promise you, Emeranne."

Slivers from the wooden door's blistered red paint fell off like blood-soaked snowflakes. Dad painted the door one pleasant summer while I'd sat nearby, drawing in the sunshine, my crayons soft and warm.

I looked through the doorway. Unlike the misleading dilapidated exterior, Bear Paw Lookout's one room cabin was immaculate and dust-free. I inhaled distinct, sweet scents of

208

burning sap on dried pine logs. I stepped inside the cabin. The double-sided fireplace was still surrounded by a beautiful field stone hearth in the middle of the cabin. Framed maps and faded Forest Service posters hung on knotted timber walls. Smokey the Bear, the same one hanging in my bedroom next to framed prints of fireflies, butterflies, dragonflies. Survival skills in the wilderness. A guide to the numerous hiking trails twisting and turning through Snow Valley National Forest.

Spartan hand-hewn furnishings were arranged neatly. I ran my hand along the thick timber mantle. Assorted pictures were arranged on the beam. I picked up one frame, traced the rough wood with my index finger. Dad, Moe, Luke and I smiled at the foot of the lookout. Moe's oldest brother, Huron, took the photo. I remembered that day, a perfect summer day.

Framed, too, was my crayon drawing of stick man Dad surveying the expansive valley using oversized binoculars. Instead of lenses, the binoculars were drawn with big, green eyes. Dad's eyes.

Swiftly, I was transported to another time, long ago, when I'd come to Bear Paw Lookout as a child. Dad's friendly voice filled the cabin. So, too, Luke's infectious laughter and Moe's whistling to the chopping beat of his axe, and my own voice, young, piercing, and giggling.

Dad, look! I fed a squirrel! I heard myself squeal.

Ems, watch out for the poison ivy, Dad warned.

Wanna race up the ladder, Ems? Luke was always competitive. I noted the tip of a tree Luke had climbed. The tree had grown a lot since then …

What's for lunch, Jack? Moe never missed one of Dad's delicious meals.

I'm certain I saw a younger version of myself in the kitchen, standing on a small stool and reaching up to the chipped wooden countertop where I prepared peanut butter and jelly sandwiches.

Luke mixed grape Kool-Aid with spring water pumped from a large plastic bottle.

I'm sure I saw myself watching Luke throw pieces of stale bread and unshelled peanuts from the wooden railing outside for the chipmunks, squirrels and birds.

These happy memories made me smile, even the roaring fire, red and orange and pink and yellow and blue, that fire raging fiercely, even that brought back pleasant memories, flames prancing before me.

The scent of chocolate teased my nose and taste buds, bringing me back to the present. Standing next to a potbelly wood stove, Ben stirred with one hand and kept the other in the kangaroo pocket of his purple and silver Snow Valley High hoodie.

Ben was full of surprises today, both good and bad. "Hot chocolate?" I stared at him wordlessly. I didn't think hot chocolate could make up for the bad part. "I'm always prepared," he explained. The backpack he carried up the mountain was unzipped. He piled foil pans next to a hand basin on the kitchen counter. The last items, art supplies, seemed useless to me now. How was I supposed to sketch anything?

Ben busied himself in the tiny kitchen where he stirred the hot chocolate and unwrapped foil pans. I walked around the cabin, beneath its slanted roof. Dad never finished building the sleeping loft. A ladder stood on the left hand side of the cabin, leaning against a beam where planks of wood lay neatly stacked. Encased in a sleeping bag on the floor, I'd stayed overnight many times when violent rainstorms washed out the dirt road. There was no electricity or plumbing. An outhouse with a crescent moon window on the door was located behind the cabin. Chamber pots were likely still hidden under the beds.

I absorbed a surge of memories, joyful and fresh. Two wooden rocking chairs with red and black tartan pillows faced westward, on the cabin's left hand side. Behind the rocking chairs, several items were piled neatly on a small table. Faded novels. Hardcover books, tattered and worn. Leather bound journals. A large sketchpad. Pencils short and long. Dark blue ink bottles. A fountain pen.

I picked up one of the books and read the spine. "Veurçon Aramis Delacroix," I whispered. My gut wrenched and twisted. "Delacroix," I repeated again, and replaced the book on the table.

One of the journals was open. I couldn't help myself. I had to see. See what Ben wrote, if anything, about me. It's not as if I'd opened the journal, strewn upon the table right in front of me. My eyes darted and skimmed and skipped over pages and pages of handwritten prose, over pages filled with words created in a beautiful script, from another time, another era.

> *how many lifetimes*
> *how many sunsets*
> *would you wait*

I flipped forward a few pages…

> *oh who am I to brighten the mourning indigo nightfall?*

My heart raced. One after the other after the other after the other, pages and pages and pages. I mouthed the words to one short poem.

> *and of love*
> *what does the heart say?*
> *it beats its silent wings*
> *before it flies away*

It was Ben. He'd left the poem in my locker…

One after another, *flip flip flip.* Heart thudding racing beating breathing fast faster faster faster…

> *to be with the one you adore worship*
> *dream about*
> *love*

Ben sketched in the journal. And the sketches looked familiar.

Like me? Except, without facial details, a blank face, like the boy in my dreams.

How could Ben be a killer and write about love? Write so sincerely, so deeply, so eloquently? Or sketch as though his pencil caressed, embraced, touched as though his hand was a gentle and warm and soft summer breeze?

With the leather bound journal open in my hands, palms sweaty, heart thumping, slowly slowly I lifted my eyes. Turns out, the journal filled with poetry and sketches was a taste of what was to come. Every inch of wall space was covered with more sketches, some discolored, torn at the edges, some winter white, some newly bleached. In pencil, charcoal, sepia.

But with one common denominator.

There weren't any details on the face.

I gasped and covered my mouth, then dropped the journal and clenched my fists and placed my hands, shaking with anger and fear and confusion, on my hips.

I didn't see Ben standing next to me. He picked up the journal and read quietly.

> *who are you?* the voices always ask
> *i don't remember,* I say
> *we do not know,* one voice says
> *he is dying,* another voice pleads
> *we do not know his wishes,* says the first voice

who are you? the voices repeat
we do not know he would want this, says a third voice
i don't remember, I say
we do not have the authority, says the first voice
i don't remember, I say
he would want to live, the second voice begs
i don't remember, I say
and then the burning sun vanishes
and the world is dark
and I am cold
and I am lost
and I am alone
and I am dead

"Ben," was all I could say through trembling lips.

"Emeranne, are…are you all right?"

I held my hand out, touched the journal, then the sketches on the wall. "What…when?"

"Forever," he replied quietly.

"Who was she?" I asked again.

"I don't know. Let me explain. How about we sit down, over there," he said, pointing to two rocking chairs in front of the windows. Ben sat down in one of the chairs.

Trembling, I managed to walk to the chairs and cautiously, drew a long, halting breath and moved closer to Ben, to the chairs overlooking the panoramic view from the livingroom. He patted the seat next to his chair.

Taking a seat, I clasped my hands nervously until I rested them on my thighs, shaking as much as my hands. Handing me a blue tin cup of steaming hot chocolate, Ben held out his other hand, tenderly untangling mine. We sat in silence, my hand trembling in his protective one, enveloped in the cabin's warmth, rocking back and forth in unison. And we sat rocking, holding hands for a long time, without saying another word, staring out into the mid afternoon sun. I hadn't realized so much time had passed.

Ben's voice broke the emptiness. "I've sketched her for so long, but her face was never clear to me."

"And?" I prompted.

"And I kept sketching and searching, forever searching for her face."

"Have you found her yet?"

"No. Maybe. I don't know."

Like one of Ardelle's storm knots, our hands remained tied together. Ben raised his hand and pressed mine to his lips. He closed his eyes and sighed. Until now, Ben and I were just friends. Part of me realized we'd never be friends and yet, another emotion rose inside me today on Snow Valley Mountain. I didn't pull my hand away from Ben. I should have, but didn't. I should be repulsed by him, but wasn't. In fact, I liked being close to him.

What was wrong with me? *He's your enemy*, I scolded myself.

I stared ahead, afraid to look into his irresistible, sterling silver irises. The fire continued to fizz and snap behind me. As the sun hovered above the tree line, I gathered enough courage to ask Ben the most burning question of all.

"Who are you?" I lowered my voice to a whisper. "Or should I ask, 'What are you?'" I couldn't stop the shiver that ran through me. Did I really want to know?

Chapter Eighteen

Boundaries

BENNETT

Emeranne's hand dropped from my cold lips. The windows framed a spectacular canvas, casting shadows on a tabletop of navy blue clouds. The loud, crackling fire raged on, throwing shadows on the windows. Panes of frosted glass flickered with muted images of Emeranne and me rocking back and forth. Back and forth. The sky darkened when the sun hid beneath thick sheets of frothy mist.

I wanted to lift those wispy sheets of mist. Wanted to see what lay beneath them. Wanted to face the sun's mysterious gaze. To dive into the mist and discover its secrets. I'd never seen the mountainside quite like this before. I saw the sprawling valley below for the very first time, with a different set of eyes, perhaps getting a glimpse through Emeranne's eyes, a tiny taste of her world. Could we ever share that world? Her world, my world? *Any* world? The worlds of an immortal witch hunter and a witch?

Who was I kidding? How could we ever come together? How could she ever trust me?

My body rocked back and forth with the steady tempo of Emeranne's breath, at first in unison until she rocked out of synch with me.

Was I destined to move in an opposite direction to Emeranne? Or could I somehow, against all odds, against the laws of nature, of my laws and hers, could I ever reconcile our impossible differences?

Drawing a long, hesitant breath, I formed the words on my lips. But nothing came out. I tried and tried to say three words. Immortal. Witch. Hunter.

"I am your worst enemy. I am the hunter."

Emeranne stopped rocking abruptly. She seemed to be processing what I'd just admitted. For an eternity, she just sat there and said nothing. Not a word.

Three words filled my head. *Venefici Venator Immortalis.* Three words escaped my mouth, over my lips, into the silent, lonely world. "Immortal witch hunter." Still, she was far away. Again, I offered those words, hushed and apprehensive. "Immortal witch hunter."

At long last, turning to me, she spoke. "Tell me something, Ben. Where does a conversation lead after an admission of immortality?" Stunned by her calm reaction, I stayed silent. "What year were you born?"

"As far as I know, in thirty-one," I replied casually.

"Interesting. And what century would that be, if you don't mind elaborating?"

"Fourteenth," I said, maintaining my gaze on the mauve sky.

Emeranne stopped rocking, put her hot chocolate down and broke my firm grasp, needing her second hand to count the number of centuries I'd been alive. "So…that means…"

She turned, locking eyes with mine. "Seven? You've lived for seven centuries?"

"More like existed for most of those seven centuries. After all, I'm not really alive."

"You weren't joking at my birthday, were you?"

"No, I wasn't."

"When did you…you—?" she stammered.

216

"When did I die?" She nodded. I gritted my teeth, knowing I'd risk losing her trust if she knew more about me. But, in fact, there wasn't much to tell. The worst part was out there.

"My rescuers found my body washed ashore. A ship, *La Tempesta*, sank in a terrible storm. I was dying. And then, by some miracle, I was alive. Or so I thought. I was told that the crew had all been accounted for, so I must have been a passenger. The ship's manifest was not found among the wreckage, and by the time my rescuers and I visited the port where the ship set sail, that manifest had disappeared. I never discovered my real name or place of birth. The only detail my rescuers remember is the shipping company's record of the boy's approximate year of birth, based on his estimated age. The year, so I'm told was thirteen thirty-one. Coincidental date, huh?"

I forced the corners of my mouth into a smile and moved my head slightly to peek at Emeranne.

She picked up her mug. "Coincidence?"

"Your home address is the same number as my birth year."

Emeranne reflected on this fact, perhaps recalling the mysterious grin I'd worn the day of the snowstorm, the day I'd driven her home. Staring at me, she caught her breath. "And how…"

"How did I become immortal?" She didn't answer, so I said, "Are you sure you're ready?" She placed her hot chocolate down again and looked at her hands, rested her chin on her chest, twiddled her thumbs rapidly. I reached out again, gently took hold of her hand and held it tighter.

Eventually, she spoke. "How do I know you're not lying? That this isn't a sick prank? To cover your tracks? After you killed—"

"I didn't."

She huffed. "So you say."

Into the cabin trickled twisted sunlight. Emeranne's forest green eyes asked me, asked over and over and over again, *What are you saying? What do these jarring words passing through your lips and these moments together in these colliding worlds of ours, what do they all mean?*

Wordlessly, I stared into her eyes, asking her to believe me. After extended moments spent staring at the lanterns of clouds, I wanted her to hear my thoughts, reassuring her. *Don't worry. Please don't worry. Never worry.* And she seemed to know what I wanted to say.

Tears ran down her cheeks, trickled under her chin and settled near her collarbone. I reached out to that tiny brook through which a single tear carved a new path toward her heart.

"Mrs Kerr?" I guessed. She said nothing, but I knew her tears were for Leland's mother. I knelt and turned to face her and extended my hand. With my back to the muted sunlight visible through the long windowpanes, she would see my graphite eyes reflecting tangerine and fuchsia and faded denim, the shades of burning logs and simmering embers imprisoned within the fireplace.

"Are you afraid of me? Of what I am?"

She looked at me through her eyelashes, nodding apprehensively. I held her eyes with mine. I felt ashamed.

"I know," I whispered in her ear. "I've always known what you are, and your friends, too." Slowly I lifted her chin and said, "Witches." Without moving a muscle, I crouched, one knee still on the ground. Emeranne looked terrified, as she should have.

"Just out of curiosity, how does this work?" she asked.

"The immortality?" Emeranne nodded. "From the moment a mortal is converted into an immortal witch hunter, blood is replaced with serum—*argentum vivum*—a serum comprising —

"Liquid mercury," Emeranne interrupted.

"How did you ...? Oh. Selene and Carlton."

"Yes."

"This serum is administered as a potion during the transformation." I frowned, turned away from the fire. I knew what was about to happen. My eyes—I could feel it happen—changed from a raging bonfire to a dreary, rainy afternoon and then to a sad, stormy night sky, mirroring my emotions. My despair.

"Over the centuries, many talented scientists and alchemists have tried in vain to decipher precise ingredients of the elixir of immortality. To date, the only discernable ingredient is mercury extracted from cinnabar ore. The rest remain a mystery. The alchemical explanation for how or why this serum works is unknown."

Emeranne reflected a few moments, then said, "Your ring is snowflake obsidian."

"You remembered."

"You *have* to wear it?"

"Yes. It masks our identity from—"

"Witches. Me. The Coven."

"Yes," I admitted. "From witches."

"And the serum, too?"

"The serum too."

"So who did it?" Emeranne asked me.

"The conversion?" She nodded. "Allora, her husband, and son."

Emeranne looked incredulous. "Allora," she said. "Your aunt?"

"She's not my aunt," I told her.

"And Philippe?"

"Not my uncle, either. His children aren't my cousins."

"But you look so much like Wallis."

"Yeah, that helps with the cover story."

"So," she paused, "Allora is—"

"The oldest of us. Never, ever, ask her age, by the way. In time, she'll tell you her life story."

"Really? Do you honestly believe I can trust you're going to spare my life? Please don't kill me so I can ask another witch hunter to tell me her life story?"

I closed my eyes. She was right. I knew it, and couldn't argue the point. "After my transformation, the early days of my death are a blur. I...I...don't know much about that time. I was created to destroy witches, and at first I did what was required of me. And yet—during our last assignments, I've hesitated. I've struggled with doubts."

She gasped. "About killing witches? Why now? After all of these centuries?"

"Even the best elixir of immortality can't alter a person's values. The serum changes our mortality, not our morality. It changes the color of our eyes, but not our values. For me, killing witches never came naturally. Or easily."

"How could killing witches come naturally to anyone? Unless, of course, you're an immortal witch hunter." Her tone was caustic.

"After Mrs Kerr's murder, my family's pretty much in agreement, not to kill any more witches. With one exception."

"Miranda," Emeranne muttered.

I laughed. "How did you guess? She's utterly committed to her destiny as an immortal witch hunter. Miranda is bitter for many reasons, which I won't get into now." I drew a long, slow breath. "Assimilate. Infiltrate. Eliminate. The immortal witch hunter's creed. She reminded my family, the other night, of who we are, what our task has been, over the centuries. And she texted it to me the night of your party. 'Assimilate, infiltrate, eliminate.'"

Emeranne mouthed each word slowly. "Miranda really hates the Coven, doesn't she?"

"Yeah."

"How many other immortal witch hunters are there?"

"Hundreds. Thousands, maybe. No one really knows for certain, except the Varangian Guard—"

Emeranne interrupted me. "What's that?"

"The Varangian Guard is made up of ruthless legions of immortal witch hunters. Their Supreme Pack Commander has been responsible for sending hunters to the farthest ends of the earth."

"Pack Commander. As in—"

"A pack of hunters," I said matter of factly.

"A *pack* of hunters," she repeated, choking on the words. "Like wolves?"

"Yes. And the Pack Commander assigns us the next—"

"Coven to kill," she choked out the words.

"But one Varangian Guard, a brave Templar Knight from the twelfth century, defied his pack, and saved Allora during the Crusades."

"Allora again," Emeranne said mostly to herself.

"Yes. Emeranne, not even my family, not Allora or Philippe, nor any of us, could detect the hunters, the filthy poachers who killed Mrs Kerr."

"Poachers?"

"There are different categories of hunters," I explained, ticking them off on my fingers. "Stalkers, poachers, trappers. Poachers don't respect *any* boundaries.

"Is that what you were doing at Bellavista Lookout? Stalking?"

"Yes, but not in the creepy sense. It's not what you think."

"Really, Ben? What part of stalking *isn't* creepy? What would *you* think if you were me?"

"That I've stalked you," I admitted.

"Is that what you thought I'd assume? Or is that the truth?"

"Both," I said.

"Why?" she cried, impassioned. "Why would you do such a thing?"

"I'm not a poacher, Emeranne! Poachers kill witches, *any* witches, anywhere at any given time, regardless of whether another hunter or group or hunters has been given the assignment."

"Assigned," she said plaintively. "Your family was assigned to kill me? To kill the Snow Valley Coven?"

I nodded. "But we didn't kill Mrs Kerr. I saw the smoke, that morning, that's why I went to investigate. When I found Charlsie, it was too late—far too late—and I'll never forgive myself for not getting there in time to save her. To make matters worse, I watched you find her. Watched you go through hell."

"So that was worse for you? Imagine how *I* felt? And Leland! And my Coven!" I dropped my head. "So, who murdered Mrs Kerr, if your family didn't?"

"Poachers. You know what they look like."

"The sketches on the picnic table," she said, shaking her head. "Who are they?"

"The pair in the sketches? Octavia and Ulric. Poachers. Witch hunters gone rogue. Until recently, the Varangian Guard has managed to contain them, but obviously that's no longer the case."

"Contain them? How? What difference would that make?"

"Even witch hunters have rules, and a chain of command."

Emeranne stopped rocking. "So you think—"

"I don't think. I *know*."

"When we saw them, it looked like their eyes were on fire."

"We're Fire Born, and our eyes glow orange when…" I couldn't finish the sentence, couldn't say, *it happens when a witch hunter is about to kill a witch like Violet or Charlsie or like you, Emeranne.* How could she forgive me for centuries of violence against witches?

"Your eyes turn orange when you're about to—"

"Please forgive me, Emeranne. Please, I'm so sorry."

"No, I can't, Ben."

"I don't blame you. I wouldn't forgive me either."

We sat in silence until the brilliant colors faded in the fireplace.

Emeranne hugged her knees to her chest. She rested her feet, fitted with thick wool socks, on the rocking chair. "Ben," she mouthed softly. "Ben," she repeated. Would saying my name make any difference, I wondered, to how she now saw me? Did she see me still as a monster?

I stared ahead into the glittering sunlight, sitting next to Emeranne, a witch. Glued to the rocking chair, watching fluffy snowflakes dance by the frosted windowpanes, she closed her eyes. After an extended silence, she raised her eyelids. I looked outside where flurries hung motionless. Emeranne stood up, faced the fireplace, staring at the flickering flames, splitting the motionless flames in half, as if chopped with an axe.

"My powers," was all she said to me.

"Your powers," I said back to her.

A field trip to sketch the scenery had turned into a nightmare for Emeranne, all because I slipped up, said the wrong thing, and now she knew about me, my fake family, and the poachers. Why did I have to say anything about her helmet?

And yet, maybe this was for the best, that Emeranne knew my secret. After all, I'd always known she was part of the Snow Valley Coven, and now she knew everything about me, that I'm not human, not Ben the high school junior who made deliveries for his family's pizza parlor.

I was fear and danger and death and sadness.

And now Emeranne knows exactly who and what I am.

monster
hunter
executioner
murderer
fiend

fraud
liar
enemy

Emeranne was everything in an instant: lying on a pine needle bed, sketching in art class, cheering at the football game, dancing at Homecoming, Dopey sitting on the dunk tank, walking home in the blizzard, trapping snowflakes on her long, dark lashes, eating Pizza Margherita, cutting her birthday cake, opening presents, making a secret wish.

And I was nothing more than this: gray eyes and frozen memories, icicles of truths, flurries of lies, and a thousand moments of perpetual regret.

After a long silence, I broke the tension. "Hungry?" I asked. Emeranne didn't reply, didn't even look at me. How could she?

"A bit," she replied hesitantly.

"Well then I know a great place on the Left Bank. I saw Hemingway there, scribbling away, many times," I grinned.

"The Left Bank? Of the Roars Hack River?"

"No, Paris."

"You're not joking, are you?

"Nope."

"About Paris or Hemingway."

"Nope, neither one."

Emeranne leaned forward and put her forehead in her palms.

I got up and left her alone for a bit. Without exchanging further words, I busied myself in the tiny kitchen, where on the little cast iron pot-bellied woodstove I warmed pizza, and assembled several slices on paper plates.

When I came back, I said, "Can you smell it? Your favorite." Her face lit up for the first time since, well, I didn't want to think about what happened earlier today.

"You remembered," she said, and in return I gave her my best *I'd never hurt you in a million years kind of smile.*

I handed her a plate. "There's more," I said.

"Thanks," she replied quietly.

We ate in silence, with only the raucous voice of an irate wind filling our ears.

The cozy cabin's foggy windowpanes frosted over as dipping outdoor temperatures pushed against the warm glass. Afraid of what I might see in the glittering reflection of my own ashen eyes, I avoided looking at Emeranne.

"Violet Grimesby," she said under her breath. "Did you?"

"No."

"Who?"

I sighed. "I don't know."

She shivered. I reached out to hold her trembling hand, brushed the top of her head with my lips, drew her hand closer, positioned it over my heart.

"I don't understand," she said. "How can you be immortal, and at the same time, grow up just like the rest of us?"

"Good question. In a mortal's eyes, we age. But in fact, we don't."

"Never?"

"Never. And there's more." She didn't say a word. But her eyes said to me, in disbelief, *What more could there possibly be?*

So I just blurted it out. "My heart rate isn't like a human's."

"What?"

"My heartbeat is far slower than a human's. Yours beats around seventy beats per minute, but mine averages one tenth as many—seven per minute. Maybe it's the serum that changed our heart rate. I have to give myself regular injections to maintain it, or…"

"Or what?"

"Or I'd cease to exist," I said, lowering my voice.

"You skipped CPR. And flu shots," she gasped, shaking her head.

"Yes, and now you know why."

"Have you ever thought about, well, about *not* injecting the serum?"

"So many times I've stopped counting," I admitted.

"But you didn't. Why not?"

"Allora, Philippe—everything they've done for me, taking me in, accepting me as one of their own. I couldn't do that to them."

Emeranne bit her lip. "The Ice Born didn't detect the poachers, the ones named Octavia and Ulric," she told me. "And you're Fire Born. Why didn't you know the poachers were in this region?"

"Wallis concluded that our serum was likely altered. That may be why we couldn't detect Octavia and Ulric. The worst part was knowing Mrs Kerr would still be alive if we had known." Emeranne's face froze. "What is it?" I urged.

"Nothing," she blurted nervously, then inhaled and spoke in a hushed tone. "We couldn't detect you or the poachers. Neither could—" she stopped.

"River." It was all I needed to say.

"Yes. River and the rest of the Den Born."

I didn't press her for more details. "There's something else, too." But I couldn't say it. The thing I'd most dreaded. I was a heartless monster.

"I can't kiss you, Emeranne," I admitted.

The dark forest in her eyes disappeared. "I don't understand, Ben. Why would you tell me this?"

"Because I like being around you, Emeranne. And I think you like being around me too. Except you won't admit it."

"You do? I do?" she asked. I smiled at her. "Even knowing I'm a witch? And you're a witch hunter?"

226

"Yeah, I have this need to protect you, since that day on the mountain, realizing you were in danger."

"I can take care of myself," she snapped.

"I know you can. Even so, I need to make sure you're safe, like that morning of the fire."

Emeranne massaged her temples with her index fingers. "It was you, wasn't it? You dragged me from the fire. I don't remember crawling away, but I do remember there were two lines of drag marks though the pine needles."

"Yes, it was me. If I'd wanted you dead, why would I save you?"

"True," she said and added, "I guess I should say thanks."

"Anytime. I only wish—"

"I believe you," she said to me.

"You do? Really?"

She nodded. "Yeah, really."

"So, back to the kissing," I started to say.

"The kissing," she repeated nervously.

"This sole boundary will keep our relationship vastly different from a mortal one. I can't blame you, after everything you've learned about me, if you never want to speak to me again. But I'm still hoping you'd like to be more than friends."

Emeranne raised her chin to the wooden peaked roof and closed her eyes. "Why can't you—"

"Sir Terence, Allora's first husband, never anticipated the fatal toxicity of mercury vapors in the *argentum vivum*, given that he and Allora were both immortal witch hunters when they fell in love. The *argentum vivum* or *hydrargyrum* or liquid silver in our veins where blood used to flow, regularly releases toxic vapors through saliva."

"Toxic. Vapors," she repeated calmly, slowly.

"Vapors cause *hydrargyria*. Fatal mercury poisoning."

A million competing feelings seemed to flood her mind. After a long pause, her face reddened. "You can't? Or won't?"

"I'd kiss you in a heartbeat, but I can't. It's a critical boundary."

Emeranne shifted uncomfortably. "Can we talk about something else?"

"Like what?"

"Like the art project we're supposed to be working on," she replied.

"Oh, right. I brought supplies."

"I saw them," she pointed, "over there."

"Do you still want—?"

"Might as well, since we came all this way to sketch."

Emeranne picked up a sketch pad and pencil. I did the same.

The sunlight slowly faded, transforming the sky into shades of tangerine, red pepper, royal blue and grape. The colors deepened as the sun gradually disappeared, and the sky filled with a million fireflies dancing in the shelter of the clouds.

"Can you see them?" I asked.

"See what?"

"The fireflies. Over there."

Emeranne looked through the window and stared for a few moments. Then she lowered her head and continued sketching. She put her pencil down and held up her sketch book. "What do you think?" Emeranne drew what looked like clusters of snowflakes in the sky. The sun was barely visible behind the mountain peaks. A few rays from the setting sun reached out and touched each cluster. She made the clusters appear illuminated.

"Do you see snowflakes?"

"As much as I love fireflies, I've only seen them in my dreams. Not in Snow Valley."

I thought I saw a glimmer in her eyes, as though there was something more she wanted to say, but let it go. "You're right. Fireflies don't live in Snow Valley."

My mind wandered. Another flashback I couldn't control invaded my thoughts. The voices repeated the same words again and again.

you were dying …
we did what we thought was best …
what was your name
was your name
your name
name
we had no choice we had no choice we had no choice we had …
but I'm scarred forever scarred forever scarred …
no
choice
scarred
forever

Emeranne leapt out of the rocking chair. "What time is it?"

Disoriented from my flashback, I hadn't heard what she said. "Huh? What? Where?"

"Time. What time is it?"

"Oh, uh, later, later than I'd realized."

"Time stands still here, like magic," she sighed.

"Magic," I echoed. "But it won't be magical when Aunt Allora sees me. I was supposed to be at the Matterhorn two hours ago. We better leave."

"I wish we didn't have to."

Her admission took me by surprise. "Really?"

"Yes, really."

"I could talk all night," I confessed sheepishly.

"Me too," she said.

"Me too, Emeranne." I smiled. "Me too."

Chapter Nineteen

Missing

EMERANNE

£ike a snow globe shaken furiously, a million thoughts swirled in my head. I had to tell Carlton about the serum. I had to tell River about the Bassetts. I had to tell my Coven…

I *had* to tell. Tell them everything, I thought as Ben cautiously, hesitantly withdrew a silver-filled syringe from his hoodie's pocket. Pushing up the sleeve of his left arm, he clutched the syringe in his right, pierced his skin with the long, thin needle, until the shimmering liquid was gone. I stopped breathing and held one hand to my mouth, whispering so low I was certain Ben couldn't hear me. "*Argentum vivum.*"

Ben nodded. "I didn't eat enough," he explained. "So my energy was low."

"Does this happen often?"

"Not often, only when I exert a lot of energy. It's the price I pay for what I am."

By the tortured look on his face, I knew my reaction wasn't what he'd hoped for. Though I don't know how else I could have reacted, when you see someone injecting liquid mercury into bloodless veins.

Possessed with renewed life, Ben rose from his chair. A blur of black and orange light streaked out the door. The room went

230

eerily dark. Moonlight flooded the cabin seconds later, when Ben returned, wiping his hands.

"I buried simmering embers and charred logs under a snow bank, away from any trees."

My disbelieving eyes processed the scene that had unfolded seconds ago. I pointed my quivering index finger back and forth, from the faded red door, to the fireplace, to the door.

"You were here…then you were there…and then you came back here…"

"Don't look so shocked," he teased me. "The witch who froze fire, split flames, felled pine trees."

"Yeah, but I don't have asbestos hands," I said. "And probably can't outrun you."

"No, probably not," he admitted with his warm, rare smile, the one that took my breath away time and time again. "But you already experienced that."

"Do you always move so fast?"

"No," he said, lowering his voice to a near whisper. "It takes too much out of me. On that morning when, you know, at Bellavista Lookout, after I pulled you away from the fire, I waited for emergency services to arrive. As soon as I saw the fire trucks, ambulances, and smokejumpers I was relieved. You were safe. After that, I followed you down the mountain to the police station and home."

"You stalked me," I said mostly to myself.

"Yeah, like I said, to make sure you were okay, which I doubted you were, after what you saw that morning." He cleaned the kitchen, filled his backpack with empty foil containers, and carefully rolled our sketches.

We threw on our parkas, mittens and snow boots, preparing to confront the cold mountain air, then began to clamber down on snowshoes to the overlook where Ben had parked his Silverado. Above our heads, like a shimmering summer pond, the evening sky filled with water lily clouds, glistening stars, and a bright full moon. The milky garden's canvas provided a magical backdrop, as though lilacs were strewn on a deep green lake. I felt alone in the universe with Ben. Alone, and surprisingly safe.

Ben led the way, occasionally checking to make sure I hadn't turned around or run off again, though I now realized he'd always catch up with me.

As we reached Ben's Silverado, I sank to the ground, my legs burning slightly, my stomach aching, my mind reeling.

Ben. Immortal witch hunter. Ben. Immortal witch hunter. Ben...

"Emeranne? Are you okay?"

Defensively, I leapt to my feet. "Yeah."

"I don't believe you," he said. "If I were you, I wouldn't be either."

Shrugging, I bent down to remove my snowshoes.

"Let me," he said.

"No," I objected rather sharply.

"Emeranne," was all he said, so softly. I didn't object again. Kneeling, Ben untied the laces attaching the snowshoes to my boots. When he finished untying his own, he pointed to the truck with his remote to unlock the doors, clapped our snowshoes together until most of the snow fell off, slid the shoes behind the driver's seat, and asked, "Wanna drive?"

I laughed. "I already told you, I don't have my license."

"You need to practice." He chuckled.

"No, I don't."

"C'mon. There's no traffic up here and my truck's snow tires won't slip and slide around," he urged, handing me the keys. "Besides, you're sixteen, remember? It's every teenager's dream to drive."

"Not mine."

"Just try, only for a few miles, then I'll drive, okay?"

Ben stared in to my eyes. How could I say no to those ashen eyes? So I climbed into the driver's seat. Ben closed the door and got in on the passenger side. "Ready?"

"Not really. Guess I have no choice."

Ben tossed his head back and laughed. "No, you don't."

I put the keys into the ignition. "What now?"

"You have to start the truck." Ben suppressed a grin. "I'll be late for my shift."

"You already are," I said in a low voice, mumbling, "Mr Immortal Witch Hunter."

"I heard that," he said. I started the truck. "Hands at ten and two. Good. Step on the brake, shift into drive, move your right foot to the gas, and press down slowly. Yeah, like that. Turn the wheel slightly and…"

"Crap!" I screamed. The truck lurched forward. I was saved by the seatbelt when I hit the brake. "Oops."

"Relax and breathe slowly. Now try again."

Unbelievably, I managed to turn onto Roars Hack Falls Road without a mishap. But then, there wasn't any traffic at this time of the night.

Ben placed one hand on my shoulder and squeezed it softly.

Navigating the curvy, narrow road was tricky. I concentrated so hard I hadn't heard Ben's voice. "Emeranne?" I think he'd repeated my name a few times. "Wanna continue a bit farther?"

I nodded, afraid speaking would break my concentration. He squeezed my shoulder again. I wished he didn't do that. It made it harder to do what I'd expected my friends and the Serranos would want me to do as soon as we got back to civilization: stay as far away from Bennett Bassett as possible. But right now, I couldn't think about that or anything else but driving down the mountain road. When snow began to fall, Ben leaned over and turned on the wipers. "Thanks," I said to him.

Everything was going smoothly, until my breathing slowed. A thick blanket of fog surrounded me. Sound receded, leaving me with a sense of detachment and deep concentration. The clock on the dashboard was out of focus. I turned to Ben but could barely see him through the heavy fog. The clock and Ben faded away. Once again, I broke through the mists to another space beyond my own world, a space where time and motion seemed suspended. When the mists lifted, I saw her face: Ardelle.

Ardelle writhing in pain. Screaming for help. Calling my name. And Carlton's, Leland's, Morgan's, Selene's, Gareth's, Byron's, River's...

Beware, I heard the voices of those faces from the fire, the poachers, warning *for one of your Coven shall be next...*

When the mists shrouded me again, I floated within, as though I'd called the mists to return and carry me to Ardelle. As the fog slowly fell away, I wandered back to my own world, heard Ben's frantic voice and saw the clock come back into focus. My Ice Vision ended.

I braked suddenly, skidding to the side of the icy road. A snow bank five feet high stopped the truck from sliding into the tree line.

Startled by my sudden stop, Ben held on to the dashboard. "Careful!"

I parked the truck and turned to Ben, my voice trembling. "Ardelle's in trouble."

BENNETT

I didn't understand how Emeranne knew Ardelle was in danger, but I didn't question her. "Let me drive," I said. Quickly, we changed places.

I raced down the mountain, not knowing what was happening. "Emeranne, how?"

She sat silently for a long, long moment, rubbing her forehead. "Ice Vision," was all she said to me.

"Ice Vision?"

Emeranne nodded. "It came to me. I don't know why. Because I wasn't warned about Mrs Kerr. None of us were. And then…and then it was…it was…it was too late."

The only light came from the Silverado's high beams, sweeping left and right as I turned the wheel to hug curve after curve after curve.

In a trance, Emeranne fumbled for something in her coat pocket. "I forget. I lost my cell phone," she said to me.

"Use mine," I urged. "It's in the glove compartment"

Frantically, Emeranne tapped the screen. "Morgan? Morgan!" she cried. "Me too…I must have lost it…he did?… when?…oh, he was so close…Bear Paw Lookout…uh huh… he's here," she said, lowering her voice, turning to me. "Can't talk right now…at my place?…Okay okay see you soon."

"Ben," she said calmly, "Ardelle's been abducted."

I stepped on the gas and sped down the mountain road as fast as I possibly could without getting us both killed. Well, only Emeranne. I was already dead. "What did Morgan say?"

"That the Coven experienced the same Ice Vision: Ardelle. Writhing in pain. Screaming for help. Calling out our names. And…" She choked back tears and buried her face in her hands.

Her pain was too much for me to bear. "Emeranne, we'll find her, I promise, just like I promised I'd never let anyone hurt you."

Holding her breath, she turned to me. "Promise me, Ben. Promise me!"

"I promise," I repeated softly. "What else did you see?"

"Ardelle. Tied to the base of a lookout. Weak."

"Aconite," I murmured under my breath. "It's in the manual, his formula."

"Delacroix," she sighed.

"Delacroix," I confirmed. "It's them, it has to be."

"Who? The hunters in the sketches? What did you say their names were?"

I clenched my teeth and said, "Octavia and Ulric."

She gasped. "The poachers. And what about this, acon... aconite?"

"The poison of all poisons, disguised in gardens as a beautiful perennial, and commonly known as monkshood. But deadly, and distilled to disable a witch's powers. So that...that—" I couldn't say it, admit it may be too late to save Ardelle, her fate probable. "That's what likely blocked your sensory powers, the Serranos' too. Even ours, if our serum sourced from the Varangian Guard had been tampered with, it would prevent us from sensing the poachers' presence."

"It might be too late!"

I had to reassure Emeranne and give her hope even though I knew, felt it may be too late.

Certain Emeranne was going to vomit, I turned the corners as carefully as I could without losing momentum. The distant, tiny lights of Snow Valley grew larger and larger by the second. Swerving, I sped along the last stretch on Snow Valley Mountain Road until I turned into her driveway. All of the lights were on in the log cabin. Several cars were parked outside, including Chief Walker's black and white cruiser and the Fire Chief's red SUV.

Ardelle's father. How he must feel, I couldn't imagine, except, I wondered for a moment. What did my parents feel about my disappearance at sea? Were they still alive when I'd drowned in the storm? Did they look for me?

you were dying...
we did what we thought was best...
what was your name
was your name
your name
name

Emeranne opened the car door and jumped out before I could park behind the long line of cars. She was half way to the front door where Morgan waited before she turned back. Wordlessly, she told me what she needed to do. Find Ardelle. And I said to her, unspoken but sincere, that I knew what I, too, had to do, once and for all.

Somehow, I knew where they were, the filthy poachers, even without Emeranne's Ice Vison. I knew where they'd carry out the next murder. There was only one place, one way they'd kill Ardelle.

> near a mountain cliff there stands
> caressing the black sun
> the clockwork moon
> the choking stars

I backed out of the driveway, spun the truck around on Snow Valley Mountain Road, and raced to the Matterhorn, hoping Ardelle was still alive, hoping that another monster, another witch hunter, hadn't killed her.

Hoping. Hoping. Hoping…

I'm not sure I ever arrived at the Matterhorn. Without warning, the evening turned darker than the raging, angry night sea that took my life away so many black suns ago.

i

    i

        am

i am

    a

      a

mon—

Chapter Twenty

Betrayed

EMERANNE

Mayhem descended upon the log cabin. Maps were spread all over the kitchen harvest table. Gareth sat in the kitchen with Dad and Police Chief Walker, surrounded by the rest of our parents. Mr. Kerr was visibly shaken.

Nearby, Chief Curry, distraught, yelled into his cell. "I don't give a crap! Just get out there and look, damn it!"

Mrs. Hurst put one hand on Chief Curry's arm, reminding him that he needed to contain himself so this unofficial headquarters wouldn't be discovered. The regular villagers didn't need to know about our unique methods of search and rescue. Nor did Coop the Scoop need to get wind of Ardelle's disappearance. He'd be all over the story if he found out.

Mrs. Curry sobbed. Her hands shook so badly she could barely help Selene work the Spirit Board. Using my bloodstone, Morgan scryed on the map I'd drawn of Snow Valley County, the same one Carlton borrowed, the one that hadn't worked to keep track of me. Leland threw a mixture into the fireplace, but nothing happened. Not a single clue. Not on the Spirit Board. Not on the map. Not in the fire. Ice Visions didn't present any updated images, either.

We'd all seen and shared the same vision of Ardelle. It could have been any one of us, but it was Ardelle. Beautiful, kind Ardelle with her thick, flaming red hair and freckles and horn-rimmed glasses and happy green eyes.

I didn't have much time to explain what I'd discovered about the Bassetts. I wanted to gather the Coven in my bedroom as soon as possible. I jerked my head toward the stairs.

"Mrs Garcia? Could you sit with Mrs Curry for a bit? We'll try more spells upstairs," I said, lowering my voice, "away from Mrs Curry." Mrs. Garcia nodded and waved her hand, urging us upstairs. Quickly, I looked at Gareth with a knowing smile. He raised one thumb.

I closed my door. "Where's Byron? Carlton?"

"Looking for you. Byron went to Moonridge to alert River and see what, if anything, the Den Born Elders might be able to do, even though the Scent didn't warn them," replied Leland.

Morgan drew a long, deep breath. "Carlton left to astral project around Snow Valley. He traveled to your cell phone signal, but found it buried in the snow."

"Dropped it. Running from Ben," I explained, launching into a rapid summary of my date. My friends were horrified. "And that's all. He drove me home."

"Without harming you?" a bewildered Selene asked.

"Without harming me."

Leland pounded his fists on my desk. "I don't believe that bloodhound!"

I took his hands in mine. "He promised me, Leland. Promised he didn't hurt your mom."

Leland stared at me incredulously. "And you believed him?"

"Yes, I did. I do. I can't explain why, but if he'd wanted to hurt me, or any one of us, he had the opportunity today."

"And, after all, he was with you when Ardelle went missing," Selene said.

"It could've been another Bassett," argued Leland.

Morgan had been silent for quite some time. When a long pause descended, it was Morgan who broke the silence at last. "We can't worry about the Bassetts at the moment. We don't have the time. Ardelle is our only concern. And these, these… what did you call them? Poachers? Ben knows who they are?"

"We don't stand a chance without Ben," Selene rationalized. "We need to take a chance, trust Ben with Ardelle's life."

I nodded. "And speaking of Ben, he's just sent me a text message."

"Meet me outside at 8," was all he wrote. I read his message out loud. Time had passed so quickly since Ben dropped me off. It was now seven o'clock.

"What are you going to do?"

"Look for Ardelle, with Ben, and his family can help us too." With the exception of one family member, a fact I wasn't about to reveal at the moment.

"Ems, he's here. His truck just pulled into the driveway," Leland reported.

"Leave from your deck so your dad doesn't worry. We'll cover for you," Selene said.

Morgan shook her head and said, "I don't like it. Not one bit. This feels all wrong. All wrong."

"We don't have time!" I argued. "Ardelle doesn't have time!"

Leland stepped away from the window. "Okay, but take my cell and please try not to drop it this time."

Still in my parka and boots, I dashed through my bathroom door and climbed down the trellis. Ben waited for me in his truck with someone else.

"Wallis!" I cried.

"At your service," she saluted.

Before I could stop them, Geneva and Matt ran from the porch where they'd waited to go inside after being let out one more time for the night.

240

"Geneva! Matt! Go back! Go back!" I urged.

Geneva and Matt growled at the truck as they backed away, tails between their legs. Looking over their shoulders and snarling, they slowly made their way to the front door. Strange, I thought to myself.

"Good girl, good boy," I said to them through the open window. Ben backed the car out of the driveway. Geneva and Matt howled so loudly that Wallis closed the window. The truck was filled with frosty night air.

"Where to?" I asked Ben. I noticed he removed his parka. Both sleeves of his hoodie were rolled up to his elbows. *Fire Born*, I thought. He must be warm.

"We got a reliable tip, more or less," Wallis said.

"And?" I prompted.

"We think Ardelle was taken to Hunter's Point Lookout," Ben replied, twisting his snowflake obsidian ring nervously.

"I'll text Carlton. He's astral projecting all around Snow Valley. Then I'll text—"

Wallis held her arm in front of my chest. "No," was all she said. Her obsidian bracelet dug into my ribs.

"Why not?" I gasped.

Ben and Wallis exchanged uneasy glances. "Because if it's truly Ulric and Octavia, it's best the Coven stays away. Who knows what they're liable to do? Look what happened in the summer—" Ben left the rest of the sentence unspoken, but I knew what he didn't say: What happened to Mrs. Kerr.

"Ben's right," added Wallis nervously. "Don't worry, Emeranne, we'll protect you. The rest of my family is helping, too, in case this lead is a false one."

When I looked over my shoulder, I saw a car following Ben's Silverado.

An old yellow Mustang convertible.

Coop the Scoop. "We're not alone," I whispered. "Don't worry. I know what to do." Closing my eyes, I visualized a mountain of snow blocking the road behind us. And cutting Coop the Scoop off.

It worked. Once again, Ben and Wallis traded uncomfortable looks.

I turned to Ben and snorted jokingly, "Like you've never seen that before."

For the third time, surreptitiously, Ben checked Wallis' reaction. "Oh, oh yeah," he said uneasily, nervously. His reaction was unsettling, but I had to file this away for now.

Ben sped up Roars Hack Falls Road and parked on the side of the road nearest to the lookout. This time, we didn't snowshoe to Hunter's Point Lookout. Before I had a chance to say anything, Ben swept me up into his arms. "We have to hurry," he said, following the flash that was Wallis.

The crescent moon rose high and shone bright. The Snow Moon of November, according to Selene, a powerful time for any spells cast. From within the depths of snow-clad emerald boughs in the dense forest, the crunching sound of footfalls broke the eerie silence, then stopped abruptly. A sinister stillness returned, filling frigid gaps in the cold alpine air.

In the distance, beneath the lookout, a lantern flickered. I wanted to scream out, but covered my mouth instead. Blood pumped through my veins with all the power flowing down from Roars Hack Falls.

A breeze swung the black and yellow lantern like a beacon in a raging storm or a bee hovering above a peony. My heart thrilled with the thought that Ardelle was alive. That she was beneath the lookout just as my Ice Vision presented. That, with Ben's and Wallis's help, I'd saved her. What I'd failed to do for Mrs. Kerr.

"Ardelle!" I shouted. "Ardelle!"

"Em…"

"Ardelle!"

"Em…"

"I'm here!"

"Ems," spoke her fading, faint voice.

I ran to the base, through deep snow and thick ice. Daggers of clear icicles ran down the lookout's posts. Vapors rose from my mouth. I nearly reached Ardelle, who was tied to one of the posts just as the Ice Vision had shown. Weak, bloody, bruised, Ardelle was bound in a thick rope.

"This was one…one…one knot I couldn't…couldn't," she struggled to say to me.

"Shhhh! I'm here now," I said reassuringly, wiping away sweat and blood and snow caked to her face and hair. A lantern swung above Ardelle's head and added more light to that cast by the bright Snow Moon. Frantically, I untied Ardelle and began to unwrap the rope. "It'll be okay," I sobbed. "You're safe now."

Suddenly, I felt the force of Ben's powerful embrace. He held me for several minutes. And then the unthinkable happened. Ben pulled me away, his silvery-white eyes now a flaming shade of orange, eyes on fire.

Orange eyes. And flames. Flames Morgan had scratched into flesh, tongues of fire on skin, coiling black chains binding bone, appeared on Ben's wrists. Snakes of fire. Snakes of red and orange and black, around his wrists, up his arms, as far as his elbows. I looked around at Wallis. Her eyes were on fire, too. I couldn't see her arms, hidden beneath her parka, but I knew the snakes of fire burned.

Like steel shackles, effortlessly Ben locked one hand around my wrists.

"What…what are you—?"

"Don't bother yelling," he sneered. "No one will hear you."

He dragged me by my hair on the fluffy snow, like a Christmas tree cut down to adorn a cozy livingroom. I struggled to free myself from his grasp. But it was no use. He was too strong. And my powers didn't affect him.

On my knees, I glared at Ben. "I trusted you! You said… you promised you'd never hurt me! You gave me your word and…and—"

"'*You said…you promised*'," he mocked. "You believed me."

Why wouldn't an immortal witch hunter turn on a witch? It was his nature, his instinct, after all. Besides Wallis, was the rest of his family aware of what he was doing?

"Ben, do you need more *argentum vivum*? Is that it? You mentioned earlier…needing it sometimes. Maybe a glitch in the potion?" I said soothingly, grasping at straws, at anything, anything at all to explain his violent behavior.

"Shut up," he snarled.

I screamed louder. "Wallis! Help!" She didn't respond.

Ben kept walking. "Obey and do exactly what I say."

"As long as you let Ardelle go, I'll do anything. My life for hers."

"You're in no position to negotiate," he shot back.

Wallis cackled. "I told you she'd take the bait!"

Ben agreed. "Anything for her Coven."

"Why are you doing this? You said you didn't kill Mrs Kerr! And I believed you!"

"That's because you're a stupid little witch."

"No, Ben, I beg you to stop this," I pleaded through a stream of tears that froze into icicles on my cheeks.

"Get up, fiend!" Ben yelled. His booming voice echoed like thunderclaps all around the valley. "Now! I don't have all decade!"

In a fog of tears and confusion, I stood up and thrust my hands in my parka, fumbling for Leland's cell phone.

"Give that to me," Wallis screamed and snatched the phone out of my hands.

Who could save me now? I couldn't even save myself, a hopeless witch. My hand felt something else in my pocket. The note I'd given Selene in science class. I remembered the words:

please help me

do you think Ben is a hunter

I couldn't write by magic, but I could remove the graphite of the pencil. I concentrated on deleting KGZVNZ and YJTJPOCDIF. Perfect. If I could warn the others, I might save the rest of the Coven.

"Let me say goodbye to Ardelle," I begged, hoping my plan would work.

"Why not," Ben said.

I gave Ardelle a silent message, hoping she'd understood what I'd asked of her.

"Ardelle, I'll miss you. Don't forget me," I whispered in her ear, pressing the altered note in one of her hands, bloody and cold.

Wallis pulled me away from Ardelle. "That's enough."

Instead of leaving Ardelle alone, Wallis threw a match toward the lookout. It wasn't until the match set a fire that I'd noticed Ardelle sat on a pyre. So I visualized snow extinguishing the flames. It worked. Covered in snow, Ardelle shrieked, but at least she was still alive. And I didn't extinguish the lantern. "Leave! Her! Alone!"

"Listen very carefully," said Ben, his voice disturbingly quiet and calm.

I kept my hands in the deep pockets of my parka, awaiting Ben's instructions.

Ben pointed toward the cliff's edge. "Walk to that ledge."

Slowly, I walked toward the cliff's edge. Took small steps, hoping to drag this out as long as possible. If there was a chance, any hope...oh, who was I kidding?

Ben was an immortal witch hunter. And I, a mortal witch, his prey. I was the hunted.

"Hurry up, witch! We don't have all night."

"So much for wanting to change!" I said, having nothing left to lose, now that my life was almost certain to end.

"Whatever," he chuckled darkly. "Shut up and walk, stupid little witch."

I kept a slow, steady pace, using the moonlight to guide me.

"Take off your parka and throw it over the ledge. Now! I don't have all night, witch!"

Ben's commanding voice frightened me so much that I didn't hesitate for a second. I shrugged off my parka and tossed it without looking down. My jacket disappeared over a frozen precipice. Down a deep, dark crevasse. Into my pretend icy grave.

Walking toward me where I stood shivering from fear, Ben laughed in a sinister way. "Now trace your steps backward, can you do that vile witch?"

I looked down at my footprints in the snow and did as Ben ordered.

"The police will find your footprints here," he said, pointing to the cliff's edge. "Your death will be viewed as an accident…you fell over the cliff trying to save your witch friend."

I was furious. I summoned as much courage as I could. Why not? I had nothing to lose. "You're nothing but a cowardly murderer. And to think I believed you! All that talk about how you don't want to be a monster. I should have trusted my instincts. Instead, I trusted you!"

Ben struck me across the face. I fell on the snow, stunned by the force of his blow. "You've hurt my feelings." He pouted, wiping crocodile tears from his fiery eyes. "That was a warning. I held back my powers, struck you as lightly as a feather would caress your evil skin."

Ben whipped out his pocketknife from the purple hoodie. Slashing through my jeans, blood gushed from a large vein on my right leg, creating a crimson pool of blood. I screamed, the pain excruciating. "Stop! Just kill me…end it now! But leave…leave Ardelle alone! Let her go! Please please please let her go let her go let her go…"

Wallis shrieked with delight. "Did Ben hurt you, witch?"

"My name is Emeranne Sophia Goode."

"Shut up, witch. You're all the same. *I have a name. I have a family. Oh please don't hurt me. Kill me quickly.* Blah blah blah." Wallis waved one hand dismissively.

"My name is Emeranne Sophia Goode," I repeated.

Wallis hissed. "I'll call you whatever I want, understood?"

"My name is Emeranne Sophia Goode," I yelled at the top of my lungs.

Ben slapped me across the face again, harder this time. "I told you to shut up!"

He was crazy, after all. A crazy immortal witch hunter determined to torture me.

How could I rationalize with an irrational undead being?

"M-m-my…n-n-ame…is Em-mer-er…S-s-o—"

Ben pushed me down. I fell on the frozen ground. He ripped a strip from the bottom of my jeans and soaked the strip in my blood before throwing it into the abyss.

"Maybe your dad's stupid dogs will pick up your scent," he growled.

"Don't *ever* call Geneva and Matt stupid," I hissed, directing a tree at him for good measure.

"As if that'll hurt me," he scorned, shielding his body with one arm.

"They're smarter than you think and didn't like you when you and Wallis picked me up. I should have known then. I was so blind to believe you were sincere."

Having lost a lot of blood, I felt dizzy. My head spun. I limped on one foot before fainting. When I came to, I glared up at Ben from the snowy ground.

His eyes, enraged and smoldering like embers, stared down at me when I regained consciousness. "You never clued in, did you witch? Get up right now."

I staggered to my feet. My right leg was too weak. I fell again and again and again. Ben violently seized my arm and dragged me on one foot, covering our tracks.

I didn't know how he'd explain the blood, but I guessed he had a plan.

As it turned out, Selene was better at reading Tarot cards than I'd imagined, for here I was, The Fool, walking near the cliff's edge.

Without warning, Ben picked me up, threw me over his broad, muscular shoulders, the ones that had once comforted me, protected me, enveloped me...

I must have passed out. When I woke up, I found myself alone in the unheated cabin of Hunter's Point. Chains wound tightly around my wrists and ankles, all raw, cut, bleeding. And held within an iron cage, chained to thick bars.

The lookout wasn't burned to the ground. I hoped that meant Ardelle was still alive.

In case Ardelle couldn't send the message, I had to send another. If my powers couldn't save me now, or be used against Ben, I could still move things. I put aside my debilitating fears to search the cabin's dim light. Shards of moonlight sliced on a small table in front of me. I looked for a set of keys. Ben knew my powers. He wouldn't be stupid enough to leave keys lying around. I am a stupid witch, I moaned. Maybe I could move other things...remote things...like the Etch A Sketch I gave Morgan, who'd left it in my bedroom. I had nothing to lose now.

I concentrated with all my might, pictured the red and white contraption and moved both knobs with my mind, spelling Hunter's P. Then passed out from mental exhaustion. When I awoke in the sparsely furnished cabin, I pictured Selene with her Spirit Board in my bedroom, pictured her, hands above the planchette, holding my bloodstone, waiting for a sign. With the rest of my energy, I sent Selene a message, visualizing the planchette and bloodstone in my mind, and pointed to each

248

letter. Within minutes, I finished the message, again exhausted but managing to spell: Ardelle alive. It's all I could send.

There was one last thing to do: share an Ice Vision with the Coven. My breathing slowed. A thick blanket of fog surrounded me. Sound receded, leaving me with a sense of detachment and deep concentration. The chains on my wrists faded away. Yet again, I pierced the mists.

I shared images of where Ardelle and I were held captive, as many images as possible until I could no longer concentrate. And the pain. Oh, the pain.

The mists shrouded me. When the fog slowly fell away, the chains on my wrists came back into focus.

With difficulty, I managed to rip another piece of fabric from my jeans. With my bound hands, I wrapped the strip above the trickling wound on my throbbing right leg. My hands trembled. Forced to use my teeth, I was unable to tie a decent knot.

"Ardelle, where are you when I need you?" I sobbed. After fainting again, I awoke to the sounds of muffled voices outside. Ben and Wallis sauntered through the door, dangling keys in their hands.

"Ready, stupid little witch?" Wallis taunted me with her burning eyes.

"How can you live with yourself, Wallis? I thought we were friends?"

"Don't you get it, witch? I can't live with myself. Because I'm not even *alive.*"

Wallis cackled wickedly as she opened the cage door, unlocked the shackles on my wrists, and dragged me out by my hair. I couldn't walk. My ankles were still wrapped with chains. "Don't worry, it won't be long before it's over. And Ben," she cooed oddly, "don't leave any rubbish or personal items behind, not like the last time…"

They'd done this before. Obviously. Violet Grimesby. Mrs. Kerr. And so, so many other innocent witches. Ben placed an Angels baseball cap on his head, the same one I'd seen in the town square, on a homeless man with flaming, orange hair.

I lay on the cold, bare wooden floor, curled up in a ball. My lips were chapped, raw.

Wallis kicked me in the ribs. "Get up, witch, this isn't nap time at boarding school."

I tried to breath. My lungs were still deflated from the force of Wallis's kick. "I…I can't…can't…my ankles…bound…"

Wallis kicked me again. "Oh, shut up!"

Until tonight, I'd adamantly refused to believe someone I'd trusted, someone who confided in me, in whom I'd confided my own secrets, in the end, would betray me.

Both eyes raging wilder than a bonfire, Ben scooped me off the floor and threw me around his neck like a ragdoll. My head dangled on his left shoulder, my legs on his right. He scaled down the lookout's ladder. Nearby, Ardelle lay on her side, passed out but still breathing, still alive. On the far side of the mountain, flames shot from a massive bonfire. A long cable was attached to a pole. The cable stretched across the mountainside, ending directly above the fire.

At that moment, I knew exactly how I was going to die.

Chapter Twenty-One

Chameleon

EMERANNE

Wallis raised her hands high above her head as though summoning a blustering wind. Dramatically, intensely, she swung her dark hair around her glowing orange eyes, deftly jumping to the long, thick cable. Flames licked the cable like sinewy fingers.

"Ready for the one and only zip line adventure of your short life, wretched witch?"

Circles of black smoke puffed from the fire's dark belly, reaching higher and higher, threatening to burn through the cable suspended nearby on another tall pole. The pyre was almost completely engulfed. I glanced down at my chained feet. Pain shot through my useless, sliced right leg. The cable ran from smoke to flames. Ben carried me to the nearest, and highest, end of the zip line. I knew what was about to happen. And prepared myself. If my plan worked…maybe there was still a chance I might live.

"Attach her feet," ordered Wallis. Ben obeyed. "And bind her hands with this." Wallis handed Ben what appeared to be frayed wire with tiny spikes.

Ben obliged and tied barbed wire around my wrists. Excruciating pain and agony escalated. My hands, pierced by dozens of sharp thorns. My shredded palms oozed blood.

I dangled upside down from my stocking feet, having lost my boots somewhere on the mountain. Chilly, frosted air hung around me in halos of cool, white light. Blood immediately rushed to my head. Could I slow my heart down? Stem the blood rush? I imagined blood flowing slowly in my veins.

It worked.

Wallis sneered. "Ready for the ride of death, vile insect?"

Ben pushed me toward the roaring flames, where I'd crash land in the middle of the bonfire. Even though my leg was in unimaginable pain, I concentrated harder, as I'd done at Bear Paw Lookout, visualizing the bonfire frozen and split in half. And when the zip line neared the flames, I closed my eyes.

Speaking seven names out loud, I petitioned for help from my friends.

"Ardelle. Byron. Carlton. Gareth. Leland. Morgan. Selene. Please. Help me."

The zip line came to an abrupt stop. I'd done it. The bonfire froze.

Next, I had to get myself off of this wretched cable. But Ben had other ideas.

"What a clever vile witch you are. Freezing flames. I'll have to teach you a lesson for being so clever. Wallis, what do you think?"

Wallis carried a long piece of wrought iron resembling a fireplace poker. From my reversed position, I saw what she handed Ben. It wasn't a poker. It was a brand. A brand with the letter B. "Recognize this letter?" she asked.

"It looks like the letter on a hankie Coop the Scoop showed me," I said.

"What a clever little witch you are," Ben said again.

"Who do you think tipped off Coop the Scoop on your whereabouts? Or contacted him during that farce of a dunk tank? Or this ruse to rescue Ardelle?" Wallis said.

"What?" I started to hyperventilate.

"We promised him an exclusive, and a front row seat to the witch executions. But you had to use your powers, didn't you, and ruin everything," Ben said.

"Why? Why would you do that? And risk revealing your identity?"

Wallis slapped me across the face. "That's none of your business, vile sorceress!"

My pulse escalated. I knew what Ben planned to do with that branding iron. To mark me. Mark me as a witch. A witch marked for the vicious Varangian Guard. Ben held the heavy rod in the fire, split and frozen on either side of me.

Wallis waved a white handkerchief with the letter B. "Here, you might need this to wipe human tears from your eyes, witch." She snorted. A hankie like the one I'd seen in art class. Ben's hankie, just like the one Coop the Scoop showed me. Now I knew who gave him evidence from the Lookout Murder.

I licked my parched, cracked lips but didn't react.

"Thirsty? *You vant drink?*" she said, shoving the hankie in my bloody fingers. "*Pleeze to come up. Pleeze to hurry.*"

"It was you. In, in the square," I blurted, "and, and the flu clinic!"

"Of course it was, witch. I was already watching you and your Coven. So was he," she laughed, making strumming motions with her hand and jerking her thumb toward Ben, in the midst of removing the glowing iron from the fire. Snarling, the Angels cap secured on his head, he turned to face me, twirling the brand in one hand. He glared into my frightened face with his flaming eyes. Too weakened to summon my telekinetic powers again after I spilt and froze the flames, or shield myself from Ben, he circled around me, laughing, until he stopped behind my back. Without hesitation, he ripped my shirt and stamped my right shoulder, digging deep, burning my flesh.

At first, I didn't scream. It felt like a dream. Someone else's body, scorched with a sizzling branding iron. I concentrated on breaking the cable from the pole. Adreneline rushed through my body and gave me strength. And when I heard the cable snap and felt my hair tossed by the biting wind and smelled my flesh burning, it was only then that I screamed. And screamed. And screamed. But never begged Ben to stop.

He had his fun. Now it was my turn. *"Something wicked this way comes,"* I whispered.

As my body fell toward the snow-covered mountainside, I imagined a colossal pile of snow extinguishing the fire, burying Ben and Wallis, pushing them toward fingers of icicles that clutched the cliff's edge, rows of sharp frozen nails pointing down the mountainside.

With my hands and feet still bound with barbed wire, I reached out for a piece of dangling cable, hoping against all hope to pull myself away from the cliff's edge.

Through a curtain of smoke, my eyes strained, filtering the smog for a glimmer of hope. I struggled to free the wire and chains wrapped around my lacerated wrists and ankles, visualizing the wire snapping in pieces.

It worked.

I staggered to my feet and steadied myself after a brief dizzy spell, knowing my powers wouldn't work on Ben. Maybe I could try moving snow again, just to buy some time, though for what I wasn't sure. Still, a few more minutes might make a difference. I gazed into the sky where, had Ardelle done what I'd hoped, the message would have been formed by a handful of the billions of stars in the universe.

But I saw nothing. Absolutely nothing. My broken heart sank.

Then I heard Ardelle's voice in my mind. *Don't be silly*, I heard her say. *Never know when a good storm will come in handy.*

Storm knots! I could cast that spell. Give myself more time.

Drawing a deep, long breath—my last, perhaps—I visualized the ropes that had bound Ardelle. Then, I pictured three knots on one rope.

The spell worked. A huge storm circled Ben and Wallis.

Next, with my hands, raw and bloody, I pointed toward the mountainside and swiped the air with my arms, directing a mass of ice and snow to the jagged ledge.

It hit Ben first. Wallis outran the mini avalanche and rushed to the ledge, where Ben's hands gripped a rocky outcrop.

I must have been hallucinating, because Wallis's face switched back and forth. Back and forth. Like a hologram. First Wallis's face. Then the face of the woman in the sketch, Octavia. Next, the face of a strange looking woman wearing a long black dress and a black veil draped around her head and spilling around her shoulders, pulling a cooler in Hastings Square. A fourth face, the nurse from the Flu Shot Clinic.

Wallis. Octavia. Strange woman. Nurse. Wallis. Octavia. Strange woman. Nurse…on and on it went.

Wallis screamed. "Don't let go! Don't let go!"

And the same thing happened with Ben's face. Ben. Ulric. A homeless man with a twisted upper lip, orange hair, and a filthy Angels baseball cap. Ben. Ulric. Homeless man. Ben. Ulric. Homeless man…

Back and forth.

Back and forth.

Back and forth…

Dizzy and confused, near death, I was certain I was seeing things. Seeing double. Seeing faces from Hastings Square, faces from Snow Valley High. Seeing the sketches come to life. The faces from the fire. The faces I'd wanted to see so I could drain my powers on them, for what they'd done to Mrs. Kerr.

Fair is foul and foul is fair…

Nothing was as it appeared to be.

Unexpectedly, Carlton hovered right before my eyes. Or an image of Carlton.

"Ems, hang in there," he pleaded. "Get Ardelle out of there!"

I turned my gaze to the sky. A faded message was written in the stars.

help me
Ben is a killer

The torn, coded message I'd left with Ardelle. She'd done it. Cast the spell, higher than a flare, notifying the Coven of our location. As the message faded, like a million fireflies the stars reassembled to form a huge, bright pentacle.

"Carlton," I gasped. "Why isn't help here yet?"

"Not enough time to reach you, because the road was blocked with a pile of snow. You have to hurry, Ems, get Ardelle, escape using Ben's truck. The keys are inside. Go, now!"

The last time I saw Ben, his orange eyes glared at me, his mouth smirked rudely. Abruptly, his face changed from triumph to shock to anger, and lastly, pain. He writhed in agony, just as I did when he branded me. When his Angels baseball cap disappeared, Wallis screamed, holding on to Ben's arm. "I can't!" I hoped her serum hadn't been topped up and her powers were weakened.

"Hang on to the mountainside, I'll rappel down," Wallis said, then jumped off the ledge after Ben. *Good riddance.* I couldn't think about either surviving the fall, as Ben had told me he'd tried to commit suicide by jumping off Mount Everest. I hoped both were so weak they'd be destroyed. Carlton would astral project later to find their bodies.

To be honest, I really didn't care at this point. Ben could fall and burn in hell for all I cared. In fact, hell was too good for him. He'd killed Mrs. Kerr. Probably Violet too.

How could I have trusted an immortal witch hunter?

I was a stupid witch, after all. Alive, but stupid.

And so, so let down. Let down by Ben's lies.

Clouds appeared suddenly, shrouding a pale silvery moon behind a misty veil. Lightning bugs flashed before my puffy, teary eyes…a thousand tiny fireflies.

Inhaling, each breath more painful than the last, the dryness in my throat, the aching in my pierced heart. I struggled to my feet and willed my body toward the base of Hunter's Point Lookout.

"Ardelle?" I whispered softly. "Ardelle?"

Slowly, slowly she turned her head around. "Ems?"

"I'm taking you home now, Ardelle. It's over."

Somehow, I helped Ardelle to her feet and balanced her against my side, even though my right leg throbbed. Inch by inch, step by painful step, I walked with Ardelle toward Ben's Silverado. Panting, out of breath, we reached the truck. "Almost home," I said to Ardelle while I helped her up and buckled her in. Limping, I climbed into the driver's seat and found the keys in the ignition just like Carlton said.

Moments before I started the truck, I heard Ben's voice.

"Wallis! I can't hold on!"

A bone-chilling howl haunted the cold night air.

Then everything went silent.

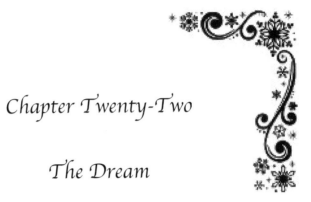

Chapter Twenty-Two

The Dream

EMERANNE

I drove the Silverado down the twisting mountain road, knowing it was blocked as a result of my actions, preventing Coop the Scoop from following us to Hunter's Point Lookout. Before I reached the huge pile of snow on the road, I visualized it in my mind and blew it away as effectively as a stick of dynamite. There was no sign of the yellow Mustang convertible. I doubted Coop the Scoop gave up and went home, wherever that was.

I dropped Ardelle off at her parents' house, as instructed by Carlton. To avoid questions or raise suspicions, Chief Curry thought it best to deal with Ardelle's condition discreetly. Leland attended to her immediately, his healing hands on her wounds, gashes and burns not nearly as bad as his mother's, whose wounds he'd never had the chance to heal. Now, at least, he could make use of his powers to save Ardelle.

Ardelle could be dead. I could have died. At this point, I really didn't care about my own injuries. Ardelle was alive. That was good enough for me.

But what happened to Ben and Wallis? Were they alive? Scaling the cliff, coming after us to finish what they'd started? I shivered at the thought.

I drove Ben's Silverado home, having forgotten I didn't have my license yet, though doubting Chief Walker would give me a ticket tonight. I'd been through enough.

I turned on Snow Valley Mountain Road and began to breathe normally, until I spotted a black tow truck parked on the side of the road closest to my home. A familiar yellow Mustang was hitched to the truck. Coop the Scoop stood next to the truck, chewing on a cigar stub. I slowed down and pulled Ben's truck into the snowy driveway. Coop tipped his scruffy hat, stroked his moustache, and wore a grin that only meant trouble. I drove on, and glanced into the rear view mirror a few times. He stood as still as a frozen ice sculpture. I lost sight of him when I parked the truck. I couldn't deal with Coop's nonsense at the moment. I vowed to teach him a lesson. Now was not the right time.

Dad, Matt, Geneva, Morgan, and Selene waited outside for me. The porch light illuminated their tortured, sad, exhausted, relieved faces. The dogs' snowshoe-sized paws covered their eyes, their breath formed circles of white mist around me. With whimpering Geneva by his side, Dad helped me out of the truck and carried my aching, limp body into the house. Matt walked around the Silverado, growled, and lifted his leg against one of the tires. Despite all that had happened I couldn't help laughing. "Good boy," I said.

Distraught, Dad didn't know what to say. He didn't have to. The pain and anguish in his bloodshot eyes summed up what he couldn't say to me. After what happened to Violet Grimesby and Charlsie Kerr, he'd guessed what I'd been through. I was too tired to explain. I'm sure Carlton had already told them what he'd seen, skilled astral projector that he was.

I was just glad to be home. Safe. Alive.

Selene wrapped her black shawl around my shoulders. Carlton waited in the livingroom where he stared in to the fire, stabbing it with a poker. As soon as he saw me, he threw the poker down and ran toward me. "Ems, thank goodness."

I fell into Carlton's arms. Morgan and Selene helped Carlton support me. Matt and Geneva pushed their way into the group hug, deciding it was their turn. With Carlton's help, I knelt down and let them lick my face.

Dad helped me to the sofa. He and Morgan sat on either side of me, with Carlton perched on the coffee table. Selene disappeared in the kitchen and returned with a steaming mug. "Witch hunter antidote, New Orleans style."

Selene prepared one of her special herbal teas to rid my body of aconite, to give me strength to use my powers, drained as I was from this evening's use of witchcraft. I took a few sips from the mug and felt some of the pain subside. I put down the mug and caught up on what had happened while I was at Hunter's Point Lookout.

Carlton discovered the flu shots had been tampered with, weakening our powers. "Monkshood," he said. "Moonridge's wells were contaminated with monkshood, too."

"With Carlton's discovery, Selene and I concocted a rudimentary antidote for our Coven and the Serranos," Morgan said.

The poison of all poisons. I turned to Carlton and said to him, "Distilled to disable a witch's powers, and the Den Born's powers, too."

Carlton pressed his fingers together. "How did you—?"

"Ben told me. That aconite, or monkshood, blocked our powers. He didn't know about Ice Visions until I experienced one in his truck,"

"And you told him?" Carlton asked.

"I told him," I admitted. "Ben also said the Den Born's Scent would be blocked, too, and prevent all of us from sensing the poachers' presence."

"Poachers?" Morgan and Selene said in unison. I filled them in on what else I'd learned from Ben.

"Why did I see Ardelle, if aconite blocked our powers?"

"Do you remember the Homecoming football game?" Morgan asked. I nodded. "You were drained the most. Carlton and I have a theory. Your Ice Visions seem more intense than other members of the Coven. That could explain why you could fight through the aconite sooner that the rest. Eventually, the aconite wore off. That's when we received the message you shared, where you and Ardelle were located, through an Ice Vision."

I turned to Selene. "River?"

"Furious. The Elders vow to avenge Ardelle's abduction and your torture."

"There's more, Ems," said Carlton. "About the Bassetts."

"I've heard enough about the Bassetts and hope I never hear that name or see their faces ever again."

"Well, you need to hear this," Selene said.

"Yes," Morgan said. "Philippe and Henry found Wallis tied up in the Matterhorn's walk-in freezer, her powers further weakened from long exposure to sub-zero temperatures."

"Fire Born," I mumbled.

"Philippe assumed Wallis was drugged and dumped there, presumably by the two poachers, as you called them," Carlton said. "She's recovering with the help of the same antidote."

"I don't understand, so let me get this straight. Wallis was tied up in the freezer and weakened so she couldn't break out. Ben is missing. That doesn't make sense. I was with Ben and Wallis," I argued, "in the truck and on the mountain. I saw them fall off the cliff."

"It wasn't them, Ems. Somehow the two hunters, or poachers, were disguised as Ben and Wallis. Allora suggested the potion could have been altered to create an illusion," explained Selene.

"Their names are Octavia and Ulric," said Morgan.

"The faces from the fire and sketches," I said. "Ben told me their names."

"He did?" Morgan said.

I nodded. "So," I drew the word out for a moment, "Ben wasn't Ben. Wallis wasn't Wallis."

"No," Morgan confirmed, "I mean they weren't the *real* Ben, *real* Wallis."

"Things are beginning to make more sense, and I didn't think that was possible." I recounted the uneasy glances Ben and Wallis exchanged, how Matt and Geneva growled at them, and what I'd learned about Coop the Scoop.

"The poachers tipped off Coop the Scoop?" Morgan said.

"Did the poachers say why?" Carlton asked.

"Yes, Morgan. And no, Carlton. Only that Coop was offered a front row seat at the witch executions, according to Ben, or the poacher."

Selene shook her head. "I don't understand why the rogue hunters planned to expose the Coven and the Bassetts. I'll pass this information to the Den Born."

"Revenge? Rivalry? Orders?" I said.

"Whatever the reason, the Ice Born, Den Born, and Fire Born aren't safe in Snow Valley," Morgan said.

I processed this new information. "Wallis is recovering." Everyone nodded. I was afraid to ask. But I did anyway. "And Ben?"

"Still missing," Carlton told me.

"Still missing," I repeated.

"Henry was certain Ben was drugged too, with the tampered serum," Carlton said.

"But he's confident Ben will show up, Ems," added Selene.

"He's strong," said Morgan, wrapping one arm around my shoulder.

I screamed when her hand touched my shoulder.

"Ems?"

"It's just, I was—" I folded my arms across my chest and slumped forward. Morgan removed Selene's black shawl, saw the wound through my ripped shirt, and gasped. Carlton moaned. Selene ran to the sofa.

"Ems?" Dad spoke at last, having been silent the entire time. "What the—?"

"Get her upstairs," instructed Morgan.

"How bad?" Dad said.

"Selene, you know what to do," Morgan said. "Mr Goode, move her carefully."

I was in such shock I'd forgotten how badly hurt I was. Countless scrapes, burns, and bruised ribs would heal in no time. And the worst of my injuries—the brand—would heal, though my skin would be marked forever with a scar in the shape of the letter B.

Dad carried me upstairs to my bedroom and carefully placed me on my bed. "Ems." His voice cracked and he left the room.

Selene drew a bath and added medicinal herbs and essential oils. By the time I was bathed and bandaged and tucked beneath warm blankets, I didn't know if the past day was real or not...*fair is foul and foul is fair*...nothing appeared to be what it was. Black was white. Night was day. Except, a witch hunter was still a witch hunter.

I wasn't going to be fooled ever again.

With Morgan and Selene by my side, I drifted off to sleep. Selene's herbs, Morgan's tender healing powers, worked their magic. But their healing touch didn't stop my recurring dream. The Dream arrived slowly this time, carried into my mind like a fading leaf on an autumn breeze.

I looked out my bedroom window. Strings of glowing fireflies hovered near the dark forest behind the log cabin. I tiptoed downstairs, mindful that the last step creaked. Dad was fast asleep. Geneva and Matt snored on the rug in the tiny livingroom. Always alert, they lifted their heads, saw me, wagged their tails, resumed snoring. Silently, silently, I opened the side door through the kitchen, careful not to slam the springy screen door.

Barefoot, I walked outside. The weather had changed.

The soles of my feet didn't feel soft, wet grass beneath them. My lungs didn't fill with scents of sweet clover and musky earth and damp pine cones. Tall, wild grass didn't floss my toes or tug backward or hold me or warn me. Instead, I slid across ice and snow, cold and hard.

I couldn't help myself. I must know, must discover where the fireflies have gone, why they beckoned me so, how they survived, even in the dead of winter. They swirled behind the stand of massive pine trees. I took one deep breath and stepped into the forest. Without piercing my arms, I moved pine boughs away from me, aided by the moonlit sky. Left and right and left again, one foot in front of the other, snapping twigs or stabbed by sharp broken branches. I didn't make a sound. Didn't flinch. I wandered quietly, deeper into the dark forest, guided by pure light of a full moon and the sparkly glow of the fireflies.

The perfect circle of fireflies entered an apple grove enclosed within the thick woods. Even in winter, red apples and ballerina pink blossoms filled the grove. Squirrels, their winter coats thick and tails extra fluffy, flitted and scurried up and down tree trunks and nestled on snowy boughs. Pale blue waters drifted gently beneath a smashed windowpane of thin ice.

After a few blissful moments standing still within this improbable grove, I moved on, my bare feet cradled by the cold snow, my skin brushed by tender moonlight drizzling through thick limbs.

Moonlight disappeared behind a dusty cloud. In the darkness, lightning bugs spun and spun and spun around and around and around. After drawing a quiet breath, I wandered toward the fireflies, spinning and dancing in one spot.

I nearly tripped. A rotten log or branch or mound of moss. I adjusted my eyes to see what I'd stumbled upon. A boy, sprawled on his back, asleep or unconscious or dead, his face obscured, out of focus, except for his eyelids, closed and still. I fell to my knees. Afraid and exhilarated, cautious and reckless, I examined him. Tall, six feet or more, a teenager. Kneeling, I leaned over his shoulders, watched his chest, placed one ear on his heart, touched his wrist. I saw, heard, felt nothing, nothing at all. No breath or heartbeat or pulse.

And he was cold. So, so cold.

The clouds disappeared. Moonbeams struck his body like stage lights.

I wanted to scream, but couldn't. I wanted to run, but couldn't. My bare feet were frozen, my stomach ached with fear, my heartbeat was rapid. I just stood there, watching the boy sprawled on his back, beneath the moonlight, glowing like the thousands of fireflies dancing above his head.

I woke with a start, my heart still pounding. I was awake, yet I still saw the Dream.

At last, I saw his face. The boy's face. The boy in the Dream. It was him. Ben. All along, part of me knew, sensed Ben was the boy in the Dream, his face always obscured, but now it glowed beneath the moonlight. Then I knew it wasn't the Dream I was seeing. It was an Ice Vision.

"Ben," I whispered to him. "Ben, my firefly."

Deep down, I knew Ben was gone forever. Maybe he'd gotten his wish, after all.

No need to wake the others. Just as in the Dream, I crept down the stairs and past the sleeping dogs. At the door, I grabbed Dad's parka—something big enough to cover both of us—and slipped my bare feet into an old pair of boots I found by the door. Silently I left, echoing the Dream. Following the Dream. Tracing the Dream path…until I found him.

I lay down upon the cool snow, soothing and inviting, never wanting to leave the dark forest.

Never leave Ben, my firefly.

I didn't have to run from fear, knowing I'd confronted the monsters in the dark forest. Instead of monsters, I found the boy in the Dream, the boy who attracted fireflies where there were no fireflies, beneath the moonlit sky, knowing I no longer needed to wonder what the next day held in store. Because my time on earth was almost up. I could say goodbye without fear or sadness or regret. Say goodbye to the Coven, Dad, the Den Born, Matt and Geneva.

Finally, I'd found him, found the boy, so the Dream, my story, could end forever.

Stay away from the dark forest, I heard a voice say to me again.

I wasn't afraid of the dark forest anymore.

Because this was the place where I'd come to live, to laugh, to love and now, to die.

I leaned over Ben's body and cried. Tears flowed as gently as the nearby brook. I cried, I sobbed, I wept for a long, long time. I wept so much that I'd shed endless tears upon Ben's chest, where I lay my head, certain I heard his heart beating beneath my tear-soaked ear. Ben believed he was a heartless monster, but he was wrong. He did have a heart. A good, kind heart.

It was that heart, his heart, that destroyed him in the end.

So I kissed him. How long I couldn't say. I kissed his lips. Kissed and kissed and kissed his lips, brushed mine, wet with my salty tears, on his, cold as stone. Stroked his cheek, stained with more of my tears, and his forehead, caressed his dark, curly hair, threading sections of strands between my fingers. Trembling, I ran the tips of my fingers down his arms, over his scars and his wrists where I'd seen snakes of fire.

Not *his* wrists, I'd realized far too late.

I whispered in his ear. "It was you I searched for in the Dream, Ben. I am safe now. Safe with you, forever at my side."

I lay down beside Ben and covered us with the parka. I held his hand, my own bandaged hand lost within the safety of his palm. He didn't wear his ring, but I knew where it was.

When I closed my eyes, for the last time I heard the warning I no longer needed to fear.

Stay away from the dark forest
Stay away from the dark
Stay away from the
Stay away from
Stay away
away
away...

Chapter Twenty-Three

Two of Cups

BENNETT

I opened my eyes. I needed living silver to regain my strength, drained and lost. Why I was weak, I couldn't explain.

My memory was fuzzy. Did I imagine Octavia stabbing Wallis with a syringe? Did I imagine Ulric, his face, glaring at me, his hand, ripping my hoodie over my head, pulling my snowflake obsidian ring off my finger, before stabbing me with a large syringe?

And then, nothing. No sound. No touch. No memory.

I pictured another fire in my mind, just like the one that took Mrs. Kerr's life.

Like a tolling bell resounding in my ears, the poachers recited Delacroix's words.

> near a mountain cliff there stands
> caressing the black sun
> the clockwork moon
> the choking stars
> an enchanted tower
> high above the magical valley
> an enchanted tower
> a tower on fire

on fire
fire…

Beneath thin layers of ice, heaps of snow surrounded me. Curiously, instead of chills, a loving warmth drowned my body, no longer aching or frozen or immobile. I wanted to discover the source. Backtracking from my lips, caressed and satisfied, my resurging emotions passed down my throat to my chest, moist and comforting, my shoulder to my arm and down to my hand. Still weak, I forced myself up to see why my hand was so full of love and tenderness.

Next to me, I found Emeranne asleep and beautiful. Her still hand, wrapped in gauze, lost within my palm. I didn't want to unclench my hand. Stretching out my other arm and hand, reaching out for her, nearly touching her, closer and closer, until I stroked her arms, her chin, her lips. I leaned over, caressing her face, tracing her eyebrows, nose, cheekbones and at last, her melodious lips with my fingertips, singing to me, humming, *Kiss me*, Ben.

"Emeranne, wake up," I said to her, shaking her gently.

So quiet, so silent, so peaceful. Emeranne, sleeping next to me in the broken snow.

"Emeranne, wake up," I said to her again.

Beneath her T-shirt, I noticed gauzed wrapped around her upper arm. I followed the gauze, up her short sleeve, felt a large bandage under the gauze behind her right shoulder.

And I knew. Oh, I knew. I knew how Emeranne suffered. I covered my eyes, hung my head. I'd failed her, failed to protect her, broke my promise. *Oh, Emeranne. I'm so so sorry.*

…the spirits cry out
pleading, bleeding, needing
air and earth and water
a pine needle bed

pierces naked flesh
a flowing river weeps
red tears on tender skin
branded with orange iron
held beneath silver stains
on a lifeless navy sky

Gently, I lifted her off the snowy ground, wrapping her in the parka, cradling her in my arms. Cradling and rocking and holding back tears until I gave in and let them flow.

"Emeranne."

Her eyes didn't open. Her breathing was shallow and labored.

Within minutes, nothing. Nothing at all. No light, no breath, no melody. A smile, only her smile, peaceful and starry and joyful. I never thought death could appear this serene. I'd only witnessed death as pain, agony, violent.

"Emeranne," I whispered softly in her ear, rocking her as though I'd held her in the rocking chair at Bear Paw Lookout, where I'd confessed and she'd forgiven me for sins I wished I'd never committed, sins I'd wished I could erase. She should have hated me. Instead, she forgave me. Me, a monster.

I held her like that day on her porch, when she stumbled into my arms. And the night we danced together.

"It wasn't me. It wasn't me. It wasn't me," I said to her, even though I sensed it was too late, knew she wouldn't learn the truth, never know it wasn't me, never learn that Ulric, the poacher, was a decoy, who along with Octavia, drugged Wallis and dumped her while they executed their murderous plot.

A throbbing, cutting pain, a pain shared silently as if an invisible string stretched from her heart, a string tugging my body, my hands, my arms, my legs, my feet, drawing me toward her, toward the fading ballet pink on her lips, still and cold, her chest no longer rising wherein her heartbeat no longer thudded, the string linked us irrevocably with what, if anything, survived of my deceased soul.

I rocked Emeranne in my arms, rocked her and held her tear-stained face to mine. And I realized why my chest was moist. It was her tears, her loving warmth, her sadness that saved me.

After seven centuries, everything became so painfully, so agonizingly transparent to me. The sketches. The poems. The face I'd sought for centuries spent waiting, longing, searching, searching for her face her voice her touch her smile.

At last, I learned whose face belonged on all of my sketches. *You will know*, the strega had told me.

Emeranne's face…it was her face I sketched, for her alone I'd written poems about and for and to. Her and her alone.

And when you find her, you must make a difficult choice. Eternity or death. Live forever or die with her. There will be strife, there will be much pain and agony, there will be sorrow and loss, there will be separation and reunion. Until then, you will not leave the earthly world for the next.

"I choose death," I said to no one.

"*I choose death*," I said louder.

"I CHOOSE DEATH," I screamed.

No one listened.

You will know, the old strega had promised.

She was the one. At last, when I'd found her, the one I'd been searching for, I'd always feared I'd lose her, knowing what I was, knowing she was the hunted and I, the hunter, knowing what the strega had read in my palm and the Two of Cups.

There will be separation and reunion.

Yes, strega, you were right. But a reunion? When? In the after life? Must I make a choice now? I could stop injecting the serum. I could throw myself into a volcano. I could…

I'd waited so long for her. At last, I felt her. *The heart's shadow remembers.*

But I don't deserve happiness, I'm a monster, I reminded myself. I'm a killer. I'm the hunter and she is the hunted.

I couldn't finish Emeranne's poem because I never wanted the poem to end. So I left her poem unfinished, clinging to the last lines, wishing for a reunion, wishing that our story didn't have to end.

…and still you wait
believe she will appear
if only in your dreams…

You will know, I heard the old woman say to me, as if she were nearby, watching me, watching while I cradled Emeranne in my arms, her body cold and still.

I looked around, confused. I must have passed out. Where was I? Near Emeranne's home? My gut feeling said yes. How long had we been lying in the snow? The scattered clouds had disappeared. The moon shone high in a clear sky full of stars when I woke.

Was it too late to save Emeranne? No, it couldn't be too late. There was time, I told myself over and over again. Although I was weak from the injection of the altered serum only hours before, I summoned what little energy was left and stood with Emeranne in my arms. I swayed on my feet until the spinning pine trees decelerated before starting my trek. Through the dark forest and toward snowy pine boughs reflecting starlight, flaming like a thousand tiny suns, I carried Emeranne. Through golden flames, blurry and pale. Dizzy spells came and went in waves. Weakened by lack of serum, I dragged my boots through the snow. Emeranne didn't stir.

I gathered strength for Emeranne. Only her life mattered. What might happen to me from the extended delay without living silver was of no concern to me. For the rest of my existence, should I survive, I vowed to the Coven that I was not a monster, that I would protect them. Even my family, with one exception, could be their allies.

So I pushed ahead, willing myself forward, while the forest transformed into one giant spinning top. Emeranne's home appeared through my squinted eyes. My instinct was correct. Almost there. I staggered past a tree house, a dog house, and reached the kitchen door. The thick winter air carried a number of voices toward me. There was still time, I hoped, to save Emeranne's life. I shifted my quivering right arm to support her, and braced the other arm to steady myself against the cabin's wall next to the door. Drawing one last burst of strength, white puffs swirled in front of me, I faced the door and kicked the aluminum bottom half beneath the screen. One, two, three kicks. Snow and ice fell from the frame and screen. No one answered. I turned sideways to shift Emeranne into my left arm. I made a fist to hit the door frame with my right hand. There was no need. The inner wooden door swung open. Indoor light spilled out, casting a long shadow of a tall figure on the illuminated snow.

"What the…"

"Mr G…"

Emeranne's dad caught his daughter as I fell to my knees.

"She's…she's…" I pressed my hands onto my thighs, leaned forward and gasped for air. The long shadow disappeared from the ground and gleaming snow replaced the silhouette. I remained kneeling for a long moment and stared at the snow-covered ground. Emeranne was home. I couldn't help her now.

The snow turned to charcoal. Another shadow appeared, a miniature version of the previous outline. I turned my head to see who stood at the kitchen door.

"Bennett."

The last thing I heard was Allora whispering my name.

End of Book One

What's Next for the Coven?

Butterfly

Ice Born: Book Two

Dragonfly

Ice Born: Book Three

For updates about *Butterfly*
follow P. M. Pevato:
pmpevato.com
pmpevato.tumblr.com
twitter.com/pmpevato
facebook.com/PM-Pevato

Emeranne's Playlist

Act I: Flower Duet – Delibes: Lakmé
Waking the Witch – Kate Bush
In the Woods Somewhere – Hozier
Firefly – Ed Sheeran
Things We Lost In The Fire – Bastille
Half A Person – The Smiths
National Anthem – Lana Del Rey
Dance This Mess Around – The B-52s
Kiss Me – Sixpence None The Richer
Hey Now – London Grammar
Hurricane – MS MR
Now Is Not The Time – CHVRCHES
Aquarius – Digital Daggers
Neighbourhood #3 (Power Out) – Arcade Fire
Run – Snow Patrol
My Immortal (Alternate Version) – Evanescence
Shadow of the Day – Linkin Park
Missing – The xx
Beat and the Pulse – Austra
Line of Fire – Junip
Love the Way You Lie – Eminem (feat. Rihanna)
Somebody That I Used To Know – Gotye
Glory and Gore – Lorde
Icarus – Bastille
House of Smoke and Mirrors – Matthew Good
Born to Die – Lana Del Rey
Be My Baby – Snowhill
Asleep – The Smiths
Angels – The xx

Bennett's Playlist

Intro – The xx
You Know I'm No Good (feat. Ghostface Killah) – Amy
It's A Fire – Portishead
Little Hell – City and Colour
Give Me Love – Ed Sheeran
Creep – Daniela Andrade
Hurt – Nine Inch Nails
Demons – Imagine Dragons
Cure For The Itch – Linkin Park
Fireproof – The National
Snowflake – Kate Bush
Afterlife – Arcade Fire
Wasting My Younger Years – London Grammar
Music of the Night (Theme Music) – Phantom of the Opera
Wintermezzo – Chilly Gonzalez
Lost Parts – Forest City Lovers
Secrets – OneRepublic
Exile Vilify – The National
We Found Each Other in the Dark – City and Colour
Enjoy the Silence – Denmark + Winter
Overjoyed – Bastille
What I've Done – Linkin Park
Hot Like Fire – The xx
Radioactive (feat. Kendrick Lamar) – Imagine Dragons
Bring Me to Life – Evanescence
The Spell – Tchaikovsky: Sleeping Beauty
Here with Me – Susie Suh & Robot Koch
Dark Paradise – Lana Del Rey
I Need My Girl – The National
Black Black Heart – David Usher

About the Author

A flâneur at heart, P. M. Pevato constantly seeks new experiences whilst strolling down the boulevards of life. A global free spirit, the author studied and traveled extensively. She completed an LLM and PhD in public international law at the London School of Economics and worked for the United Nations in Geneva.

For more on the author, visit: pmpevato.com or her tumblr page pmpevato.tumblr.com.

About the Cover Artist

Henrique de França lives and works in São Paulo, Brazil. An award-winning artist, his work has been exhibited in solo exhibitions and in select group exhibitions internationally. Henrique's graphic art captures the essence of each story. So, too, do his unique drawings and paintings, inviting one inside the expression of his variegated narratives.

For more on the cover artist, visit: henriquedefranca.com.

41671609R00169

Made in the USA
Charleston, SC
04 May 2015